He'd alm̶o̶s̶t̶ ̶m̶i̶s̶s̶e̶d̶ ̶h̶e̶r̶

Absolutely not what he needed to be thinking about five minutes after a gunshot rang out. But Harc's gut was telling him that the shot hadn't been meant for them.

Someone whose operation was sophisticated enough to avoid international agencies with the best agents on the case wouldn't blow their cover by shooting unless they were absolutely certain they had the target in sight.

And someone dealing in illegal arms would have a sniper rifle, which would not only bring the target clearly into focus.

The next shot could be aimed at them from a sniper's nest and Nicole would be dead. She still had time to get out.

They had no idea where to put her to keep her safe. Not now that she'd breached at last some of his security walls. In a way that would have told him that she was the one doing it.

No one else could dismantle her coding. He needed her aware of the danger. Constantly alert. It was the only way she'd have a chance of defending herself if the need arose.

Dear Reader,

Welcome to Sierra's Web! If you're new to us, the firm is made up of a group of college friends who bonded over the death of their friend and consists of seven experts in various fields who work to solve crimes, help families and make the world a safer, happier place. They've given us twenty books so far! If you've been with us before, we fondly welcome you back!

This particular story really hit me hard, as it deals with two really good people, a true hero and heroine, who were led astray. People who wanted to do good, believed they were doing good, but one choice at a time, ended up involved in things that shame them. People with consciences who hurt, every day, for the pain they caused. I've made mistakes in my life, some that cause me pain, and as I wrote this story, these two people not only found their own redemption, but they helped me to find mine, too. Turns out that sometimes we are our worst critics and condemn ourselves where others do not.

It's also a story of a woman who had twenty-four years of her life robbed from her. She was kidnapped, her identity was changed, and at twenty-five, she finds out her entire life was a lie. I wasn't sure how I helped her on the page. In the end, I didn't have to. She showed me the way.

Tara Taylor Quinn

HORSE RANCH HIDEOUT

TARA TAYLOR QUINN

ROMANTIC SUSPENSE

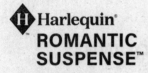

Harlequin®
ROMANTIC SUSPENSE™

ISBN-13: 978-1-335-47152-9

Horse Ranch Hideout

Copyright © 2025 by TTQ Books LLC

 Harlequin Enterprises ULC
22 Adelaide St. West, 41st Floor
Toronto, Ontario M5H 4E3, Canada
www.Harlequin.com

Printed in Lithuania

Recycling programs for this product may not exist in your area.

MIX
Paper | Supporting responsible forestry
FSC® C021394

A *USA TODAY* bestselling author of over one hundred novels in twenty languages, **Tara Taylor Quinn** has sold more than seven million copies. Known for her intense emotional fiction, Ms. Quinn's novels have received critical acclaim in the UK and most recently from Harvard. She is the recipient of the Readers' Choice Award and has appeared often on local and national TV, including *CBS Sunday Morning*. For TTQ offers, news and contests, visit tarataylorquinn.com!

Books by Tara Taylor Quinn

Harlequin Romantic Suspense

Sierra's Web

Tracking His Secret Child
Cold Case Sheriff
The Bounty Hunter's Baby Search
On the Run with His Bodyguard
Not Without Her Child
A Firefighter's Hidden Truth
Last Chance Investigation
Danger on the River
Deadly Mountain Rescue
A High-Stakes Reunion
Baby in Jeopardy
Her Sister's Murder
Mistaken Identities
Horse Ranch Hideout

The Coltons of Owl Creek

Colton Threat Unleashed

Visit the Author Profile page
at Harlequin.com for more titles.

To Rachel Reames Stoddard—
you are who you need to be, I am honored
to have raised you and I love you more than life.

Ma.

Chapter 1

"Here you go, Nicole. It's official!" The clerk smiled as she slid some paperwork through the open bottom of the glass partition through which she spoke. "These tell you how to change your birth certificate, driver's license, and social security number..."

Blinking through her tears, Charlotte Duran... *NO... Nicole Compton*...glanced down at the sheet on the ledge in front of her, her gaze following the woman's blunt-tipped finger over a series of web addresses.

She continued to watch that hand as it reached out further, covering hers, giving her fingers a gentle squeeze. "Good luck," the woman said.

Charlotte—Nicole—nodded, then looked up and smiled. "Thank you," she said, meeting the woman's big brown eyes briefly...for just a second...before she took her paperwork and headed for the courthouse door. Back and shoulders straight, head high, she stepped outside into the warm spring air.

It was done.

She'd taken control of her life. Reclaimed the self that had been robbed from her. She couldn't remember the first year after her birth—the year she'd been Nicole—but she'd seen all the proof. Legal documents, photos that were a one hundred percent match for facial recognition when compared to Charlotte's year-old pictures, DNA.

Seeing pictures of the mother she'd always yearned to know holding her close, the look of love on the beautiful face she couldn't remember... Nicole swallowed at the thought. Blinked back more tears.

And Savannah...her somewhat intimidating and wonderful, loving, selfless older sister...she'd kept all the photos of Nicole's first year. A lot of which had included seven-year-old Savannah.

Sniffling, she climbed into the brand-new to her blue midsize American-made SUV. She wasn't a naturalized citizen, as she'd grown up thinking. She was American born. From American parents.

She had a heritage. A place where she belonged.

And a world to protect.

The thought brought her up short. She glanced in the rear-view mirror to see the tip of the suitcase visible in the far back of her new vehicle, and it strengthened her resolve.

She'd told Savannah she was going to a dude ranch in Colorado for a couple of weeks. That after three months of intense debriefing, biweekly meetings with the best of the best in the psychology arm of her sister's firm of experts, and her own exploration into possible futures for herself, she needed some downtime where no one knew anything about her. Where she could just be and let the dust settle.

She'd done the one thing she and Savannah had promised each other they would never do to each other. She'd lied.

Sort of.

Pulling onto the Phoenix bypass that would take her to the interstate leading north, Nicole gave verbal commands to set her global positioning system to an address outside Durango, Colorado, and took a deep breath. She *was* going to a ranch in Colorado. And a dude lived there.

As much as she adored her newfound older sister—and intended to stay close to her for the rest of her life—Nicole had to find her own place in the universe, too. No more living in a protected world where she felt safe and where she'd allowed herself to depend on another person to define her.

The only way she moved forward, became a person she could respect was to create a sense of independence.

Changing her name had been a huge step. One she hadn't yet shared with anyone but the court system. Savannah would be thrilled. At least Nicole figured she would be. Hoped she would be. Though maybe hurt that Nicole hadn't let her share the process.

But she was establishing a sense of self. And that was something she had to do alone.

Well…alone except for the help of a total stranger who she hoped to God she could convince to partner with her in her attempt to pay atonement. To obliterate a creation from her past.

To save others instead of herself.

Herself.

On the freeway headed north through the mountains toward Flagstaff, Nicole pulled off at the first scenic viewing point and parked in front of a vista that stretched as far as she could see. Showing mountains and valleys that were so much larger than her billion-dollar world had been.

With the strength of the mountains within her, she grabbed the paperwork from the seat beside her, setting it on her lap. Pulling out her phone, checking to ensure that she was close enough to towers to still have full service, she typed in the first website.

Only when all the websites had been visited, all of the official work was done did she let herself look up again.

She saw grace in the massive beauty, along with the

dangers inherent within the rugged slopes. Saw hope when once upon a time she'd had little conscious need of it.

Charlotte Duran and her privileged existence had just been legally and officially wiped off the face of the earth.

But the deeds she'd done, horrible crimes her innocent work for her father had contributed to...those were still living and breathing. Some of them hiding right there in that vastness, from what she'd been told. Illegal arms didn't hang out on popular highways, on display at roadside stands, waiting to be purchased. They switched hands under covers of darkness, even in broad daylight and in plain sight.

Like the trail she'd tracked through the Arizona mountains, up to Utah and over to Colorado. A trail with which Harcus Taylor was very familiar.

Eduardo Duran, the man whom Charlotte had grown up adoring as a father, the only family she'd ever known, was extinct. But a portion of his business lived on.

The one appendage that authorities hadn't found enough evidence to stop. Or prosecute.

Nicole had thought that watching the powerful billionaire and philanthropist be stripped of his identity and exposed as the criminal fraud he was would give her closure. That seeing him forced to face charges as ex–IRS paper pusher Hugh Gussman, the man he really was, the one who'd fathered her and faked his own death before kidnapping her as a baby, fleeing the country with millions stolen from the federal government, and lying to her about who she was, would put her past to rest. She'd been wrong.

She wasn't going to rest, establish legitimacy in her own mind or feel as though she belonged in her big sister's family until she knew that the damage she'd done had been eradicated as completely as the Duran family had been.

With resolve cemented by the certainty of that last

thought, Nicole put her new vehicle in Drive, and headed back onto the freeway.

Praying that Harcus Taylor was as driven as she was.

Seated on a fallen log, Harc Taylor sipped coffee still hot in his travel mug and surveyed the valley below him. Then the vastness of peaks in the distance.

"You know it all, don't you, sir?" He spoke aloud to the once-wild mustang bearing his saddle and currently munching on the forage Harc had stopped at for their afternoon snack. "All the secrets these hills keep?"

Imperial lifted his head long enough to snort in Harc's direction.

Nodding, he took the response as an affirmative and hoped that the regal horse had seen all the good the natural beauty that had been his home had to offer.

And little or none of the bad that Harcus imagined as he sat there.

Hoping, too, that one day he'd look out and believe in the peace that seemed to lay before him. To know its existence, not just view the mirage.

Someday he wanted to walk into his barn of once wild horses and consider himself worthy of their acceptance.

Wanted to trust himself enough to be able to assure them that he would never again be a man who'd compromise his ethics, who'd get so caught up in eliminating the wrongdoing he witnessed that he'd bend laws to the extreme in order to succeed.

He was done with shades of gray.

And, noticing the downward angle of the sun shining on the mountains, had to be done with his afternoon ride, too. Cutting the usual daily activity off an hour earlier than usual.

"We've got a visitor coming," he told Imperial. Grabbing the horse's reins, he lifted himself expertly into the saddle and turned the horse toward the small ranch they called home.

Nicole Compton.

She hadn't said why she wanted to see him. Had just asked for an appointment, an hour of his time.

He figured he knew, though. His horse-therapy program. People who were struggling, especially those with emotional issues, didn't always like to reveal their challenges to perfect strangers on the phone.

Whether Nicole had set the meeting for a matter concerning herself or on behalf of someone else, he was eager to meet the woman. Every single step he took to get his fledgling business off the ground was a step in the right direction.

The few successes he'd experienced had helped him get his big toe out of the dark world into which he'd sunk. But he had one hell of a long way to go before his full body emerged and he could stand tall and clean. Be proud of himself again.

He saw the unfamiliar blue SUV parked in the circular dirt drive in front of the house as he rode in from the back of the property. Figured his appointment had turned up a bit early—and instead of stabling Imperial, he rode the gelding past the barns and down the drive toward the house.

The white wood-sided two-story structure was almost fifty years old and a lot more than he needed, but it had come with the ranch—one of the few that was small enough for him to be able to afford. And kept him from view as he approached.

Whether Nicole was there as a potential client or on behalf of one, there was no better way to introduce her to Crimson Ranch than through Imperial.

He saw her first. Out of her car, Nicole had her back

to the house, was facing the mowed green acres of front yard, separated from the road by nearly an acre of thirty-foot-tall oak trees.

His first impression—the woman wasn't dressed for horseback riding. So, maybe representing a potential client.

In a black skirt that ended just above mid-thigh and a form-fitting short-sleeved top, she might have fit in at a barn dance. If not for the footwear. Two-inch heels on leather sandals bearing an over-abundance of bling. Her hair, dark and silky looking in the sun, hung almost to her waist, completely uncontained. And yet…perfectly sculpted, too.

All about the haircut. He'd had enough experience with human disguises to have that one down pat.

The bag slung over her shoulder—thin strap, small, black—also bore bling.

She reeked money.

Yet the SUV, while a recent model and bearing temporary tags exposing it as a new purchase, was a mid-level vehicle from a common manufacturer. Not a high-end brand.

Imperial's clip-clopping gave them away before Harc was close enough to see the woman's expression clearly as she spun around.

But it wouldn't have mattered. He was down off his horse, facing away from the woman, walking Imperial to the barn before anyone had a chance to call out a greeting.

The woman on his property was not Nicole Compton. Nor was she welcome there. As soon as he had Imperial secure, he lifted his flannel shirt enough to pull out his Glock. Checked it for ammunition, though he knew full well the chamber was loaded. And with the weapon raised, headed back outside.

No way in hell was Charlotte Duran taking another thing from him.

The woman and her father had already cost him his soul.

* * *

She'd heard the man was a tough one. Intimidating as they came. Nicole had not been prepared, in any way, to meet her host with a gun pointed straight between her eyes.

Raising her arms above her head, she realized, too late, that she had no idea if the gunman steadily approaching *was* Harcus Taylor. And quickly called out, "I'm Nicole Compton! I have an appointment with Mr. Taylor."

She was half an hour early.

The man obviously had tight security. Something she'd lived with her entire life.

And based on what she knew about Taylor, something he'd be wise to keep for the rest of his.

But while the gun boded well for her in a future association with the CIA agent, she couldn't take her eyes off the barrel as the dangerous-looking man approached.

"What's your business?" He barked the words as a challenge. As though if he didn't approve of her response, she'd be dead in seconds.

"I have an appointment with Mr. Taylor," she said again, pulling on the bravado Eduardo Duran had trained into her from her first memory of him.

As long as she didn't have a bullet between the eyes, she could hold her own with the best of them.

The man with the gun didn't lower his weapon. Nor did he slow his advance on her. At the moment, she was just thankful that the shakiness taking over her insides hadn't been apparent in her voice. The cliché Eduardo had been fond of came to mind. *Never let them see you sweat.*

She'd been through a lot in the past few months—too much. She had been in critical danger. But she'd never in her life had a gun pointed at her.

She'd only ever seen them pointed at others as part of her protection.

And had never witnessed an actual shooting.

The threatening man stopped a few feet in front of her. "I'm asking you one last time to state your business," he said menacingly, speaking through gritted teeth.

She had nothing but the truth. Looking the man straight in his slitted dark eyes, she repeated, "My name is Nicole Compton. I have an appointment with Mr. Taylor."

Always speak with authority. Another one of Eduardo's oft-repeated life lessons came to her aid without forethought.

When the gun lowered slightly, Nicole's chin started to drop. She quickly shut her mouth. Duran had gone from pauper to billionaire. Of course he knew how to manipulate people to make things happen.

Thankful for the rules he'd taught her, even while she hated that they were a part of her, she continued to maintain eye contact with Taylor's watchdog.

"If you'd just let Mr. Taylor know I'm here," she said politely but in a tone she'd heard Eduardo use every time he was speaking to someone in his employ.

The gun was no longer pointing at head, but it drew Nicole's gaze as it moved to point at her chest, as accents to each word the man spoke. "Show me some ID."

Four words. Four distinct points of the pistol.

His hand was big. The knuckles worn. No mistaking the strength there. At such close range, and with her unarmed, the man didn't need to pull the trigger to kill her.

He could drop the gun and just do her in with his bare hands.

Bury her out there.

And no one would ever know.

Because she hadn't let a single soul know where she was going and why. Taking a note from her wise sister's playbook, she'd chosen not to involve her far-too-generous older sister, or Savannah's expert friends, in finding her absolution. Just as Savannah had set out to find Charlotte on her own just a few months before.

Rescuing her from the nightmare she hadn't known she'd been living in.

Savannah had used a cruise as her cover. Nicole's was a dude ranch.

Which meant she had to get past security and have her hour to ingratiate herself into ranch life. Leaving one hand up, she lowered the other, palm out, to the small clutch she wore everywhere, at all times.

"Don't move!" The voice was gravelly, and Nicole's gaze shot to her aggressor, seeing the gun aimed at her chest.

"You asked for my identification." Eduardo would be proud of the even tone.

Nicole hated that she was thankful for his tutelage.

"I know who you are, Charlotte Duran. And I'm giving you one more chance to state your purpose for trespassing on my ranch before I pull this trigger."

He wasn't going to shoot her. The impression hit as the man's voice faltered over those last words.

He knew who she was. The second fact hit and rocked her more.

And the third… "You're Harcus Taylor?"

He'd said *his* ranch.

And was clearly ready to order her off from it.

Not at all an auspicious start to what might be her only chance at success.

Chapter 2

"I am Nicole Compton." The woman's gaze didn't waver as she repeated, again, the lie she'd been telling.

Harc wanted her gone—but not until he'd figured out her game. He had a life load of unanswered questions where the Durans were concerned. There would be no more. Their ingestion ended there. Then.

Which was why when she reached for the inside of her purse a second time, he didn't shoot.

He'd have gone to the right of her left arm. A bullet intended to scare, not make contact with flesh. If he shot her, he could argue that he'd been defending himself—that she was a trespasser on his private property, threatening him—but there would be no more skating the lines between right and wrong.

If a weapon appeared from that shiny black leather all bets were off.

She didn't pull a gun. She pulled out an official court document. Handed it to him.

Nicole Gussman, also known as Natalie Willoughby, had legally changed her name to Nicole Compton.

"I was born Nicole Gussman," the woman said. As though that explained everything.

Raising his eyebrows, Harc shook his head. She was going to have to do better than that.

"My father is Hugh Gussman," she said then, her face losing all expression at the words.

Again, nothing. And Harc was out of patience. "Look, Charlotte, whatever you're after—just state your business so we both get out of this alive."

He didn't attempt to hide the threat in his voice. She was beneath contempt. To have the balls to invade his space, to disrupt the tiny piece of quiet he'd found inside himself...

Her gaze met his again. The emotion there...was unexpected. As were the words coming out of her mouth. "I need your help."

He turned his back. If she pulled a gun and shot him, then she did. His instincts told him she wouldn't. And he was done. He walked back down toward the barn where he'd left Imperial tied to a post. The part-time staff who helped him out had all left for the day.

He heard her steps behind him before he heard her cry. "Please!" He kept walking.

"You're in on it with him." Her words weren't loud. Or in accusation.

They seemed to be more like dawning awareness.

Which stopped him in his tracks. Spinning around, his nose flaring, his teeth clamped tightly together, he barely had enough time to reach out and keep her from walking into him. She'd been that close.

Her eyes, widened in fright, stared up at him. Glancing at his hands on her shoulders, feeling the tension in himself, he let go abruptly. Stepped back.

And saw her spin, running toward her car, darting to the right and left, as though she feared a bullet in back at any moment.

The sight struck him to the core. The fear. The helplessness.

It told him that he was missing critical pieces. He didn't want them. He'd left that world behind him. No going back. Period.

But what if it was coming after him and she'd come to warn him? "Wait!" he called, hurrying after the fleeing woman. A feat made a little less plausible for her based on the two-inch heels she was wearing. "Nicole," he called. "I'm sorry."

Always. Forever. For so much.

Most of all, for not having what it took to nail her father to his deathbed.

She'd almost reached her car. Could lock herself in and speed away.

He had her legal identity. Could find her. The photographic memory, or whatever helped him call up every detail, had served him well during his career and was still in fine working order. Even if his choices had become skewed.

She didn't get into the car. She turned to face him.

At which point, he slowed. Shoved the gun dangling from his hand into the waistband of his jeans where it belonged. Let his shirt fall back over it.

Figured the move was his at that point. "What did you need my help with?"

Her gaze tentative, she studied him. Shook her head. Reached for her door handle.

"I was told Duran was arrested," he said, the first thing that came to mind.

She frowned. "You were told? Of course you were told. You were a huge part of making that happen. If he'd gone to trial, you'd have been a star witness."

Her tone was off. All expression gone from her face again. So…what…she blamed him for her father's fate?

Or was she still considering the possibility that he was in with a conscienceless fiend like Eduardo Duran?

Because…he could have been. He'd gone where the FBI couldn't go. Had done things no one wanted to know about.

And…her words hit hard. "He's not going to trial?" He'd never felt the blood drain from his face before. Had heard of it happening to others. Stood there, feeling his skin get clammy, even as he tensed for battle.

Her frown of confusion confused him. "You had to have been told about the plea agreement," she said.

He relaxed some at the words. And shook his head. "I don't know what you've heard." He said the obvious. And then added, "I left the CIA six months ago. Other than a brief text on a burner phone that said, 'We got him but not on arms' I've had no contact with anyone connected to the Duran case since I walked away."

Her face paled. "You walked away? From the files I read you're the only one who…" She stopped, shook her head. Looked like she'd just lost her best friend.

Like she'd pinned some kind of hope on him. Which was ridiculous; he'd told so many lies he wasn't even sure he could believe himself anymore. He was most definitely friend to no one.

Except, he hoped, his stable of horses. He'd never lied to them.

She looked up at him again. "You didn't follow the case in the news?"

"Nope. News tends to be prevailingly bad, and I specifically don't avail myself of it." Couldn't risk getting riled up and thinking he had to get out there and do something about that over which he had no control.

He couldn't save the world.

Hell, he had moments when he wasn't even sure he could save himself.

Nicole… Charlotte Duran… Compton took a tentative-looking step forward. "Would you be willing to keep our meeting as planned?" she asked him. "It's important to me."

She'd said that last like he had a heart that could be swayed into letting sympathy guide his course.

The moist, almost lost look in her gaze got to him more. People could lie with their eyes, certainly. Actors did it all the time.

He'd made a career out of it.

But the brown-eyed gaze watching him wavered even as it held his. There was a depth to it he wasn't used to see-ing. In others. Or in the mirror.

And…she might know something that he should be privy to, to protect his horses. Just because he'd walked away didn't mean that Duran's players had done the same.

Because he knew damned straight that there were some left.

That *some* had driven him to the verge of being just like them. One of them. Just playing for a different team.

Holding an arm toward the sweeping front porch on the house, the one place he'd spent money to dress completely, he said, "We can have a seat up here, if you'd like."

And was a bit shocked at the relief that flooded through him when she smiled.

Charlotte Duran would have been halfway to the high-way. Nicole wished she was as she followed the cantanker-ous and clearly dangerous man up the three steps to a lovely front porch. From the braided oval rug that covered nearly twenty feet in length to the table and padded chairs on one side and matching couch and rockers set on the other to the lovely red-flower-filled planters set around the space, the area screamed against a presence like that of the man who owned it.

Standing on the top step, she took another glance around, finding beauty in the ugly moment. "This is nice," she said, not sure what to do next.

Did she claim the seat that appeared to be most advantageous to her, as Charlotte would do, or did she wait for him to lead the way?

"I saw it in a magazine," he said, shrugging as he headed over to the table. Pulled out a chair for her.

Not the one she'd have chosen. He was putting her back to the road. But she most definitely preferred the table over the couch or rockers.

She was there on business. With a very serious matter to discuss. Not lounging around having casual conversation.

As she sat, she thought about what he'd said. "You saw the furniture in a magazine?" she asked, more to be polite, to accept the second for them to regroup that he'd offered than because she cared who'd furnished his porch.

Sitting across from her, he kept a very clear eye on the yard, the drive, the front of the property. And she felt a little better about his choice of seating arrangement. She might not be able to have her own back, but if he had his, he'd have hers.

And he was armed.

"I saw the whole thing in a magazine," he told her. "Down to the planters."

Looking around again, she frowned. "And then you, what…called the magazine to find out where to get everything?"

With a sideways nod of his head, he said, "I'm a CIA agent. I didn't need some publisher to put me in touch with a photographer who'd put me in touch with the photo-shoot designer to get what I wanted."

Right. But… "You *were* a CIA agent." She repeated what she'd been told. Watching him.

Not trusting him.

But needing him.

"*Was*," he acknowledged. Sitting back, his hands folding on his stomach, drawing attention to the flatness of that part of his physique, he asked, "What's this meeting about?"

She'd rehearsed that exact moment during the many hours' drive she'd just taken from Phoenix to southwestern Colorado. Had her speech all planned out. Memorized to every pause she'd take.

But that was before she'd found out he hadn't seen the news.

"I'd like to give you some context, if you can humor me long enough to do so," she said, calling on her years as a guest lecturer at some of the most prestigious universities and private schools in California, speaking to packed auditoriums. She could be so many different people.

Was only just discovering how many guises her father had raised her to wear.

And was feeling like she was somehow marked with big red x's floating in a circle in the air around her.

Her normal had just been obliterated off the face of the earth. Or, more accurately, had simply evaporated into the ether.

Leaving…what…behind?

"You have an hour," the man finally said, after almost a minute spent silently studying her. "Use it however you think best."

An hour and not a second longer. The message in his words came through loud and clear.

She was good with that. Had grown up with clear expectation. Knew how to live within its boundaries.

Harcus Taylor might've been one tough dude.

For all but three months of Charlotte's lifetime, Eduardo Duran had been able to best all the Taylors who'd been after him. From multiple countries.

And in the end, for all the work the best investigative and enforcement agencies in the world had done, she and Savannah had been the ones who'd bested Eduardo. The two daughters he'd fathered and then betrayed had been his downfall.

There was irony in that, if nothing else.

"Until a little over three months ago, I believed I was born Charlotte Duran, in El Salvador. I believed my mother, an American, died giving birth to me and that she had no other family. Because my mother was American and had spent the months before my birth in America, I was able to apply for and receive American citizenship and did so, at my father's behest, when I was a teenager. I'd been aching to know more about myself and longed to be in America more than anything. At least that's how I remember it. I now know that he used me to get us back to the States under the assumed names he'd managed to obtain when he faked his own death and kidnapped me just after my first birthday."

She wouldn't bore him with all the details. Wouldn't waste the hour. But if she had a hope of convincing him to help her—a much steeper climb than she'd imagined now that she knew he'd walked away from the case before Eduardo had been caught—there were some things he had to understand about her.

"As of today, Charlotte Duran's fake identity has been permanently deleted."

"You said your father's name was Hugh Gussman."

He'd been paying attention. She took that as a positive. "It is." She swallowed, her throat dry in the dusty, seventy-degree early May air. And had to press on with what he'd missed in the news. "He was a supposedly happily married man, working for the IRS. A man of above-average intelligence who, in reality, was bored stiff at his job but couldn't leave it because he had a family to support and no other training."

"He'd grown up poor?"

Nicole blinked. Shrugged. "I have no idea how he grew up. I just know he was an only child whose parents died in a car accident when he was twenty. He'd just finished his last year of college and was already dating my mother." To her way of thinking, none of that mattered. And the hour was hers.

"He found a way to hack into various accounts and siphon money. At first he'd just done so to see if he could. To expose leaks. But had obviously found the thrill of succeeding far more heady than being a husband and father to two. He had almost two million put away when he figured out that someone was onto him. He came forward, said he'd hacked into a hacker. Said he knew who was taking the money and would testify as long as he and his family were protected because he was accusing a very powerful person. He was stepping up, putting himself at extreme risk to do the right thing. From what I've been told, my mother went to her grave believing in him one hundred percent. Loving him with her last breath. The day he was due to testify, he took me from my day care, then faked his own death, leaving in a deserted dirt field a body so badly burned that it was indistinguishable except for traces of epithelial found in the heel of a tennis shoe nearby. There was evidence of a body having been lying where the shoe was found. And a hole dug in the dirt that fit the heel of the shoe. The theory was that he'd been being tortured, had been moving his foot back and forth in pain, before they threw him on the fire… When really, he was living as Eduardo Duran."

She stopped. Feeling the cold sense of helpless fear creeping up on her again. A weakening sensation she hadn't known until the night she'd gone with FBI Agent Mike Reynolds, known to her as her bodyguard Isaac Forrester to arrest her father.

"I was never seen again," she said then.

"And your mother and sister?"

"They were put in witness protection. And my missing person's report was as well, with DNA evidence to identify me if I was ever found. I became Natalie Willoughby, as far as the US government was concerned. At the same time, my father identified me as Charlotte Duran."

Her host had been watching the area behind her back as much as he'd had eyes on her. She kind of appreciated his lack of piercing attention while she, a person who'd grown up having her body—and information—guarded by professionals, laid herself bare.

She'd come with one thing to give Taylor, hoping that it would convince him to see through the job he'd started. She had time left in her hour to get there.

And wanted to get through everything that had to be said. Once done, she wasn't going to revisit the conversation again.

Ever.

"Is it true that you're just twenty-five and have three college degrees? Or is that just part of Charlotte's fake identity?" The question didn't carry a cruel tone.

Nicole felt the slap just the same. Her whole life had

been a sham. How did someone ever find a person who was real in that?

"You did your homework on me," she said. She'd known he'd been privy to a particular program she'd written.

He shrugged. Waited.

"Yes, it's true. I imagine everything you found was true. Duran managed to amass billions in those twenty-four years he robbed from me. He had the wherewithal to make certain that there were no weak links." She stopped and then, looking over at him, said, "I'm as smart as, or smarter than, he was. He knew that there could be no falsities in my life or I'd find them."

"You owned the home the two of you lived in."

"He told me that the house went in my name for my protection. So that if anything ever happened to him, my home life wouldn't be interrupted. There wouldn't be probate or any question that the home went to me. He'd said that if he got in a car accident, for instance, and it was his fault and someone else in addition to him died, his estate could be sued. As long as I had the house, I could always sell it if I had to and be secure for the rest of my life."

The man had manipulated her down to the last speck of dust. "As Charlotte, I adored my father," she admitted then. "And because he was all I had, I worried a lot about being alone. I yearned for other family. His reasoning played right into that weakness."

Harcus Taylor nodded. Believing? Agreeing? Accepting? Seeing how she'd been manipulated?

Realizing that she might never recover from that enough to have a normal existence or any kind of committed partner relationship? How could she ever trust another enough to be able to commingle emotionally again?

Or was he thinking the entire situation was too bizarre and she'd made the whole thing up?

"It sounds to me as though he loved you." Taylor's words cut through her. Sharply.

Unendingly.

She'd made a mistake coming to the man.

Had to find another way.

Even if she died in the attempt.

Her meeting with the ex–CIA agent hadn't gone in any way that she'd planned.

It had made one thing ever more clear to her, though.

She could change her name. She could love her new-found sister. She could yearn for a real life of her own.

But she was always going to be Eduardo Duran's daughter.

The woman who'd been conceived by—and then spent her entire life loving—a man who'd been committing heinous crimes since before she was born.

And she was done talking.

Chapter 3

Harc saw the change come over Nicole Compton.

Compton. Why?

He needed more, and based on the emotionless gaze, the straight face, and the sudden stillness about the woman, he sensed that his last question had lost him her interest. Which was what he'd been seeking, wholeheartedly and nonstop, since he'd first recognized Charlotte Duran on his property.

He'd wanted her, and anyone she might have brought with her, gone.

Right up until she'd started talking about her life.

Lifting the skinny strap of her thin black purse to her shoulder, the woman stood.

He couldn't let her leave. Not until he knew more.

Most particularly, knew what part she'd seen him playing in her day.

Taking a breath, Harc said "I'm sorry" for the second time in the few minutes he'd known the woman. Because he was.

And also because she'd given him another chance the first time he'd admitted to a mistake. Then, without forethought, he continued. "I can't imagine waking up one morning to find out my entire life has been a lie," he said. She deserved to be heard. To be understood.

Even if she was up to no good or intended to use him.

Whatever she was into, whatever she'd hoped to include him in aside—what had happened to her, the way she'd been raised was just not right.

She didn't pause in her retreat. Was almost at the stairs.

He remained seated. "I'm just saying…you were a kid who loved a parent who loved you. That was real." She'd given him the details for a reason.

He had to know what that was.

And it was clear that force wasn't going to do him a damned bit of good at the moment.

The fact that it had become his immediate reaction to getting things done was one of the reasons he'd walked away from the only career he'd ever wanted.

She turned. Holding her purse strap with both hands, she said, "I was driven to find more connection like I had with him. To find my mother's side of the family. Last year, without my father's knowledge, I entered my DNA into a family-finder database. But because we were so close, and I trusted him implicitly, I felt guilty and told him what I'd done. And unknown to me, he put an immediate watch on the company's databases."

Her tone held no inflection at all. Her face was turned toward him, but she seemed to be looking through him more than at him.

A well-played ruse? One of his fortes.

This didn't feel like that. But even if she was as good at acting as he'd become, he needed to know where she was leading him.

"My older sister, Savannah, has been looking for me my whole life," she said then. "She grew up in witness protection, believing that our father had been murdered by whoever he'd been about to testify against in his job with the

IRS. And believing that I'd been kidnapped. She's a lawyer now, and partner, heading up the legal department, in a nationally renowned firm of experts. She'd spent her whole life worrying about me and entered her DNA, but not her contact information, into the same site as I did, allowing her to be notified if she had a match, but not notifying the other party. She knew of the danger, of which I was unaware. Her partners were unaware she'd ever had a different identity. But now in the know, they're in full protective mode."

The way she'd delivered that last statement, as though a warning, had his attention. He took note of the fact. He'd know all there was to know about the firm before he slept that night.

"But back to where I was, when Savannah came to California to find me, her partners didn't know that she was part of the witness protection program. Like me, she'd been forced into keeping secrets for twenty-four years. But she risked her own life, risked leaving protection, risked losing the partners who are her friends and only family to travel to California to make certain that I was okay. She thought I'd been adopted by a wealthy family and just wanted a glimpse of me, to know I was happy, and then she was just going to go. She had no idea who Eduardo was—criminally or biologically." She paused then. Shook her head. Clearly remembering things she wasn't saying. She just stood there like a statue, as though she wasn't real.

A sense of urgency washed over him. He waited for it to pass. But he couldn't let go of the fact that he needed Charlotte Duran… Nicole Compton…to stay a while longer.

If what she was saying was true…

Then what?

He was done.

Out.

But he had a stable full of horses—and the people they were being trained to help—to protect. If there was any chance his past life could bring evil to his doorstep, he had to know about it. To prevent it from happening.

"You mind sitting back down?" he asked her. "I'm getting a crick in my neck." More like he didn't want her swaying on her feet. He saw the woman's strength. Admired it.

But she looked like she'd had enough.

Maybe even too much.

She didn't immediately do his bidding. Seemed to be weighing pros and cons of whatever was on her mind.

He wasn't sure if it was a good thing or very bad when she finally took her seat.

He was going to find out why she was there. How she thought he was involved. But it had to be some pretty bad news to keep her from getting the hell away from him, when clearly that was what she most wanted to do.

He didn't blame her. He spent a lot of his time wishing he could get away from the man he'd become.

Nicole raised her gaze to his, and he saw life there again. And a boatload of regret. Something he'd seen in his mirror far too many times. "Eduardo was onto her," she said. "He put hitmen on her. Fortunately, the first bullet missed. After that, she knew to protect herself."

The firm of experts. Meant the sister was better than just good at her job. "You said she's a partner in this firm...and a lawyer what does she do, exactly?"

"She travels all over the country, taking on specialized cases. She has a team of lawyers who work with her as well, on a case-by-case basis depending on specialties."

Good to know. Or not.

Lawyers weren't at the top of his list of potential people he wanted getting close to his life. He'd always worked under direct orders. Was protected against prosecution.

The thought of jail time wasn't what bothered him.

It was the much larger judgment and form of justice— the opinion of society, largely shaped by lawyers—that was the problem.

"So she got her firm involved, and they brought Eduardo down?" He needed to get to the end of the tale. Her hour wasn't up yet. He felt like his time was.

When Nicole shook her head, Harc settled back. Wholly analytical again. For the moment.

"You know a guy named Mike Reynolds." Statement, not question. Still not a connection he was free to admit to.

"Why do you say that?"

"I first knew him as Isaac Forrester. My bodyguard."

Harc was privy to the information. Hadn't been sure she was.

Now she had his full attention. Would have had it an hour ago if she'd started there.

He'd done it, then? Mike had succeeded where Harc had failed? He'd be damned if he wasn't happy for the guy. He'd respected Mike. Had trusted the FBI agent more than anyone in his own agency.

"Mike had no idea about Savannah's relationship to me and wasn't sure how she was involved with Eduardo, but after she was shot at, he had her under FBI protection. Without her knowledge. She just thought he was a bodyguard helping her."

Harc knew the drill. Had been undercover in various forms since he'd graduated college. Was under guise right then, as he sat back as though just a rancher at the end of his day, listening to story. When, in fact, she had his full focus.

Critically.

He was filing pieces in places where they might or might not fit yet, but he wouldn't know unless he tried.

Puzzle building was what he did.

"She eventually told him that I was her sister. That I'd been kidnapped. She didn't tell him about being under witness protection, though, thinking she was protecting us all from whoever our father had been about to testify against."

But Mike wouldn't have told this Savannah woman who he was.

Yep. Been there, done that.

Mike had had a job to do. He'd been there to bring down Eduardo Duran. Not to reunite long lost sisters.

"I...unfortunately...chose then to rebel for the first time in my life and rigged security so that I could sneak out in the middle of the night just to have a day or two of alone time."

He almost sat up straight. Maintained his relaxed position through instinct borne of years of life and death training.

Right when her father was on the verge of being brought down—though she'd yet to tell him how her sister showing up had helped Mike get the job done—she suddenly decided to slip away?

Too much of a coincidence.

And he'd figured out how Savannah's presence had been the missing piece that had allowed Mike to bring down the guy that multiple US agencies, and international ones as well, had been after for two decades. Savannah had told him about her father's murder and sister's kidnapping, and Mike had put it all together with the ages and timeline of Eduardo's life as they knew it.

The FBI agent had detected another "too much of a co-incidence" situation.

In another life, Harc and Mike might have made good work partners.

And none of what he was hearing was leading him to understand why Charlotte Duran had sought him out.

Unless…was Mike in some kind of trouble? Was someone holding him hostage? Or worse?

No way Harcus Taylor could turn his back on that one…

His thought was interrupted as Charlotte—he just couldn't stop thinking of her as such—said, "My disappearance put everyone in a panic, for very different reasons. Eduardo thought I'd been taken to get to him. Savannah thought she'd brought the past to my doorstep as well as her own. Mike thought Eduardo was behind my disappearance…"

He got the picture. Had heard enough of the blow by blow. Needed to know the end.

"In the end, Savannah and Mike worked together to find me. At an FBI safe house Savannah told me who she was—who I was."

Right. Too clean. "And you believed them?"

"Hell no!" The woman's tone, the look in her eye might have been part of the act. His gut told him it wasn't. "But once I was facing the DNA evidence my sister showed me…no," she shook her head. "Backing up… Savannah told me I'd been kidnapped… I knew I wasn't. When we first came to the States, I told Eduardo that I had to visit my mother's grave. When he told me that the cemetery had been vandalized and my mother's grave was no longer there, I freaked." She stopped, looking at Harc, this time as though she was really seeing *him*. Talking to *him*. As though him being the one listening to her made a difference. "I insisted that we get a DNA test. I had to know he was my real family. That I wasn't really alone in the world.

And I took it one step further. I took things out of his bathroom for DNA samples and paid out of my own money to have my own independent test run, too, in addition to the one he had done for me."

She'd known. Some part of the girl had known that something wasn't right. She'd been fighting then.

Had finding out that Eduardo was really her parent—conceivably the only family she had in the world—turned her? Was that when she'd become his partner in business? Using her skills to help her father's illegal dealings remain invisible to authorities looking for proof to arrest and prosecute him?

Because he knew she'd done so.

No matter what she had to tell him, he'd seen the proof of her work himself.

"When I told Savannah and Mike that Eduardo was my biological father, all hell broke loose. Mostly within Savannah. She'd adored the father who'd been murdered when she was seven. Had spent her life grieving him.When it became apparent that not only were Savannah and I sisters but that our father had faked his own death and somehow become billionaire Eduardo Duran, I knew what I had to do," the woman continued, not batting an eye as she held his gaze. "While Isaac, Mike, and Savannah got in touch with Sierra's Web, my sister's firm, I called my father, told him how I rigged the technology to get out of the house on my own. I said that I was sorry, that I wanted to come home but would only do so if he'd quit trying to control my life so completely. He agreed immediately, and I was back home that night. With Sierra's Web's involvement, along with local police and the FBI, Eduardo was in custody by morning."

Wait. What? "You turned in Eduardo Duran? They let you go back in there, knowing the danger…"

She shrugged. "It's like I told Mike—I wasn't under arrest. I was a free agent. And if I chose to go to the home I owned, there was nothing anyone could do about it."

Harc's respect for the woman rose another notch. Even while he looked for the hook, the hole in her logic. And found it. "You made a deal…"

Mike had accepted Charlotte's help with an agreement that she wouldn't be prosecuted.

Harc would have done the same.

Watching the expressions flash quickly across the woman's face, there and gone, Harc didn't know what to think when, ultimately, she shrugged and said, "I don't blame you for thinking so, but no. I didn't know, at first, that I was a suspect in Eduardo's dealings, but quite frankly, I wouldn't have cared one way or the other. When you're faced with finding out that your entire life had been a lie, having people think wrong things about you seems like child's play. Of course, people aren't going to believe in you. You don't even have anything to believe about yourself."

You don't even have anything to believe about yourself.

Her words cut deep. Not aimed at him at all. But hitting him directly in the heart.

And Harc had to ask, one more time, "Why are you here?"

Then, before she could answer, he got up and walked away without looking back.

He didn't believe her.

She didn't blame him.

But she was pretty sure he was going to help her. And after recounting her story, telling it aloud to a stranger who hadn't followed the case over the past three months, Nicole was more convinced than ever that she had to pursue the course she'd set.

It was her only hope for life ahead.

Using Mike's name had been a last resort. Something she'd promised herself she wouldn't need to do.

Something she didn't have his permission to do. Not that, technically, she needed his nod to tell her story, but if she hoped to be in his good graces in the future, she should have given him a heads up.

Same with Savannah and Sierra's Web.

But she wasn't changing her mind. She'd made her choice to put herself on the line, not them. The world wouldn't lose a whole lot without her. But without Sierra's Web and agents like Mike, a whole lot of people's lives would be one hell of a lot harder.

A couple of minutes passed before Harcus Taylor returned and sat. Saying nothing.

He'd asked why she was there. "I'm getting to my reason for seeking you out," she told him after running her self-check to make certain she was still happy with her previous decisions.

Finding a confidence she hadn't known was still within her, she rested her forearms along the chair in which she sat and said, "First, you should know that Hugh Gussman, my father, took a plea agreement. There's not going to be a trial."

The ex-agent's brow rose, his eyes widening. "The night that I went home, he agreed to turn over all his files, to testify to what he'd done in exchange for his right to life." He'd been a bit more verbose in the moment. He'd needed to know that Nicole could see him anytime she needed him. Wanted to see her. To see his grandchildren.

Fat chance of that.

She'd come to a different realization over the past few months. He'd known he was cooked. Wanted to spare himself the public humiliation of a trial. And had needed to make certain that he was not only going to escape any possibility of the death penalty, but he'd negotiated terms for what he'd determined were necessary to his safety in prison, too.

She hadn't stuck around to hear that list.

"He didn't want any more investigation into his endeavors," Taylor said aloud what Nicole—and she figured others—had determined. No one had mentioned it in her presence before.

Cocking her head, she said, "Case closed."

Except that it very much wasn't.

The tall-enough-to-be-intimidating, well-muscled, and in-perfect-shape man across from her raised an eyebrow as he said, "It's not closed, is it?"

He had his guard up. Which told her he didn't trust her motive for being there. And what she was going to have to tell him wouldn't give him reason to trust her.

But first, "Does the name Arnold Wagar mean anything to you?"

The single blink of his eyes gave her her answer. No matter what came out of his mouth. "Why are you asking?"

At least he hadn't sat there and lied to her. Not that she'd have held it against him if he had.

Taking a deep breath, she forged ahead with parts of the speech she'd originally planned to deliver upon arrival.

"The night of Eduardo's eventual arrest, Isaac… Mike… stayed close to me. But there was a period of time…minutes…when I was alone in the room where he'd set me up for any further interrogation or confirmation to information agents were gaining as, in another part of the house, various law enforcement heads were getting evidence from my father. As you can imagine, Eduardo didn't immediately capitulate. It took hours of mental manipulation and weeding through tidbits of truth to find the lies beneath before they had enough to arrest him…"

"… You were alone in the room," Harcus interrupted her.

Rescued her was more like it. The nightmare was always there. Showing itself to her. Over and over. Chronic remuneration.

She swallowed. Acknowledging that she'd been putting off the next part. Had tried on all kinds of ways to get what she needed from him without disclosing what she'd done. None had worked for her, and she knew, sitting there, that Taylor was only going to give her one shot.

"I hacked into Mike's computer files. I had to know the extent of what they had on my father. Of what he'd done. I saw a report that you'd written. About a year before Savannah came to find me you'd infiltrated an illegal arms dealing ring of a scope never seen before. You were certain Duran was the kingpin, and you'd infiltrated a sect that you thought was close to the top. You were due to…"

"… So, yes, the name Arnold Wagar does ring a bell." Harcus Taylor's interruption held rudeness, for sure. And irritation. But there was more. She couldn't read him as well as she'd learned to read most people—through Eduardo's tutelage, of course.

But she knew one thing. That look, the tone, the way the ex–CIA agent's nostrils were flaring…she had him.

He wasn't going to be able to walk away.

Chapter 4

He'd been due to cross another agency's agent. To risk a good man's life. To make his next move. Not to close a case. Or bring down an international illegal-arms ring. Just to get one step closer.

Not that Mike's report would have said as much. No, it would have read more in the lines of Harc being due to meet up with his contact.

The only way to get through that gate had been to prove his loyalty to the wrong crowd. By exposing one of his own.

He could run. He could hide.

The truth was there. Known not just by him but by others.

He'd done what he'd been ordered to do. Didn't matter that he'd managed to protect the other agent as well, that he'd saved the guy's life. That had been sheer luck.

And they'd ended up gaining nothing. The meet had been a setup.

He'd lost credibility with other agencies. But more importantly, that night he'd lost total credibility with himself. He'd done other questionable things. When he looked back, he could see how he'd compromised his ethics one little step at a time. Always justifying his actions with the knowledge that, ultimately, he was saving lives. But that last one…seeing the look in his compatriot's eyes when he'd outed him…it was a look he was never going to forget.

Charlotte Duran—most assuredly the woman sitting across from him, one who'd been setting him up since she'd arrived on his property, was a Duran through and through—watched him like a hawk eyeing her prey.

A hawk that was going to be very disappointed if she thought he'd walk one more step in shades of gray to save his own ass from being exposed by what she knew. If she thought she was going to blackmail him with the knowledge she'd illegally gained, she was in for a major letdown.

"So, what do you want?" he asked. Taking the initiative was almost always good. Spoke of confidence in his ability to handle the meeting. Of strength. Both of which he had plenty.

In his case, it also spoke of a lack of patience. Something he was running dangerously low on. He didn't like being played. Or put in a corner.

Didn't like that his six months out of the field had taken away some of his edge.

"You'd been following Arnold Wagar for six months before, by your admission, you walked away."

He crossed his arms. Gave one nod in her direction.

She continued. "I didn't see enough on Mike's computer to know your full connection to Wagar or Eduardo's criminal empire, didn't have a chance to read your full report, but the date of your first mentioning the new player on the field, Wagar—I'm certain of the date because it was my birthday—was the same day I told my father about having entered my DNA into that database."

Not a coincidence. She had his attention.

"And on the same day that Savannah got notice of our biological connection, Eduardo called me into his office and told me that Arnold Wagar had asked his permission to marry me and he'd granted it."

His sudden harsh intake of breath was unintentional. And got her attention.

After a visible swallow, she said, "Over the next week after my father told me I was engaged, his refusal to accept anything but my complete capitulation to his plans, in spite of the fact that I told him the man gives me the creeps, is what drove me to leave home that night."

Wagar was why she'd come to him.

He got that.

He saw an open door. And had no intention of walking through it. Wagar had been the man he'd been supposed to meet his last night on the job.

But…

Nicole—Charlotte—whoever he was dealing with leaned in toward him across the table—interrupting his thought before it could lead him astray. "Think about it, Harcus," she said.

And he held up his hand. He knew. Didn't want to think, much less hear about it. Didn't want to get sucked back in. "I go by Harc," he said inanely.

She didn't seem to hear him as she continued in the same tensely animated tone. "Everyone thinks, and all visible records show, that Wagar and Duran just connected over the past year. That Wagar was new to the scene. His family owns a portfolio of profitable, tax-paying companies, including a family-run winery that shipped expensive and very exclusive product all over the world. He was, ostensibly, in the US to expand the family business." She shook her head, and he heard what was coming. After the official account. Heard and didn't want to know.

He shook his head. Held up his hand.

She just continued anyway. "In his testimony that night at the house, Duran admitted that he'd been shaken since hearing that I'd entered my DNA in that database. He'd begun looking for a way to secure my future. Wagar was it. He offered him a deal—marry me with a prenup that gave me half of the Wagar fortune if Wagar divorced me, and in exchange, Wagar's family got a partnership in Duran's legal entities. It all made perfect sense. Turns out, it was too perfect."

She wasn't going to stop. Was going to sit there and look him in the eye as she played her ace card. So he just said it, "They've been connected since the beginning." The words burned his throat. "And you finding your sister, her finding you was the one thing that could expose them."

"Savannah and I talked about Eduardo being so eager to marry me off to Wagar. And so urgently. They wanted me so tied to the situation that when they got rid of Savannah, I'd be forever one of them. It was Eduardo's biggest mistake. It drove me away from him for the first time ever. I left home. If not for Isaac... Mike..."

She let the rest of the sentence lay between them unsaid.

Didn't much matter. Harc could easily finish that sentence. What he couldn't do was let her talk him into getting into the fray again. Not even with the information he had stored in his photographic brain. Information that could help her.

Help her put away a lethal criminal?

Or help her help Wagar, by giving her the critical information that would let the two of them know what parts of their vast business holdings to destroy. It was possible that Duran had been successful, emotionally if not legally, in tying Charlotte to the plot. Perhaps she'd been clued in all along. Was only playing them all with the poor-lied-to-girl-in-distress act until she could join Wagar somewhere.

Had the old man taken the fall for his daughter and her partner in business?

Stranger things had happened.

Hugh Gussman had faked his own death, entered the world of crime in a hugely successful way—and he'd taken his year-old daughter with him. The fact was key in getting into the fiend's head. To understanding not only the choices he'd made but what had driven them, which would lead them to what might be happening in that very moment that they didn't yet see.

And not at all his concern.

Or his job.

Charlotte tapped the table. He looked up, met her gaze as she almost whispered, "He's still out there. Not only running what's suspected to be the world's largest illegal arms consortium, but who knows what other international branches of Duran's empire as well? We only know what Duran told us about his illegal dealings, which was far more than anyone apparently had on him."

We? Us?

A beginner manipulation tool to make him feel a part of things. Reeling him in.

No.

Or...

We, not *I*. *Us*, not *me*. Was Mike working with her? Had the agent sent her?

He sat up straight. Put his hands on the table. "What do you want from me?" Each word was distinct.

"I want you to help me stop him."

He almost laughed. She couldn't be serious.

"I'm sure your sister and her firm—and Mike, too, for that matter—would have a lot to say about that."

Her look was open and clear as she nodded. "That's why I haven't told them."

The woman might've been of above-average intelligence in some areas. Technology for one—he'd seen the results of her work, which was why she'd been on his radar once upon a time—but at the moment she sounded like an innocent, protected little kid who had no idea how the real world looked.

He trusted that version least of all.

"We have no credentials, no source of ongoing information, no team to back us up..." He started with the most obvious.

"...and that's why we might succeed where others fail," she interrupted. Then said, "Humor me just another minute."

She'd glanced at her watch. Which prompted him to look at his own.

Her hour had just ended. She'd known? Had she set some notification on her watch? Had it vibrated?

"I can't make a life or become...anybody I'd ever want to be, a decent human being...knowing that innocent people are being shot by illegally obtained guns. Whole communities are wiped out by them all over the world."

He didn't need the lecture. He knew way more than she ever would. Had seen one or two of those communities firsthand.

The women and children...

No.

He'd tried.

He'd failed.

And lost himself in the bargain.

Even if she was for real, being sincere, he had nothing to offer her.

* * *

Harcus Taylor put his gun on the table. Sat back, arms crossed. "What you have is sheer coincidence."

She was losing him. Time to clone her father, put on pressure like she'd never done it before. She would not go to her grave having done nothing with her life but be her father's daughter.

The irony in her needing to become more like him to escape the life he'd trapped her in wasn't lost on her. It fueled her in a way she didn't really even understand.

Whatever it took. She had to stop Wagar.

"Those dates being exact aren't an accident. They link Wagar to Eduardo prior to the past year. Wagar first hit your radar the day that I told Duran about the database, Harc." She might have stumbled over the too familiar way to address him if she hadn't been all Duran in that moment. "What tipped you off to him that day?"

He looked upward. Not quite rolling his eyes, but close. "We knew that large shipments of arms were flowing out of El Salvador. In ways that couldn't happen without someone powerful paving the way. An informant led me to Wagar as the paver. Said that he'd been in touch with the kingpin. Seemed viable since he was Salvadoran. And then he was suddenly relocating to the US, to San Diego, where Duran was based. When they started hanging out together, we were certain we were getting close."

She frowned, then, as a wave of sheer panic shot through her. "Isaac knew this?"

Mike. Not Isaac. Isaac was the fake persona she'd trusted with her life. The man who'd saved her life. Mike was the FBI agent who was engaged to marry her older sister.

Oh, God. What if Mike was still playing them? Watching them?

Harc sat forward, arms on the table again, the back of his hand touching his gun. "No. The CIA isn't always big on interagency communication. In this case, my call. I was deep under. We didn't want to take the chance of communications being intercepted."

Her gaze on the flesh that was touching the gun barrel, she asked, "And?"

"It turned out in the end, after six months of undercover work, to be a false lead. And during the interim, while I was doing what I do, the agency did some checking of their own. They found nothing on Wagar or his family."

Well, that explained his attitude.

"What if I told you I don't think it was a dead end?"

He shrugged. Rolled his eyes. Shook his head.

"The first time I looked at your file, I was overwrought. I'd just found out…well, you know what I'd just found out. I saw that date that Wagar popped up on your radar, my birthday, knew it was the day I'd told Duran about the DNA database, and blanked on it. Just sat there, dead inside, until I heard Mike coming back and quickly backtracked so he wouldn't know anyone had been accessing his computer."

His eyebrows raised. As she'd expected them to do. "There was more than one time," he correctly guessed.

His fingers moved to the other side of his gun.

Ready to grab it?

At the moment, she wasn't the least bit fazed. She was so het up, she didn't care what he did with the damned thing. She needed his help.

And without it, she didn't have a life to go back to. He'd confirmed that he'd really just heard Wagar's name for the first time the very day she'd told her father about the database…that the lead had turned out false six months before Savannah had come to find her…

"Six months before Savannah found me was when Wagar started coming to the house," she said then. "Right after you dropped the case. Prior to that, Eduardo and I had seen him at social events. The two were acquainted, clearly, but he was never in our home those first six months."

Taylor sighed. "All coincidence, Charlotte. Nicole." He corrected, meeting her gaze for a second as he did so.

"Right, but this isn't. Your file mentioned a series of computer backstops that prevented file originality to be discovered."

He nodded. Seemingly bored. If she wasn't noticing the way his fingers were bouncing up and down on the table by his gun. And it hit her.

The weapon wasn't there to threaten her. It was there to calm him. As though having the thing close gave him some kind of comfort.

The possibility prompted her to lean in again. And her voice was softer as she said, "I can get to the origin."

His lips pursed.

He wasn't committing to anything, but he was no longer looking bored, either. His fingers on the table had stilled.

It was time.

"When everything was first happening, I was a mess," she told him. "Trying to stay calm and coherent to help put Eduardo away forever, to be there for my sister, to somehow grasp that I even had one…but as the weeks passed and things settled down, that date in your file kept bothering me. There'd been more there. Something I'd kind of recognized. Just a couple of symbols that were appropriately placed, but…that unread rest of the file kept playing with me. I couldn't let it go. What if, you know?"

Harcus's eyes widened. No other muscle on the man's body moved in any visible way.

"I offered to program both Mike and my sister's firm's computers with extra protection against hacking, giving them all a level of security nobody but us would know. I think they felt so sorry for what I was going through that they let me do it just to humor me. I'm damned good, but they've got an entire team of tech experts that have as much skill and experience as I do."

Harc's fingers started to thrum.

Watching them, she said, "I hacked into Mike's secure files again. Well, your file. And found what I was afraid was there. You mentioned the files with no obtainable sources... but those files you refer to, weren't ever produced."

With his chin jutting, his hands still, he said, "And you think you can find out the files' source?"

Finally. He was looking at her like she had something of worth to him. "I know I can."

"You expect me just to hand over highly classified material to *you*? That's assuming I even have access to it."

Emphasis on the *you* hurt. A lot. And yet she couldn't blame him a bit. That emphasis was exactly why she was never going to have a life if she couldn't right wrongs that she'd been a part of creating.

Whether anyone would ever believe that she hadn't had any knowledge that her programming skills were being used criminally, she couldn't say. Didn't even let herself hope that far ahead.

What she'd bet her last breath on was that he had those files. A guy like him...no way he'd walk away unless something so catastrophic had happened that he'd been at breaking point. And when you reached that point—you didn't turn your back without protecting it.

"I wrote the code that's stopping you from finding the source of those files when I was fourteen years old."

He went still. As in frozen. He didn't blink. He just sat there. His eyes on her, but almost unseeingly so.

"And not that I expect you to believe me, but I had no idea that my father had shared it with anyone or used it at all. And there's no telling what other of my stuff he's shared, or more likely sold to others…" She was rambling. Needing him to offer her the lifeline she'd come for.

Without so much as glancing her way, he got up, picked up his gun, and left her sitting there alone.

Again.

Chapter 5

He had her. One way or the other, the next little bit was going to show him why Charlotte Duran was at his ranch, ruining his day—and his mood, too.

Which was precarious at best on a good day.

Unless he got back to find her gone. He wanted to believe that was the best-case scenario.

As it was, after locking himself into the fire-safe secure room he entered through the newly laid floor in his kitchen, then unlocking the first of three safes, entering that one to head to a side wall before unlocking another safe, Harc reached into unplug one of the laptops stacked neatly in a wooden tray made specifically for the purpose of holding computers. A tray that fit into the specially made leather case for transporting them, too.

He didn't grab the case. Or the shelves. Just the one computer.

Locked the safe. Double-checked it. Let himself out of the walk-in safe, locked it behind him. Checked it. And then, verifying that the scope that would show him the kitchen was all clear, headed back up to daylight.

The security could be overkill.

It wasn't that he valued his life all that much. He just wanted to know that he could save it if he had a mind to do so.

Mostly he was protecting the information that, in the wrong hands, could blow up the world. Or the equivalent thereof.

Things the agency had never known about.

And, God willing, never would.

What it said about him that he was trusting a known criminal's daughter more than he trusted the men and women who'd been on his own team, he didn't want to contemplate.

But he wasn't really trusting her.

Testing her was more like it.

He didn't welcome the slight lift of relief he felt when he saw her standing on his front porch, looking out over his property. Standing by the chair he'd assigned her. Not the stairs that would take her to her car and away from him.

She had guts.

Determination.

Whatever her reason for seeking him out—it was strong enough to be worth risking her life.

All qualities he'd have looked for in the past when assessing operatives.

She wasn't one.

And he wasn't assessing.

Old habits died hard.

His approach was silent. A talent he'd perfected.

She turned before he'd made it out of the house. Reclaimed her seat. Was positioned primly, gaze straight ahead, hands folded on the table in front of her when he joined her.

"Your shadow gave you away," she said conversationally when he pulled out the chair he'd vacated and sat.

"I didn't ask."

"You need to know who and what you're dealing with.

What you can count on. Eduardo Duran had me convinced that, because of our wealth, I was a constant target and had to be aware of all things at all times. I went through my first training course at ten. Have repeated every year since. With harder challenges added each time. I can rappel. Stay alive in the wilderness for days. Swim for miles. Walk blindfolded out of a forest, relying on my other senses to avoid dangers planted there…"

He waited for her to take a breath before interrupting. "Too bad he didn't teach you how to keep yourself from rambling on when you're nervous."

She didn't flinch. He'd give her that. Holding his gaze steadily, she said, "I'm not nervous." And then glanced at the computer he'd carried out. "Fueled by determination, I'm overeager."

He filed away the piece of information. Whether true or false, the fact that she'd rather be seen one way than the other told him things about her.

Not that he needed to know except to get himself clear of her. Permanently.

Opening the computer, he left it off. Slid it over to her.

Held out a hand to it and said, "Do your thing."

He could have signed on, taken her right to the file that would show him if she'd been telling the truth about the code. Had actually planned to do just that when he'd walked out on her and during his journey back to her, too.

But the way she hung on…made him want to push her.

He wasn't proud of the fact. Didn't like it. But he accepted it. Right along with the rest of his unpleasant qualities. Denying his faults wasn't going to help a damned thing.

The idea was to try to correct them. To improve.

Which was another reason he had to get the woman out of there. She brought out the worst in him.

She flipped on the high-tech expensive laptop without looking for the switch. Just reached and clicked. For the next five minutes her fingers flew across the keys. He lost count of how many times her right-handed little finger hit Enter.

When the game had ceased to be fun and he was spending more time picturing the beer waiting for him in the fridge than keeping his guard up, he asked, "You ready for the password?"

The glance she gave over the top of the laptop was very clearly a query as to his sanity. Or intelligence. *As if*, it seemed to say.

And then she said, "I had that thirty seconds after you handed me the device. A combination of the most worn keys. Doesn't always work. I got lucky." She spoke slowly, as though her mind was elsewhere.

At the rate she'd been typing, with him sitting there assuming she'd been trying password attempts, she could've been anywhere on the device at that point.

He'd intended to take her right to the file that could prove truth or lie to her claims. But let her glean what she could from the laptop. There was nothing there that mattered to him. It was his gaming computer.

While he'd been undercover, he'd copied Wagar's impenetrable file into a new document. Had replaced everything he understood with made up information, leaving the code as it was. And then copied that file to his gaming drive.

He'd been working on decoding it ever since.

As a game. A puzzle. On the nights when the past tried to haunt him.

Another couple of minutes passed before the laptop closed with a definitive click. Charlotte sat there, arms folded across her chest. Glaring at him.

"Very funny."

She wasn't leaving. But she looked like she wanted to. What was keeping her there?

Her life quest, as she'd like to have him believe?

How could he ignore the possibility she was telling the truth? He was on a similar, and yet very different, journey of his own.

If what she said was true, she'd been unaware of the crimes in which she'd inadvertently been involved.

He'd made conscious choices to commit his less than stellar acts. With good motive, of course, he reminded himself.

The same thing he'd told himself every single time he crossed a line the man his parents had raised wouldn't have crossed.

The justification was true. But it had become little more than an excuse to allow him to press too far. And so, it fell far short of exonerating him in his own court.

"I can show you the file you might have wanted to see," he said, knowing that she'd found herself up against a plethora of complicated gaming code.

"I found the damned file, Taylor," she said, her tone anything but sweet. "And it traced right back to you. Very funny. Ha. Ha." She hadn't moved, though. Arms still tightly folded, she remained in her chair. Glaring at him. "I'm assuming I passed whatever test you just put me through. Now, you going to help me or not?"

She'd found the source of the implanted dummy document. Something he had not been able to do. Even knowing the source.

She'd surpassed the test. Not that he had any intention of letting her in on that little tidbit. Not ever. He'd known she was good.

Had underestimated how good.

He wouldn't make that mistake a second time.

His gun was digging into his hip bone again. As it did when he sat with it shoved into his pants instead of its holster. Pulling it out, he set it back on the table. "Just for more grins, what is it exactly you're envisioning me doing to help you?"

"I was hoping you'd help me figure that out."

Uh-huh. Right. He stared her down.

Her gaze was dead serious.

"Come again?" he asked.

"If you've got copies of Wagar's files, which I suspect you do, I can get to the source. I can find where they originated from. How many various routes they traveled and maybe find specific players, too, but that last bit is less certain. From there, depending on what I find, I've got some ideas which I'm happy to run by you. I'm a women's studies lecturer, with a bachelor's degree in that as well as psychology and another in technology, who grew up playing with code to offset the boredom of being locked on a gorgeous estate with a parent who had me mastered in survival training. But I know bupkis about criminal minds or getting the better of them. From what I gathered from your file, you're a master at both."

He'd been, not he was.

She was offering him the one thing he'd needed to possibly bring down one of the world's most wanted men. Her father.

A better man than he had done that.

And he was thankful every day that Duran was done.

But was he?

The man was in prison. There for life without parole, he'd guess based on the scope of the fiend's crimes.

And if Charlotte… Nicole…was right, if Wagar had been involved from the beginning…they'd imprisoned a man. Slowed down his operation.

But they hadn't stopped it.

Putting a hand on his gun, he met the woman's gaze openly. Sincerely. "You need to get to Mike Reynolds," he said. "And Sierra's Web."

He'd heard of the firm. From multiple sources. Hadn't ever worked with them. But this one needed all hands on deck and if she had a familial in like she said...that was the time to use it.

"Today. Immediately. Tell them what you told me." His tone was growing more urgent with each word. He couldn't help it.

Couldn't pretend her missive didn't matter.

Or that the shaking of her head wasn't about to explode the top off from his.

No! No! No! She had him on board going in the wrong direction. Completely opposite to where and how she had to travel through the dangerous maze in front of her.

Quietly, eerily calmly resolved to leave, disappear, and handle things on her own, Nicole said, "I can't do that."

Just that. Nothing more.

His gaze burned with tension. "What do you mean you can't do that? You pull out your phone and dial."

She shook her head. "Let me rephrase. I refuse to do that. I'm doing this without them. And as I'm the only who can get into Wagar's records, that decision is mine to make. Either you're with me or you aren't. That's your choice here."

Hands on the strap of her bag, she prepared to stand. And go.

She'd played her cards.

If he folded, they were through.

There was no more discussion to be had.

He shook his head. Frowning as he said, "Why?"

She frowned right back at him. "*Why?*" There was irritation in the intonation of her delivery. She didn't bother to hide it. Not with him lobbing his own tension at her.

With his gun on the table, he leaned forward, forearms on either side of the weapon. Almost as though he was cradling it.

The odd posture softened her heart some, for no rational reason. She met his gaze and wanted to understand the man, not just the words, as he said, "Why are you doing this?"

"So I can live with myself. My work is being used to allow horrible people to debilitate good people, to finance criminal operations that ultimately destroy innocent lives…" She broke off at the continual shake of his head.

"Why are you forcing me to help you?"

She shook her head right back at him. Quickly. Continually, the touch of her hair moving around her a testimony that she was real. Alive. Awake. Not caught in a nightmare that just wouldn't end.

"I'm not forcing you," she told him as she stood. "I came to make a request. Period." Purse on her shoulder, she headed for the stairs.

"If you run away at every obstacle, you'll be dead before you get to the second one."

What the hell! More angry than anything, at that point, she spun around.

The man was watching her, his gaze clearly assessing. And she returned to her seat.

With his arms crossed, the gun alone on the table, he said, "Why *aren't* you seeking help from the authorities?"

"When officials get involved, things have to go through channels and protocols have to be followed."

He gave her a nod on that point.

"Gussman worked for the IRS. He managed to get away with more than two million dollars. He claims he worked on his own, but even I don't believe that one. Which tells me that there was, and maybe still is, someone high up, with an official position, involved. Maybe government officials. Maybe a mole in the FBI whose been quietly making personal investments all these years. Perhaps even someone who's being blackmailed and will continue to be until the entire operation—Wagar—is out of commission. We blindsided Gussman the night he was arrested. *I* blindsided him. I'd like to say it was because I was brave enough to face the possibility that he'd turn on me—claim that he had no idea what I'd been up to, blaming at least a lot of it on me—but that thought didn't cross my mind until weeks later…"

She paused. His gaze was softer as he waited. Not pushing her. Just…being there.

"Had he not made the deal to confess that night, others would have become involved. And I likely would have been indicted. It's also plausible that whoever had been paving his way would bury him to protect themselves. Regardless…we don't know who might be involved, so the less anyone knows about this, the better."

"The more likely you are to stay alive."

"If I don't stay alive, Wagar's illegal business ventures not only continue, they continue to grow." He wasn't going to come up with an argument strong enough to stop her course. Nor was he going to turn his back on her without consequences on the table.

He'd called her back.

The thought gave her hope. She pushed forward. "Because we don't know who else could be involved, if we go the official route, we risk someone tipping off Wagar. The more people who are involved, the more we run the risk that he finds out he's being investigated. He'll have all kinds of security protocols in place that would alert him."

"Which they'll do as soon as you start poking around."

She sat back. "Yep. That's the point. Difference is I wrote the code. I can manipulate it so that he can't figure out who's watching him."

"If he knows you wrote the code, he'll suspect you're behind it."

She nodded. She hadn't kidded herself about the risk involved in her undertaking.

"He gets to you before you get enough evidence against him, following however many trails you'll have to follow, figure your way through however many dead ends, then the whole thing is moot."

"That's where you come in."

"I thought you just wanted my files."

"I need your files most."

The man looked like he was playing a game of table tennis. He was finding sport in the conversation that was a matter of life and death to her. "Our best shot is to get him before he knows he's being looked at. Right now he's got to be feeling like he dodged a bullet. He's going to be looking for wolves at his back, yes, but also flourishing—with Eduardo gone, he has the profits all to himself."

The man just linked his fingers together and dropped them to his lap at that one.

"He knows Charlotte Duran," she told him. "He'll have a set of expectations where she's concerned. I'm no longer that woman."

His brows raised. "How do you mean?"

"I no longer have the confidence of being well established or well loved, which tends to make one feel secure and makes one soft. I have no illusions, nor am I still living under massive delusions. I don't have to keep up appearances or bite my tongue for Father's sake. To please him. Or to make him proud of me. I'm angry. And I have very little to lose."

Taylor leaned forward again, those arms around the weapon a second time. Something she believed to be a good sign. "You didn't have money of your own?"

He might've been good at assessing people. Watching the nuances. She was equally so. Him, to do his job and keep himself alive. Her, because she'd been bored a lot and had had nothing better to do than mentally dissect those around her. Different lives. Same result.

"I do have money," she told him. "I've sold a few computer programs that continue to pay me nicely."

"And your guest lecturing? I saw some pretty hefty stipends for those."

He hadn't just noticed her during his time investigating Wagar. He'd paid some pretty close attention. Rather than making her uncomfortable, the knowledge solidified her belief that he went over and above to notice everything in his effort to get the job done.

"I donated every dime," she told him. A couple of teaching gigs, with regular salaries, had grown one of her savings accounts, though.

"And Sierra's Web?" The question came at her like a slam at the tennis table. "Why aren't you going to them?"

She didn't even flinch. "Two reasons. One, I realize that I could be indicted, depending on how cleverly my code has been used. I had nothing to do with anything illegal, but it could look like I did, and while I'm willing to take the risk for myself—hoping that I'll be able to prove what is and is not my work—I will not risk my sister's livelihood, the firm, her friends' reputations by having them involved. In any way. And just so you know, Savannah made the same choice when she came to find me. She came alone. Her partners all thought she was on a cruise. Two, I will not put my sister in danger again. She's a lawyer, not a cop or a trained agent, but if she knows what I'm doing, she won't stay behind a desk."

So there. The thought was childish. Felt good anyway. She let out a deep breath for good measure.

"So that leaves Mike."

She held his gaze. "He's FBI, official. We aren't going that route."

The man's eyes narrowed.

"He doesn't know I hacked him, and I'd rather it stay that way," she admitted.

The intensity in the gaze pinning her didn't lessen even a little bit.

"And he's engaged to my sister, okay?" Information he could get for himself in less than a minute if he was half as good as he seemed. "I will not be responsible for bringing any more pain to her life or risk damaging his reputation for letting himself get hacked by his possibly criminal soon to be sister-in-law."

"And you don't want him to know he can't trust you."

The words were uttered softly. Making her feel emotions she'd promised herself were frozen. Making her weak, prone to manipulation.

Denying them made her more so. Looking Harcus Taylor straight in the eye, she said, "He *can* trust me. I did what I did to protect him."

And then, when the gaze coming at her didn't waver, added, "But I don't want him to think he can't."

The words earned her a slight nod. A softening in the looks coming at her.

And with that, she shut up.

Chapter 6

He couldn't do it. Could not let himself get sucked back in. He'd given himself his word. Any hope of trusting himself to do the right thing, trusting himself enough to allow others to trust him rested on him keeping that word.

And what about letting a determined, broken young woman venture out by herself to do something it had taken professionals around the globe years to even halfway do?

Was that right?

He could put in a call to Mike Reynolds himself. Tell him what Nicole had told him.

And possibly jeopardize the mission, and with it, the best chance they had at getting Wagar and everyone else involved.

Based on what he'd just seen Nicole do, she could feasibly not only expose Wagar's ways and means but every player in every channel connected to Wagar. Sellers. Buyers. Transporters.

Cartels.

If she had the time.

A plan to keep her safe.

And a way to draw the criminals out of the worldwide holes they were hiding in. What if he was able to not only know names—many of which would be aliases—but could convince people, in the flesh, to expose themselves?

No.

She wasn't going to seek other help. She'd forge ahead. Get herself killed. And Wagar would be full owner of the one thing that the world had to bring him down.

Unless Harcus Taylor went back to work. Albeit sans credentials. No agency backing. Without team support.

If they failed, he could end up in jail.

Worse than the prison in which he currently resided. He'd lose the fresh air. The freedom to come and go. Most importantly, he'd lose his horses.

And they, the wild and hurt, would lose him.

Unless he took them with him.

He shut the thought down before it could prosper. But not without having to acknowledge that his mind was already on the case.

He could turn down Nicole Compton/Charlotte Duran, but he'd go to bed at night and dream the case. Or worse, lie awake with it eating at him.

Because the opportunity was clearly there. Just waiting on him.

What kind of self-respect could he possibly hope to have, what kind of man could he ever be if he didn't try?

He looked up at her to see Charlotte's wise gaze watching him. The brilliant woman was old beyond her years.

Eleven years younger than him, and yet in some critical ways she'd been through so much more than he had.

Which—considering his career, the things he'd done, the drug and war zones he'd lived within—was saying a lot.

"If I do this…" He heard the words before he'd given them permission to be heard. Stopped midtrack, the sound of them ringing a warning in his ears. Loudly. Insistently.

She continued to watch him. As though his decision didn't matter to her either way. A con? Or she'd just reached the point where she was okay within herself to go it alone?

"If I do this," he started again, consciously choosing his words second time around. "It's done my way. Other than what you do coding wise, I'm the boss. When I say *bark*, you bark like a dog. Got it?"

With raised brows—as if to ask, Who didn't know that?— she nodded.

He didn't like easy capitulations. More times than not, they bit you in the butt. "I'm serious, Nicole," he told her, his hand reaching for his gun.

To shove it back into the waistband of his jeans. "The first time you go against my bidding, I disappear."

Her mouth tightened. "Your bidding in terms of our safety and how we proceed in our efforts to get Wagar and anyone else involved," she stated in that tone that held no inflection whatsoever. But a hell of a lot of steel.

Getting her point, he held her gaze as she nodded. And then he said, "You have absolutely nothing to fear from me otherwise. I have never touched a woman without her consent, unless it was to catch a body that had been shot before it hit the ground."

A bit dramatic. But true nonetheless.

"Nor do I get off on ordering anyone around." He checked himself. Then added, "What you're proposing here could lead us into a situation where one second is the difference between life and death. There will be no time to think, to discuss. You act or you die."

She didn't even hesitate, nodding before he'd finished. And then said, "I understand."

That ready capitulation…just did not sit well with him.

Assessing her, he was already second-guessing his decision to consider going back to work for one last case.

To finish his last case.

"I was raised by Eduardo Duran, Harc." Her tone was dry as she spoke to that which he'd been thinking but hadn't expressed. "I'm very well trained in doing what I'm told when I'm told in the name of my safety."

And with those words—with the seemingly privileged and so abusive life inherent within them—she had him.

Feeling as though she had a train barreling down her back with every hour that Wagar was free to change anything he was doing before she had a chance to find him, Nicole suggested that Harc turn over access to his files immediately.

And the words she'd issued so confidently just moments before, agreeing to do his *bidding in terms of our safety and how we proceed in our efforts to get Wagar*...and... *I'm very well trained in doing what I'm told when I'm told in the name of my safety* came back to bite her.

Shaking his head, he stood and asked her to accompany him, leading her down the stairs and across the yard to one of the barns.

"We don't touch those files until I've got a plan in place to deal with whatever comes next. We need to be ready to act immediately, and we don't know to whom, what, or where they might lead us." He strode laconically toward the largest barn, the nicest-looking one, though they all had what looked to be fresh coats of brownish-red paint.

"We also have to be ready in case Wagar is alerted when you access whatever your code is keeping secret. He'll have protections in place—we have to count on that."

And while she hated the sense of standing at a precipice

with the wind blowing and not being able to do a damned thing but wait before she could try to deal with the threat, he had her. On every level.

She'd given her word to him for good reason. And his explanations were spot on.

"I should get a hotel for tonight," she said then. She'd booked the dude-ranch vacation she'd told her sister she was taking. The place was only a couple of hours' drive north. She could still get there before dark if she left soon.

"It's best if you stay here."

There? Alone with him? The thought didn't alarm her nearly as much as it probably should have. To the contrary, the idea of remaining within his sphere felt better than not doing so.

"The court document you showed me, changing your identity—it's dated today."

She nodded. And noted his attention to detail, too.

"Who else knows?"

She shook her head, then looked over at him, striding beside her as she said, "No one. That's the point. I have to hit now. Charlotte is no more. And Nicole isn't yet in the global system. Everything's legally changed. Driver's license, credit cards. But it won't have registered anywhere yet. I'm told it could take a day or two and up to a couple of weeks. That's the time I have to act without being able to be traced in any way." She might not be a trained agent. But she was smart. Savvy.

And determined to succeed.

She was going to be an asset to him.

In spite of her privileged and very sheltered upbringing, her healthy bank account, she was not soft.

"I purchased the SUV last night from a private seller

with a free and clear title signed over to Nicole Compton. Paid cash. Registered the tags online today."

"What about your sister?"

Feeling a sharp pang, she almost bumped into him as she shook her head again and said, "She knows I plan to change my name. She's expecting me to change it to Nicole *Willoughby*, the last name registered to my missing person's report through witness protection."

They were almost to the barn.

"As soon as I get to work on those files, I suspect Charlotte Duran could be on some dangerous radars. And for a short time, her identity will still pop up as valid."

"And when she doesn't, it could take some time before anyone figures out she became Nicole Compton," he added, pulling open the barn door, holding it for her.

His tone had changed. Almost as though he was humoring her. Or engaging in wishful thinking. She glanced at him as she passed by him to enter the tall wooden structure, and for a second there, it was though he was giving her something she'd yearned for her entire life.

Unconditional support.

Once on the job, Harc didn't turn off. Even in his sleep he was prepared, ready to jump into action instantly upon awaking. He also had never embarked on an operation without full intel, and…most importantly…a plan.

The lack of both hindered him. It wasn't going to stop him. Undercover, plans changed in seconds. Without notice.

His plan had just changed.

Nicole didn't ask why they were in the barn. She didn't say anything as she kept pace with him on the way to the post where he'd left Imperial tied up.

Her silence as she kept up with him won her some regard.

Other whinnies greeted them, though, and until his mind found some solid ground, he introduced her around. Making introductions at every one of the ten occupied stalls they passed. "This is Scarlet," he said, rubbing a hand down the older girl's nose as he passed. Carmine, Sangria, Fire, Mahogany were all in a row and received exactly the same attention.

"Over there are Vermillion, Burgundy, Ferrari, Salmon, and Brick," he told her as he stood in front of Mahogany's stall. All his horses were used to traversing rugged territory—and staying alive in it for days, too. Mahogany and Imperial were in the best shape.

"You ever do any riding?" he asked Nicole as he led the three-year-old mustang out of his stall and over by the post where Imperial stood grazing on hay.

She'd made her way to Imperial. Was rubbing a palm along the boy's flank. "As a kid in El Salvador," she told him. "The ocean estate wasn't intended for a barn or live animals."

She said the words as though repeating what she'd been told.

Probably as a kid. When Eduardo had used her citizenship to move them to the States. Maybe if the fiend had bought her a horse, she wouldn't have been so desperately lonely. Driven to entering her DNA into a family-finder database.

Harc entertained the thoughts as he pulled a saddle off the rail and lifted it to the gelding's back. Then tightened the cinch, and pulled his mind from places it had no reason to dwell. Charlotte Duran's upbringing being a key one.

He'd taken her on. From there, all that mattered was getting the job done. Her past, her future, her name, even, didn't matter.

Except where it helped them reach their goal.

Charlotte had disappeared off the face of the earth. He had to be sure to call her Nicole.

"Here, put these on." Reaching into a cupboard, grabbing a pile from the women's small cubby, he held out the denim and flannel to her, balanced on one palm. And when she took the clothes, he nodded toward a door that led to private restrooms. With doors that locked.

He could have had her duck into one of the empty stalls. His instincts were tightly guiding him not to go casual with her, even for a second.

Maybe he didn't trust her.

Maybe it was something else.

He had no time to question that which didn't directly impact his next steps.

Imperial was re-saddled by the time Harc's guest reappeared. In jeans that were snug as today's fashions were more apt to be. She'd tucked in the hem of the flannel shirt. Let the rest flop over the waistband.

And the two-inch heels…

"There are boots in those cubbies over there," he told her, pointing to a corner several yards away. "And socks in the drawers underneath."

And when he caught himself watching her walk away, he swung around, filling with dread. Was he ready to work again? Did he have it in him to be part of a two-person team when the other person was not a suspect? Or was not believed to be attached to one?

The question gave birth to a thought that calmed him some. Nicole Compton was most definitely attached to a very bad person. More than one of them. Her father, of course. But she knew Arnold Wagar personally.

Only difference between the current case and ones from

the past were that the attached person with whom he was working knew who he really was. Knew his goal.

And shared it.

Maybe, just maybe, he was going to get one last shot at redeeming himself in his own eyes by staying solidly within the boundaries of morality. Ethics. Legality.

And still closing the case that was haunting him.

It had been years since she'd been up on a horse, but Nicole figured out pretty quickly that, for her at least, riding a horse was like riding a bike. Once you'd learned, you knew how.

Her knees pulled in against Mahogany's sides as they started up a fairly steep slope and again as the strong horse trotted over uneven area at the top of the climb.

She had no idea where they were going. Or why. Just hoped it wouldn't be too far from the ranch. There was still another hour or so before sunset, but she did not relish being out in the mountains when that happened.

Had she been anywhere else, with anyone else, she'd have said so.

Instead, she rode. Left him to his silence. Until he broke it.

"Stirrups fitting okay?"

They'd been out twenty minutes. Had covered not one second of easy terrain since they'd set out. The question was coming a bit late.

She refrained from saying so. Just called out, "Fine."

Truth be known, the ride was treating her well. Being in the mountains, in the middle of nowhere, with no one watching her felt…a little like she imagined nirvana might feel.

Except, maybe, for the silence of her companion. And

since he'd broken it, she asked, "Mahogany? Imperial? Vermillion, Burgundy, Ferrari, Salmon, Brick, Carmine, Sangria, Fire, Scarlet? And I saw a sign when I pulled in that said we're on the Crimson Ranch. You got a thing for the color red?"

His shrug was as visible from the back as the front, maybe more so with only the big broad shoulders visible in his upper back for distraction. "How do you know I didn't just purchase the ranch and horses already named?"

She'd done her research. That was how. But she said, "The ranch sign was new."

If she earned any points for observation, he didn't give any indication of that fact. If she was hoping to impress him, she'd better get herself in line damned quick.

There was nothing about what lay ahead that left room for any emotional blowback from her. That could come later. After they'd succeeded, and she was alone. They'd reached a flat land. Wide enough for them to ride side by side.

She wasn't upset when Harc slowed and waited for her to catch up with him. An evening ride to unwind was fine. If they didn't have a million pounds of work pressing down on them. Time to get to it. Even if just verbally.

"If you're going to call the shots, maybe you should get at it," she told him as she and Mahogany drew parallel to him and Imperial. The horses turned their heads toward each other, almost in greeting, and then their noses immediately pointed forward again.

He didn't even give her that brief of a glance as he responded to her comment with, "Why the last name Compton?"

None of his business. And no reason to make it an issue, either. "It's my sister's last name. Savannah Compton."

Let him make something of the choice. Poor little rich girl, still clinging to a need for family.

She glanced his way, daring him to think less of her, and watched as, with no change of expression, he just kept moving forward. Seeming to take in the expanse of miles all around them. And it dawned on her. "You knew."

Of course he had. The man would have done at least minimal checking during the couple of times they'd been apart.

If he hadn't already been familiar with the firm. She hadn't asked if he was. He hadn't said.

"You know who all of the partners are," she said, keeping her gaze on him.

His nod to the side could have been acknowledgment. Or simply a lack of caring to respond.

She got him calling the shots. He was the expert at field work. But there was no reason she couldn't be clued into some things. Like what he knew about her. Her life.

Whether or not he was even working on a plan, yet.

"Why all shades of red?" she asked him. Pushing him for no good reason. But feeling some better as she did so.

"No more shades of gray."

Succinct. Almost cryptic. But oddly enough, she got it. Agreed a thousand percent.

And rode without further question, soaking in the moments of glorious, strength inducing natural peace he was treating her to, as they turned and headed back toward the ranch.

They'd returned to flat ground, the barns were in sight, when Harc rode up beside her again. "You're good in the saddle. You'll do fine."

What the hell? Do fine for what?

And the ride? It had been some kind of test.

Obviously he hadn't just been passing time, using it to enjoy a nightly ride before they dove into work mode.

Even knowing to be on her guard where taking him at face value was concerned, she'd underestimated him.

And wasn't sorry to find that out.

Or to be there, tackling the challenge of her life, with him by her side.

Even if he was a bit of a grouch.

Chapter 7

It wasn't much of a plan. But Harc walked back to the ranch house beside Nicole with some first steps in mind.

He'd planned to tend to all of the horses alone, figuring her for heading back to the house on her own—giving her time to search whatever she could find in his home to show her that there was nothing of note. But she'd opted not only to brush, feed, and water Mahogany while he took care of Imperial but to help him check food and water for the nine other stalled horses as well.

To butter him up?

To thank him?

Or just because she was the kind of person who chipped in and helped wherever she could? One who didn't like to just sit around and do nothing?

She'd asked some about his daily routine the few times they'd passed in the barn—apparently assuming he took care of all the horses on his own, wondering why he had so many.

He'd told her about his part-time staff. A sentence about the fact that the horses were all wild mustang rescues of one kind or another. Leaving out the part about the dude-ranch weekends he was branching into with some of them.

And failing to mention the horse-therapy program that

was his lifeline at the moment. Literally. Not financially, but as a way to build a decent life for himself, contributing to the betterment of society without much chance of taking wrong turns.

"You have a lot of visitors?" she asked as they traversed the gravel drive.

The question seeming to come out of nowhere he said, "No." Then asked, "Why?"

Motioning toward her body in the dusk, she said, "The clothes. All sorted by size. Just something you inherited when you bought the place?"

He could leave it at that.

Except that it would be a lie, and he was done crossing the lines. He couldn't afford to bring any more gray areas into his life.

"I've got a couple of trained counselors bringing in people for horse therapy. Teenagers mostly. Many aren't ready to get on a horse, don't come prepared, so we keep the supplies here." Hearing himself spouting the words pissed him off even as he was saying them.

He'd just gone over the fact that he'd done well to keep his business to himself all evening. Maintaining personal distance between them.

And then he'd gone and spilled his closest beans all over himself.

He couldn't just tell her about the dude ranch? Visitors came without proper attire for that, too.

Bracing himself for a barrage of questions, he was surprised when all she said was "Who does the laundry?"

Not that it mattered, but "I do."

They'd reached the house. He wasn't sure if that was a good thing or bad. He was putting her in an upstairs bedroom. The one at the end of the hall furthest away from the staircase.

He'd be maintaining his usual position on the couch in the living area.

With the television on.

But before he could ship her off, they had to eat.

"Single-portion frozen dinners for supper," he told her as he held the kitchen door for her. Watching as she took in the old metal leg Formica topped kitchen table with four matching chairs. Something else he'd seen in a magazine. And paid too much for.

The rest of the kitchen was nothing to notice. Linoleum flooring that needed to be replaced, except that with its creases and cracks—some a product of laying separate squares, some of age and mis-care—completely hid the lines he'd cut in the floor for access when he'd had the basement re-dug five feet deeper than it had been.

Without a word, she walked to the old refrigerator, pulled open the small freezer compartment door on top. "There's nothing here."

There was, actually. Bags of ice.

He walked into the adjoining dining room, the hardwood floors that needed to be refinished completely bare but for the long freezer covering one wall.

Opening it, he was planning to just make the choices and take them out to the kitchen but heard her behind him.

Smelled her slightly flowery horsey scent.

Then felt her beside him, too.

"Wow" was all she said as she stared. "I don't think I've ever seen this many frozen dinners in one place. Not even a grocery store."

He was betting she hadn't been to all that many of those.

Duran would have had a huge household staff.

Still, she seemed game as she studied, then made a choice of Salisbury steak, mashed potatoes, green beans, and a small square of brownie.

He'd been expecting her to go for the rice-and-vegetable medley that he picked. Wednesday night was healthy-eating night. He had his rules. Didn't waver from them.

Just made living easier to know ahead what was coming.

"I had this for the first time a few weeks ago," she told him, smiling.

That momentary look transformed her. And shook him. Suddenly he was in his kitchen with a gorgeous, warm, happy-looking woman.

Instead of the beautiful but prickly genius who'd shown up on his doorstep to ensnare him.

And had been successful in doing so.

"Mike bought groceries—he's pretty much moved into Savannah's house with us—and he had had a couple of these. I was teasing him…he dared me to try one…and I've had three more since."

She was still grinning as she looked up at him. The expression faded immediately. A closed look covering her face.

She'd shown him someone she hadn't planned to share with him. Or anyone?

And he…for a second there…had he actually been jealous of the FBI agent?

A ludicrous thought if ever there was one.

Laying his dinner on the scarred countertop next to the oven, Harc turned the button to preheat the oven. Reached into the refrigerator for the beer he'd been thinking about earlier. Said, "Help yourself to whatever you want to drink." And pulled out his phone as he had a seat at the table.

He didn't look in her direction. What she chose to do was on her. He was working. Not babysitting.

Until he heard something drop hard onto the floor, and his gaze shot to where she'd been standing, leaning on the counter. Having *not* helped herself to anything to drink.

A phone lay on the floor. She was already bending over, picking up the device, and as she righted herself, he caught a glimpse of skin that had gone completely white.

His chair scraped against the floor with a rough thud, as he shot up and over to her.

Looked over her shoulder to read what was on her screen. When she held it out to make his doing so easier, everything within him tightened.

A reminder that he was on the job.

Not entertaining a guest in his home who'd never had Salisbury steak as a child and had developed an affinity for it as an adult.

He was viewing a live newscast with closed caption.

Something about a cabin that had exploded that evening. He came to the words mid-sentence, but there was something about a gas buildup in a pipe...

No indication where the explosion had happened. Even what state.

"What is this?" he asked, reaching for the phone. She didn't try to maintain control over it. Let it slip away to him as though glad to have it gone.

"The dude ranch where I was meant to stay." Her voice wasn't weak. At all. But it wasn't anything he'd heard that day, either.

It was like she'd seen a ghost. One she recognized. Would fight against. But one she hadn't expected to see.

"I typed in a search for it, to see if I could do a late

check-in online, just to make it looked like I was there…" Her voice weak, her words faded off.

With his thumb moving rapid-fire, he scrolled past the live video to read the article accompanying it. The explosion had happened a couple of hours earlier. Only the one cabin had been damaged. No one had been hurt.

And Nicole was still white as a sheet.

"I made the reservation in Charlotte's name. Because I couldn't pay cash. I used Charlotte's credit card. I'd expected to stay there tonight. It should have been safe. No one knows I was contacting you. I made certain no one followed me out of Phoenix. I made the appointment with you from a library, borrowing a stranger's phone. No one would have any cause to know that I was contacting you or what I was telling you…"

Her words fell off there. She was looking at the device in his hand. Not him.

Not panicking.

Just looking more shaken than she had in the short time he'd known her. A hell of a lot more.

"There's no way anyone could have known I saw your file…"

In between watching her, he was still scrolling. Reading. "There's nothing here that indicates foul play," he finally told her. A gas line into the cabin had exploded. An insurance and public relations nightmare for the ranch owners, to be sure, far more than that if the cabin had been occupied, but still…

"It's cabin seventeen…"

And he knew. "You reserved cabin seventeen." He stopped, watching her, then when she looked at him, when he saw the disbelief in her gaze said, "Or rather, Charlotte did." The designation meant nothing to the facts.

But his instincts had told him clearly that it meant something critical to her.

So he said it again. Just to be clear. "Charlotte was targeted. Not you."

And sleeping arrangements had just changed.

They'd be spending the night together. In the basement.

Time was of the essence. And wasting.

Someone was out to silence her permanently. Harc and
anyone else could think what they liked. She knew.

Had spent the past three months waiting for the other
shoe to drop. The one with Duran written on it. Any Duran.

And she was it.

With Eduardo in prison and all his interests frozen, those
he'd talked into investing with him over the years were all
out of luck.

She didn't blame any of them for thinking that her money
should be theirs. Lawsuits had already been filed.

And there were those who wouldn't be content to wait for
the legal system to play out. Those who didn't trust the system to work in their favor. And those who cared about what
they were owed, not about the law. Or doing things legally.

In the event that assets from Eduardo's legal dealings
were freed—which was to be expected—any monies left
after paying investors could revert to Charlotte. Which
would then legally process over to Nicole.

She'd already signed away her rights to it. She didn't
want a cent from that man. If there was a way, she'd give
him back the genes he'd given her, too.

These were all thoughts she kept to herself as she sat at
the table alone and ate Salisbury steak. Swallowing wasn't
easy. She did it anyway. She needed her strength.

Both mentally and physically. If she didn't feed her body, her mental faculties could suffer. And they were her only hope.

Harc leaned against the counter as he ate. Fork in one hand, phone in the other. At the rate his thumb was moving along the screen, he was doing nothing but scrolling. Whatever he was looking for appeared to be impossibly difficult for him to find.

He finally set his phone down to pick up his container of food and scoop up the last bite, and while his mouth was still filled with that bite, she said, "I need the files." He stopped chewing, and she sped forward. "The sooner I get to work, the more chance I have of finding what we need before he finds me. From there, it's all yours. I'll turn over all I find, help you decipher whatever you need, go deeper, anything. And when you have no more need for my skills, I disappear."

She'd turned the planning over to him.

But her job had been clear from the start, and the idea that someone could be after her was no longer just theory. The sooner she got to work, the better chance that she'd be able to finish it in time.

She hadn't considered herself to be in danger until she'd hacked into Mike's computer and had read Harc's file on Wagar. And even then, the danger wasn't inherent until Wagar got notice of a breach on files protected by code she'd written.

"It's possible that there was just a gas leak that caused an explosion," she said aloud the thoughts that kept playing in her mind. She so wanted to believe the cabin being hers had been just a coincidence. "But we can't afford to ignore the possibility that it wasn't," she finished.

Charlotte was targeted, not you.

"And the thing that's off about that is that Wagar doesn't

know that I'm onto him yet. No one does but you. So has he been watching for an opportunity to get me all along, without involving FBI agents and Sierra's Web experts—which would bring down a whole lot more heat on him—or is someone else out for me, too?"

"Who stands to benefit by you being gone?" he asked.

"Some women's shelters in San Diego. My assets are in a trust that goes to them. But they aren't privy to the information."

"Who else knows?"

"Just my sister. She's a lawyer. She set it up for me. And drew up the paperwork for me to waive any inheritance or insurance benefit I could receive from Duran, or monies he tries to gift me, if any of his legal assets are left intact. It all goes to the government to be dispersed among families who've lost members to illegal gunfire in this country."

She wished she had copies of it all on her phone. Should have thought to include them in the things she'd brought with her. She needed to know he trusted her legitimacy if she was going to fully trust him to try to keep her safe on the job.

And paranoia wasn't going to serve her or anyone else. She'd come to Harc Taylor. He wasn't out to get her.

Throwing his empty container into the trash, he reached for hers. "You done with that?"

It was cleaned out except for the brownie. She nodded. Pushed the disposable dish toward him. Watched as he took the brownie and finished it off in one bite.

Feeling a few seconds of relief, of anticipation as she looked toward finally getting her mind on the files she knew he had stored someplace, she watched from behind as he washed silverware and dropped it in a drying receptacle. Alongside what looked to be several days' worth of other utensils.

She managed to stave off a sense of looming oppression during the next minutes as Harc helped her bring in her things from the car. Even got distracted by the fact that she'd be spending the night in the same house with him.

The man was drop-dead gorgeous. If you liked the muscled, rugged type.

She never had.

But seemed to be developing a fondness for it. She took in his thick wavy blond hair, the light stubble along his jaw, and the blue eyes…which were pinning her as she stood just inside the front door with all her belongings at her feet.

The room was bare except for a couch and across the large room from there, a large flat screen television set.

A table of sorts sat at one end of the catch. It looked like an old travel trunk, positioned on its end.

Surprised at the bare-bone basics, she looked from the trunk to him.

"I found that up in the attic," he told her, as though his choice of side table was what she'd found odd.

"Your porch is gorgeous, almost to the point of elegant, but your house…has almost no furniture." And what there was looked ancient. As she said the words, the possible lack of a bed that night occurred to her. She glanced toward the stairs, leading up to what she assumed were bedrooms.

She'd just seen a partially burned cabin that she was supposed to have just checked into and she was worried about the ex–CIA agent's decor?

"I've been undercover most of my career. Rented a furnished place in DC during most of it," he said, as though that explained why he had almost state-of-the-art barns, filled with a small used clothing free store to boot, but hadn't bothered to furnish his home.

And as she stood there, waiting for his direction as to where she went with her things, she supposed the facts did explain the man somewhat. They gave her insight into what was important to him.

The realization settled a bit more of the tension inside her.

"I've spent my whole life in elegant mansions," she said aloud. A pampered, adored daughter who had only the control her criminal father allowed her. "I'd rather be here." The truth bore witness to her about herself. She was not only standing in Harc's living room of her own accord, she'd made every single choice that had brought her to that moment.

She was for real.

And…she had work to do.

Chapter 8

The basic plan had formed. Telling her about it was next on the agenda. Right after he quit putting off getting to it.

Nicole was right. With the cabin explosion he couldn't waste any more time. Nor could he leave the woman standing in a pile of her things in his sad and bedraggled living room.

"I don't entertain," he said, almost a warning to her of what was to come. He wasn't prepared for house guests.

And until he knew more about what they were facing, the few dude-ranch cabins that were ready for guests were out of the question.

"I'm not here to be entertained." Her quiet words drew his gaze to her, and he got stuck there. In the truth pouring out toward him.

She really wanted to be where she was. Danger and all. Because the wealth she'd grown up with, some of which she obviously still had, meant nothing to her. Righting the wrongs she'd helped her father and others commit was all that mattered. He got the message.

It straightened his backbone. "That's good to know because you're going to be sleeping on an air mattress in the basement tonight," he told her. "With me on one down there, too."

"You sleep in the basement?"

He considered the response a good omen for what was to come. She was more interested in him choosing the basement for a bedroom than in the fact that they'd be sharing the space.

"No, I sleep on the couch. The basement has been altered. It's more of a bomb shelter. A bunker, if you will." Other than the company he'd hired to help him build the thing, no one in the world knew it was there.

And right beneath the house.

Her dark eyes widened. "A bunker?" Her delight reached him with such force he almost didn't hear the words. "This is perfect!"

Except that it wasn't.

But he'd get to that.

Not used to sharing full details of any of his work plans with anyone—by their very nature they'd had to be fluid and had changed on a dime—he had to take things one step at a time.

He reached for her suitcase. "The actual space is quite small," he warned her. "I'm single. Didn't figure I needed much."

"I'm good with the air mattress," she told him, picking up the rest of her stuff. A couple of cloth shoulder bags that nestled with the soft-sided briefcase she already had on.

And a steel forty-ounce cup. She'd sipped out of it the second she'd pulled it from her car.

The forty-count package of bottled water she'd insisted had to come in was all that was left on the floor by the door as they headed to the kitchen.

As he carried the thing down the stairs and then the ladder that led to the actual bunker, minutes later, he acknowledged to himself that he could have saved himself the trip simply by telling her what was coming next.

He'd chosen to lug water to save himself from conversation that was coming anyway.

Because he wasn't ready to present a plan he hadn't mentally vented enough? Or because he was still…what?

Fighting the fact that any of the present was even happening?

Was still harboring some notion that he was going to back out?

Because he knew that he was in as much danger being in partnership with the striking Duran heiress as any other force he'd ever faced in his life?

The woman's intelligence, her determination, her willingness to face whatever fear, whatever danger, whatever inconvenience and hardship necessary to undo wrongs… were captivating him.

Had he gotten soft?

Was a lack of total detachment going to prevent him from succeeding with their mission?

Where Wagar was concerned he couldn't remain impartial. He'd sold his soul proving that point. Was working with Duran's daughter going to permanently prevent him from buying it back?

Dropping the water by the wall along the ladder, Harc's attention went straight to the woman sitting on an air mattress he'd pointed out but hadn't yet taken out of the box when he'd left her alone down there. The second mattress, across the small space from the first, was in the process of receiving air from the pump that had come in the box.

"I have a better pump," he said inanely, looking to the closet door to the right of the ladder. The one she was using had clearly worked just fine.

Why did everything she did right, every unexpected move she made rile him so? At a time when it was critical that he be at the top of his game?

"I'm far more interested in what's behind that door," she said, nodding toward the thick metal structure down from where she'd placed his makeshift bed. "A freezer?"

"It's made kind of like a walk-in freezer in a restaurant," he gave a second less-than-stellar response. She just looked so…okay…sitting there.

In a place he'd never really pictured sharing with anyone.

Though he'd purchased two mattresses. Two chairs for the small table. Two sets of linens and towels.

And as it had turned out, the decision had been a good one. He'd made a commitment. Had lives counting on him being at his best. "It's a walk-in safe," he told her. And then added, "We'll get to that shortly."

Pulling out one of the two armless chairs pushed up to the wooden table, he turned it to face her and sat. Bent until his forearms were on his thighs and looked over at her.

"We aren't staying here."

Alarm filled her gaze. "What? Why? What's happened?"

Shaking his head he said, "My communication skills aren't the best. I don't do this. Don't work jobs with partners."

Her gaze was no less intense as she repeated "What's happened?"

"Nothing." With a quick self-check, he phrased, "Nothing that I know of. We're here for tonight. You aren't going to be working from here."

He paused, waiting for her emotional reaction, and sat up straight when none was forthcoming. She was still watching him, he seemed to have her complete attention. And so he said, "As soon as you start in on those files, we risk Wagar being onto us."

She nodded.

"We have no idea how long it's going to take you to find everything we're looking for. How many layers of your code we're going to need to get through to even find what else you might have to decode or hack into."

She nodded again.

"If we stay in one place and Wagar pinpoints the spot, our time will be very limited."

Her expression was concerned but open, too, and he felt his first sense of a possibility that he wasn't on a suicide mission. Or sending her on one.

And he wasn't completely dreading whatever came out of her mouth as she opened it to speak. "At first, I was thinking that him coming to us wouldn't be a bad thing. We'd catch him red-handed." She paused, then said, "But after the cabin explosion…even if it had nothing to do with Wagar…we could be dead before we know he's onto us."

In the bunker, *they'd* be safe. But there were other considerations. "Anyone who is working here or is on the ranch for therapy and all of the horses would be at risk."

He could shut the place down. Board the horses. Stay in the bunker and start over afterward. Had considered the option. But… "Considering that we have no idea how high up Duran's—and now Wagar's—contact is, assuming there is one—and in my expert opinion, there had to be someone, somewhere and likely still is—or Duran wouldn't have capitulated so easily or taken all of the blame himself…"

"He was protecting me."

"Maybe. Somewhat. But why not roll on someone else? Let them take the heat? He surely had enough people in high positions within his holdings to have passed the blame…"

Her eyes narrowed. "You think his guilty plea was to protect someone else. Someone with power over him?"

The consideration couldn't be ignored. But he kept going. "With that said, our best shot at ending this isn't just finding proof to bring Wagar down but…"

"Finding the guy my father's afraid of."

"If we can." He'd thought himself capable of anything. Which had driven him to do…anything. "The point is we don't just want Wagar. We need to draw out everyone."

She nodded. Her gaze steady as she sat on that sheetless mattress and asked, "How do we do that?"

How the woman gave off a sense of inner wealth as she capitulated to a stranger, he had no idea, but he was drawn to her.

And started to consider that with her help, he actually could do the good he'd set out to do when he'd taken on the Wagar case.

When he'd joined the agency to begin with.

"I've got satellite boxes here. A dozen of them. As long as we have the southern sky visible, we'll get internet through them. The service is paid for—an anonymous blanket policy put in place a few years ago…" He paused at the lie that rolled so easily off his tongue.

"You know how to hack into the service," she said.

At which he nodded. And then said, "I also have burner phones and all the supplies needed to survive for long periods of time."

The words, which showed him for a man who did not live above board, didn't seem to faze her. If anything, they appeared to give her strength.

She was sitting up straighter. Appearing fully focused on him. Seeming to accept it all. "These mountains have been holding secrets and those who don't want to be found since the beginning of time," he continued.

Her mouth dropped open before she said, "We're going to hide out in the mountains?"

He nodded. "Not just hide out. I'm hoping, with the change in locations, to lure enforcers out to find us. And we'll know, when they arrive, who they are," he told her.

"Enforcers?"

"Every government agency in the US is protected by enforcement officers. We see who shows up, we have the best chance of finding out who sent them."

"You have a suspicion, don't you?"

He wasn't sure. Didn't disclose his ideas until he was sure enough of what he was dealing with to risk the exposure.

"At this point, I think any number of entities could be involved." Singly, or in partnership. "And because of that cabin explosion, we don't know who might be after you. I want to leave here before daybreak. And we're taking Imperial and Mahogany with us. I plan to have the ranch continue business as usual. I have employees in place to handle every aspect of what goes on here in the event of my absence."

"You planned for the eventuality that you might have to vacate."

Clearly. "I've been involved with the worst of the worst. You don't take that on, live that way, without developing a sense of possible doom."

Her expression softened. "You get that same sense when you realize you grew up with the worst of the worst." Her words were uttered softly. And completely without self-pity.

She understood.

And that was the moment when the last of his doubts fled.

Until their mission was complete, he was all in.

* * *

They were two people who had no happily-ever-after waiting in their futures. That was what she took from the conversation with Harc right before they'd packed and turned in for an early night. To get the last bit of sleep on a proper mattress they might have for a while.

He'd loaded saddle bags. Enough for both horses. Had had her load her personal things in a backpack she'd be wearing. They'd worked silently.

She didn't see any computers going into his things. But then, he'd taken a backpack into his freezer safe, so she had no idea what he was bringing from there.

All she needed from him was a flash drive with files on them.

As she lay there in the dark, she understood why the ex-agent had only the basics of furnishings in his home. He didn't intend to spend time there. Or share it with anyone, fill it with family.

Ever.

The porch was where he spent whatever relaxation time he allowed himself.

She could be wrong, but her intuition was well-honed. It came from having to vet everything in her life in terms of how it would appear to her so protective father. From the few friends she had to the lectureships she'd accepted. Even the companies she'd chosen to sell her software to had had to stand up to Eduardo's scrutiny.

And there was no way she was ever going to just be a normal person who could have regular relationships. Not with the baggage she carried.

She'd erased Charlotte Duran's name from the records. She'd never be able to erase the woman from inside of her.

One day in Harc Taylor's company had shown her the truth.

No matter if she cleared her name or not, no matter how many amends she made, she wasn't *mom, dad, and the kids* material. She'd been shaped, from birth, by an international criminal.

And couldn't ask anyone else to sign on to that stigma.

Not that anyone was lining up to do so, she reminded herself sleepily. Other than Arnold Wagar, she'd never been anywhere close to a proposal in her life. Something else Eduardo had seen to, she was sure. He'd teased a time or two that no one was good enough for his little girl.

Truth was he hadn't been good enough to allow anyone to get that close to her. As in, he'd had too much bad to hide.

"You still want to go ahead with this?" The voice came softly in the dark. She froze for a second, as though Harc could read her thoughts.

She'd thought him sound asleep, the way he'd talked about learning to sleep on the fly, to catch rest whenever and wherever he could—just before he'd headed into the tiny bathroom they were sharing after she'd done her own business there.

Debating whether she should just not answer, let him assume she was asleep, she considered the seriousness of his question.

And the fact that he *wasn't* asleep. "I do." Her tone was unequivocal. Not on purpose, but because that was how she felt.

"What's keeping you up?"

She almost laughed at that. Smiled a little. And said, "Other than the fact that I'm about to go on a dangerous mission with a CIA-trained agent in the hopes of bringing the wrath of hell to our hideout in the mountains so that I can attempt to repair some of the hellacious damage the man I grew up adoring has done?" She tried for levity.

Hardly made it to sarcasm.

"We aren't going to have a mountain hideout." He wasn't kidding. Not even a hint of humor coming at her.

He was awake because he was rethinking the plan? Or helping her altogether?

For a second, the idea of having an out brought relief. But only for a second. He could quit. There was no out for her. "What's changed?"

She'd seen no more about the explosion, but she had to believe that someone was already after her. Had probably been watching her for a while. Searching her name, watching her credit card. The first time she'd been away from Sierra's Web protective reach, and the cabin she'd rented exploded? At a time she'd likely have been in it, if she'd driven straight there after leaving Phoenix. And even if there wasn't someone on her tail, she couldn't live with herself unless she did everything she could to stop Arnold Wagar.

The guy wasn't just a partner of her father's. He'd put his hands on her after she'd told him quite clearly not to touch. Just hands on her shoulders. An arm around her. But there'd been threat inherent in that touch.

He was a man who would not be told no.

And would make anyone who tried to thwart him, suffer.

It had only been a matter of time.

Shuddering, she lay flat on her back, eyes open, seeing images of shadows where she knew the ceiling to be. Harc hadn't answered her.

"What's changed?" she asked again.

"Nothing's changed. The plan was never to stay in one

place. Hence multiple satellite dishes. We use one, leave it up and running, and move on."

She did smile then. "A trail of breadcrumbs," she said, picturing Wagar's face when the only report he got back was a photo of a small box. Or, better yet, saw it for himself.

Then he'd be as good as...her thought stopped midstream. She could not want to be with Harc Taylor because she believed he'd disregard all laws and kill the man they both hated.

"What happens at the end of the trail?" Her question held her fear. Tightly.

"Hopefully one hell of a celebration."

He hadn't known what she was asking. She purposefully hadn't made the query clear.

And in that moment, that lack bothered her most of all.

Chapter 9

Imperial was used to predawn rides. Harc had taken a lot of them in the eight months he'd owned the place. And the horse. Imperial had been his first. Purchased the day he'd closed on the ranch.

The horse had worked his magic on Harc before he'd even heard of horse therapy. That lesson had come when he'd looked into filling his barn with more wild mustangs. Imperial had been up for auction. He'd acquired Mahogany that way, too. But the others had all come from a horse-rescue operation.

They were rehabilitated animals who'd been injured in the wild.

They knew what it was to be in pain. To suffer alone.

As he pulled to the first flat ground they came to after their initial climb to get up into the range, Harc waited for Mahogany to take the couple of steps to bring himself parallel to Imperial, and then said, "How you doing?"

"Fine." No hesitation in the response. And...maybe even a note of anticipation.

"The plan is to start out slow," he told her. "In terms of my part of things," he quickly clarified. "I want the first satellite base to be close enough to civilization that our trackers think we're underestimating them."

"Arnold would simply put it down to the weakness of a pampered, spoiled young woman," she said. "I don't think he's aware of all the rigorous training my father put me through."

The words carried a wealth of information. Enough so that he knew he needed it deciphered. "Why do you say that?"

"He was certain that he could manipulate me by force." She sounded nonchalant, was glancing toward the rising dawn on the horizon as she spoke, but Harc froze.

"How so?"

"Let's just say he let me know that he could do what he wanted and I couldn't do anything about it. And I let him think that."

Ah. He kept his approval to himself, but it was there. Full force. But he focused on what wasn't. "Did he force you…physically in some way?"

"Not like you mean. We were outside on the back grounds. Isaac… Mike was watching from an upstairs window."

"And your father had cameras all over the grounds." He'd gleaned that from some of the things she'd said the day before.

"Savannah was out in a boat on the water," she said then, her tone soft again. "Watching through binoculars." She was smiling as she turned toward Harc, and in that moment, her face was lovelier than the dawn. "That was before I even knew she existed."

There was a lot more to the story. He wanted it all.

And knew that he couldn't have it. He was on a case. And could only allow himself information, awareness that pertained to it. Lest emotion skew his instincts.

Again.

Whether or not the man they were after had physically damaged her had been a need-to-know item. There could be residual post-trauma reaction showing up during the key showdown.

The rest was not pertinent to his getting the job done.

"By the way, I noticed my car was gone when we came out this morning. Where'd it go?"

He'd asked for the fob when she'd been getting in the shower. He'd been on his way up to check the grounds before he had her make the ascent.

"I had it driven up to the dude ranch you were supposed to be at, and then towed."

Eyes bugging, mouth dropped, she said, "You what?" There wasn't quite a yell in the voice, but it was close.

"If anyone gets on to you, as Nicole, they could trace it. It's best if someone finds it that they think your destination was where they expected you to be."

"You don't want them to know we're working together. That you're giving me access to Wagar's files."

He nodded.

And the subject just…dropped.

Once again, she'd surprised him.

They stopped midday. And while it had only been a few more than twenty-four hours since Nicole had left Phoenix, she felt as though she'd been away for weeks. Was already a different person.

What she was growing into remained to be seen.

They'd spent a good part of the morning crisscrossing back and forth across the same general area. Leaving plenty of evidence that someone had been there.

And that they'd gone back toward home as well.

Their stopping place had been accessed by pure rock,

leaving no tracks. The area could be pinged, but the exact location would be difficult to pinpoint.

Harc knew the mountains like a lot of people knew their neighborhoods. He'd already mapped out their daily travels, streams for water collection and fishing, stopping points, her working hours, their sleep hours, and meals.

As they settled into the cave he'd chosen as the one to protect them overnight—more of a really deep indentation in the rockface than a structure that wound back into the mountain—he pulled things out of his packs one by one.

Two blow-up air mattresses like she and Savannah used to float in the pool. "While you work, I'm going to be taking care of all other life-sustaining details," he told her. "Including inflating and deflating as necessary. I'm also going to be fishing, but I'll be within earshot." He reached into his backpack then. "I want you to keep this with you at all times." He handed her a small black electrical device. "It's a walkie-talkie so we don't burn up internet or cell battery needlessly. From this point forward, even when we're riding, I want you to have this clipped to you at all times. It runs on good old-fashioned batteries, and I have a pocket full of them." He unzipped a small pouch inside his backpack to show her the supply. "I intend to stay within bandwidth reach at all times."

Nicole was impressed, feeling stronger and safer, more hopeful that they actually had a chance to succeed in bringing Wagar down, with each item Harc pulled out of his various compartments, but she was filled with nervous tension, too. Needing to get to the files he'd promised her.

Show-and-tell was great, and probably necessary, but every minute that passed without her having access to those files was another minute closer to danger finding them.

He pulled out a couple of handheld, lightweight solar

charging packs, showed her how to use them. "We've got more of these, too," he said. "With only sunlight, it takes each one up to seven days to charge. They're all at full capacity right now. It's critical that we monitor them and keep them charging."

In the jeans she'd packed for a trip to the dude ranch, since Savannah had come into her room to chat while she filled her suitcase, and a lightweight long-sleeved shirt, with the riding boots Harc had given her bruising the sides of her thighs in her cross-legged position, Nicole stared over at the ex-agent. "You think we'll be out here more than seven days?"

He'd been reaching into one of the packs he'd hauled in, but stopped, with flannel-shirted arm still inside to look over at her. "I think being out here is our only reality until the job is done. We have no idea how long it's going to take, so we do what it takes to sustain ourselves long-term. We look to the case, every minute of every day, until it's done. We don't look toward where we go next."

He was teaching her. And she felt…honored. Ridiculous, probably, but true nonetheless. He knew who she was, what she'd come from, and he was giving her his respect, too.

The arm he'd shoved into a saddle pack came out, holding a couple of five-inch long cylinders with what looked like drinking lids on top. "These are our water filters. I'll boil water when I can, but when we can't these will work fine." He showed her how to attach them to containers that looked similar to water bottles. And how to easily clean the filters.

The next pack was filled with freeze-dried food. "Four and a half pounds and over seventy servings," Harc said, holding the pack open to show her the contents. "Just boil, let it sit for ten minutes, and you've got a meal."

She nodded. Getting a bit frustrated at the lengths he was going to stall giving her the files she needed. He'd said he was taking care of all the generalities while she worked.

He had water pouches, in the event that they were trapped and couldn't collect their own. A first aid kit that contained things she'd only seen in the survival training Eduardo had insisted on. A folding shovel. A multipurpose tool.

As he pulled out the various pieces of the tool from its base, he told her what each one did. And she stopped him, nodding. "I'm fully versed in those," she told him. "Eduardo's training, remember?"

He stopped, looked over at her, blinked, as though remembering who she was and why they were there, and then, hands on the thighs of his jeans where he knelt, he nodded. "Sorry—I've taught a lot of these classes..." He handed her the utility tool and continued with, "And I'm always on my own when I'm actually on the job."

She understood, relaxed some. "You're good," she told him. "Continue on." She was humoring him but glad, suddenly to be doing it.

His next glance was all frown. "What are you going to do if I get hurt? Or fall over a cliff?"

Or was shot. His message hit her with a force far stronger than irritation, frustration, need to get to files, or anything else that had crossed her mind as she'd been sitting there.

He hadn't been holding a seminar. Wasting time. Or putting off getting her to work. He'd been protecting her life. Potentially saving it.

The things she'd taken for granted under Eduardo's care.

"I guess I *am* a bit of a spoiled socialite, huh?" she asked with a horrible taste in her mouth.

His gaze sharpened, and the couple of feet between them

seemed to disappear as she was certain his warmth enveloped her through that glance even before he spoke. "You are nothing like that," he told her. "You're aware of those around you and of any residual you might be carrying from your past life. You care. And you have the courage and determination to do whatever it takes to repair, too."

He'd known her less than two days.

Still, some of what he'd said resonated deeply inside her. As truth.

And she knew that if she died trying to destroy Wagar's reign of terror, her life would end on a good note. Because she'd have given it up in an effort to right wrongs.

He'd saved the weapon pack for last. Nicole was clearly aware of the powerful sidearm he carried. He'd had it pretty much in her face the day before.

But he had a smaller, very powerful nine-millimeter for her, too. And plenty of ammunition. Pulling out a silencer, he loaded her gun, stood, and asked her to accompany him outside.

Untying Mahogany and Imperial from the tree he'd left them on, he walked them around the mountain a few yards, retied them, and came back. Handed her the weapon, gave her full tutelage. And when he was done, asked her, "You feel comfortable trying to shoot it?" he asked.

It was the last training session of the day. He'd planned them all the night before, while he'd lain beside her in his bunker, assimilating the job ahead. One he'd taken with no forewarning or briefing whatsoever.

The first one on which he'd have another human being, a noncriminal good person, with him at all times. A partner of sorts.

She'd nodded in response to his question, held out her

hand for the weapon. He was waiting for her to look at him. For verbal assurance.

The glance she shot him was squinty-eyed, and not because of the sun—not only was she wearing sunglasses, but the sun was behind a cloud. "You feel comfortable?" he asked a second time.

"I do." She sounded like she was making a vow.

To him.

He shook his head, clearing his mind. And handed her the weapon. Pointed out to the left of them. Across a deep ravine. "See that tree over there? The one with the fallen branch hanging by the trunk? Aim for the leaves on that downed part."

With the gun in one hand, her other hand holding her gun wrist, she held the weapon down by her thighs, looking out. Her long hair was tied back, giving him a view of the slenderness of her neck. A sight that made her appear fragile.

What in the hell was he doing working with her? Taking on her quest?

Getting her killed?

The thought chilled him so much he turned to reach for the gun. Stopped instantly as she raised it. And shot.

Not at the leaves. At the small twig to which they were attached. The entire pile of them dropped down at least a hundred feet into the canyon below.

And he almost chucked. "Let me guess—not just survival training, but target shooting, too?"

She shook her head. "Oddly, no," she said softly, looking out toward her target. "He didn't want me anywhere near guns." Surprised, he cocked his head, was going to respond when she stopped him with "See the rock that looks like an *H*? Right below the two trees that are leaning together?"

Hands in his pockets, he nodded. Then said, "Yeah."

She pulled the trigger again. And within seconds he saw the glint as flying trajectile hit rock, causing sparks.

And he had to ask, "Where did you learn to shoot like that?"

"Through one of the domestic violence shelters that I support."

That she supported. Not just that she lectured for. Or donated to.

He took another note.

Every time he thought he had a handle on the woman, a fairly accurate profile, she surprised him yet again.

"Does Wagar know?" he asked. It could matter in how they played a showdown.

"Eduardo didn't, so no. I'm sure not." She sounded positive. And he remembered what she'd said about the man thinking he could physically force her to do his bidding.

In another lifetime, he'd have needed to know more about that incident. First and foremost, how many times had it repeated itself? And how far had it gone?

He didn't have another lifetime. And the one he did have was pretty much used up. At least in terms of any interpersonal human interaction.

In his current life, he reached for the nine-millimeter. Took off the silencer—used in case someone was already on their trail—put on the safety, and handed it back to her. "Keep this with you at all times as well," he said.

She blinked. Her brows raised. But she took the gun.

"What?" The question came even while he acknowledged that it wasn't a need-to-know thing. That pursuing was inappropriate.

She shook her head.

He turned back toward their makeshift lodging for the

rest of the day and night. Letting it go. He thought. When she walked beside him, he turned his head as they stepped in unison. "You looked surprised."

She shrugged. Still said nothing.

Which, instead of shutting him up, drove him further. "Why would you be surprised that I'm arming you? I've made it pretty clear that you need to be able to take care of yourself out here in case you end up on your own." He'd thought he'd been quite clear on that one.

Needed to know that she was prepared for the eventuality.

"You'll trust me with a powerful weapon, yet you continue to stall the one thing I came for. Giving me access to the files that will lead me to Wagar."

He didn't like the *me* in that last bit but let it go. "It's not a matter of trust," he told her, impassioned and not caring if she knew it. "It's a matter of preparedness."

When she said nothing more, he stopped walking, and when she did as well, he turned to face her. "I need to know that you're fully prepared for what you're getting into here," he said. "The minute you access your code, break through it, our location becomes a potential target for some of the world's most dangerous people. Made more so by the fact that there's likely at least one high-up US government official or law enforcement agency mole involved."

She didn't break eye contact. Or even swallow hard. "I'm aware."

He peered down into her eyes. Boring into them. Needing to transmit the critical nature of what he was telling her. "Then how could you possibly want access to files without things firmly in place to withstand whatever attacks might come our way?"

"I wasn't planning to manipulate the code until we were

set," she told him quietly. "And not even then, until I'm ready. I need to study the programming first. To get a feel for language used, like...the original coder's signature. I need to see how my own code has been successfully manipulated into files. And I'm hoping to be able to see how many levels deep I'm going to have to go to get to the root before I actually head in."

Right. He had some tech experience himself. Quite a lot of it.

And, once again, he'd sold her short. "You need to do what I've been doing," he said then. And started walking again.

Relieved to find her moving along right beside him.

Chapter 10

They'd taken the batteries out of their personal cell phones and left them in the bunker beneath Harc's house. His employees had been told he was called out of the country. He'd left the husband-and-wife team he'd hired to run the dude ranch in charge of his entire place. They'd be staying in one of the non-renovated cottages on the property until he returned.

Nicole hadn't thought about any of the hundred things he'd tended to since she'd descended on him the day before.

And realized another thing about herself she didn't like. Another residue left from her upbringing. Her world was too small.

Which meant her vision beyond herself was as well.

As intelligent as she was, as much as she knew, there was so much more that slipped past her awareness.

He'd shown her how to use the four-cup propane coffee maker to boil water for their packets of lunch. And while the water had been getting hot, he'd pulled the one-burner camping stove out of the bottom of his backpack.

She'd thought they'd be building fires for their cooking needs.

"We can't risk anyone seeing the smoke," he'd told her

when she'd said so. And she'd promised herself that would be the last time she had to ask in order to catch on.

In her old life, her responsibilities and the expectations others had of her had defined her days. Real life didn't come enclosed in those easily definable statistics. There was nothing controlling what might come at her.

As she sat down on the blown-up air mattress, pulling her computer out of her backpack to finally get to work on Thursday afternoon, Nicole realized that she'd had to get away from Savannah, even without the Wagar crisis eating her alive.

Because her sister had taken over where Eduardo had left off. Probably not meaning to. And likely because she'd been following Nicole's indications of what she needed. But her sister had been sheltering her. Limiting the demands on her.

And limiting her exposure to others as well. Or rather, others' exposure to her. The press. All the people she'd known in California, the high-society circle she'd traveled in through Eduardo, the scholars and shelter workers she'd befriended on her own. Sierra's Web had arranged for her privacy from all of them.

Giving her time to heal, Savannah had said. To acclimate.

Nicole didn't think she'd ever really do either. She could move on. Or not. Those were the choices before her.

She'd chosen to move on.

Which meant taking back control of something important that was stolen from her. Something she *could* reacquire. Preventing her work from being used for ill gain.

Harc had refilled the saddle bags with everything he'd removed. As soon as he was done with something, it went back into storage. And all the bags, other than her backpack, were by the cave's entrance. Ready to go at any moment.

He'd rolled large rocks over from two separate spaces close to the cave's entrance. Had the unfolded shovel leaning against the wall. From what he'd said at lunch, he was planning to dig two separate bathroom holes. One for him, one for her. When it was time to go, the dirt would be swept back into the holes, rocks rolled back over them, to cover any sign of human activity.

Something else she hadn't given a lot of thought to the day before when she'd immediately agreed to head up into the mountains with a man she'd just met.

A man no one knew she was with.

She'd never peed in a hole before.

But she would. She had no doubt about that. The prospect was far better than holding it which was what she'd been doing since they'd left the ranch that morning.

Anticipation swirled through her as she turned on her fully charged laptop and signed into the satellite internet she'd just helped Harc set up.

He approached, his cowboy boots almost silent on the weathered rock face. She saw them, though, watched as they came closer. It was finally happening.

And she was scared out of her wits.

"It's all on here," he said. She didn't dare meet his gaze. Didn't want him to know about the fear sluicing through her. Glanced up to see the tiny, plastic-encased chip he was holding out to her.

She took it gently. Inserted it into her computer.

And focused on the screen.

Afraid. But not entertaining a single doubt. She was where she needed to be. Doing what she had to do.

And…the boots were still there.

She glanced up. All the way that time. Meeting Harc's gaze. "Last chance," he said. "You don't have to do this.

Your father stole from you. And he's the one who passed on your programming."

The words made sense. Held truth. She felt the reality of both as she got locked into Harc's intense blue gaze.

Her resolve didn't waver. But she felt better. "Thank you," she nearly whispered and then clicked to open the drive he'd just handed her.

A part of him had hoped she'd change her mind. Back out. A very small part. One unfamiliar to him. All in all, he was still the guy who, once signed on, had to give everything he had to the job. To succeed.

And apparently, in spite of nine months of seeming recovery from the at-any-cost determination that had taken over him, he was still, at his core, the guy who couldn't walk away.

He just didn't think it was right that Nicole Compton should have to give up any more of her life—or lose it altogether—for having been born.

Didn't stop him from digging holes slightly smaller than the small boulders that would eventually be rolled back over to cover them. He fed and watered the horses, moving them into a shady area just yards from the cave's opening, with growth that allowed them to graze.

Kind of shaking his head as he did so. Imperial and Mahogany knew more about surviving in the Colorado mountains than he ever would. They'd been born there, wild and free.

And grown into adulthood there, too.

Before they'd been captured and domesticated due to over-population.

Which was one of the reasons he took Imperial out every

chance he got. And was glad to get Mahogony back up on the mountain slopes as well.

Chores done, and not liking all the traits he'd seen in himself in the past twenty-four hours but accepting them just the same, Harc sat down between his horses, leaned up against the tree providing sun blockage for them, and opened a burner phone. One of the several he'd brought with him. A minute or two later he was signed on to the satellite internet and went to work himself.

He might not know deep-dive code, but he knew how to find out things. On the web. The dark web. And by hacking into places he shouldn't go, too.

In ways that would never be traced back to him.

And with permission as well. When he'd left the CIA, he'd been told, with no possibility of mistaken reference, that if, on his own, Wagar came to him or he had reason to believe that Wagar was coming after him, he should do what he needed to do.

He was just supposed to have contacted the director before doing so.

Unless, of course, he was in a position that made notification impossible.

He'd deemed his current circumstance one such situation.

Using several of his many aliases, in various ways, he worked until Nicole came out of their naturally provided rock campsite shortly before dinnertime.

When he saw her moving toward the hole he'd dug for her, he got up and walked in the opposite direction. Giving her time. Privacy.

Drawing a very clear boundary for himself between the job and personal time. There'd be none of the latter between them. Even in knowing how long she took in the bathroom.

As he had the thought, he had a flash of memory. The night before. Nicole coming out of the tiny lavatory in the bunker. At his suggestion she'd showered, before putting on the sweats, matching top and bottom, he'd brought from the barn's stash for her to sleep in. And she'd still only been ten minutes. So...too late to be spared one personal detail. She was quick with bathroom usage.

And he had far more important matters to contend with. Heading back toward the horses, he saw Nicole standing there, petting Mahogany, and picked up his pace.

"What'd you find?" he asked before he was even abreast of her.

As important, how exposed were they?

His own searches could have nudged a radar or two, but none that should put their lives in immediate danger.

If anything, he could have let a former trusted technical expert at the CIA know that he'd been online and put his own ethics in question.

A one-in-a-million chance, almost literally. The woman would have had to be searching a ten-year-old alias to spot his use of it to enter an official portal.

He didn't care a hell of a lot, either way.

"It's very clear that whoever created those files is hiding something," she said. "The levels of security and depth of walls to get to a source is intimidating. Or would be if you hadn't written the basis of the code."

He nodded. Watching her. Reading her facial expression, her body language as much as hearing her words.

She was onto something. She knew it.

And it concerned her.

"Can you break through it?"

"I can."

"Did you?"

"Not yet."

He wasn't sorry to hear that. And knew he should be. Someone who only wanted the job done, who wanted Wagar stopped and others exposed and brought to justice would be sorry.

Except that... "It's best if we find out all we can before we breach that final wall," he said aloud.

He thought he saw gratitude flash in the brown eyes that were steady on his. "I breached a basic security curtain," she said then. "It shouldn't raise any concerns, but it could. If someone was on the lookout for any hint of, say, me getting in."

He held eye contact as he said, "If Wagar has a team on the lookout for you accessing your code." He had to spell it right out. For both of their sakes.

Her nod was slow. But sure. Aware.

Adrenaline pumped through Harc. From a source he hadn't felt in a while. More than one of them. He was ready to jump from a plane without a parachute to get this guy. Could finally feel victory in his grasp.

And... God help him...he was attracted to the woman who was helping him. To her looks, absolutely. She was gorgeous, and he wasn't dead. But it was more than that. Her brain turned him on. Her ability to take a deep breath and do the hard job.

Her stamina and determination.

He'd spent almost all his undercover time with women in his sphere. Even in relationships with them when the situation required his going that far. Never, ever had the fact that they were helping him reach his goal attracted him to them.

Because they hadn't known the part they were playing in his schemes.

This one, Nicole Compton, did. But it wasn't that that

was getting to him. He almost wished it was. To the contrary, it was the hint of vulnerability that had him wanting to throw the case to the wind and get her into protective custody.

To protect her himself. For more than just a day. Or a case.

As if he was a man a woman could ever trust to have her back outside of work. Thirty-six years and it had never happened. He could keep woman physically safe all day long.

Emotionally…he was just no good at that.

Not a welcome realization.

A fact to be aware of. To guard against.

All that was required to do that was to stay focused on work. Also pretty much a given for him. "Arnold Wagar left the country the afternoon before your father was arrested." He just blurted the news right out there.

"Someone was onto Isaac and Savannah. Or me. All of us."

He nodded. It was the logical assessment. Except, "You said, and by the account I read, your father was taken unaware when you arrived home that night."

They'd reached the edge of the cave. When Nicole ducked down to head inside and then straightened once there, he followed suit. The conversation was what mattered. Not where they held it.

She leaned against the wall, closed her eyes, and took a deep breath.

Her lips tight with tension.

Signs of stress. Of fear.

And he knew.

With the afternoon she'd spent and the news just imparted, she'd felt exposed outside.

Which he translated to mean that fear was taking hold.

The enormity of the task she'd taken on, the danger involved was kicking in.

There was more that he needed to divulge. But it could wait long enough for her to catch a breath. To get on top of any panic the afternoon's work might be bringing down upon her.

And if fear won, if he needed to get her into protective custody while he fought on without her, then he'd respect that choice, too.

Reaching for the pack that held their cellophane wrapped meals, he grabbed two, and the propane coffee maker, and headed toward the door. He'd be right there.

Not for the job, but because she seemed to need it.

They'd take a break from all that was bad. Concentrate on simple things. Comforting things. Like eating. And talking about horses. He'd amassed a lot of stories on that topic in the past eight months.

Above all, he was going to stay within her sights as she hid out.

Giving her a sense of security, even if ultimately it was a false one.

She had a job to do to buy her freedom. He knew what failing would cost her. So he would do everything he could to see that she succeeded.

To stop Wagar—absolutely, hands down, no doubt there. But his quest had taken on new purpose, too.

He was too late to buy back his own future, but he was going to help Charlotte Duran segue into the life Nicole Compton was trying to give her.

No matter what.

Chapter 11

He'd brought in the bed rolls hooked to the backs of their saddles while she'd been working. Hers sat on end by her backpack.

Shaking inside, feeling weak in ways she never had before, Nicole wouldn't let herself sink to the mattress. Or head out to Mahogany and ride off into the sunset.

Both options were tempting.

She'd always believed herself a strong person. Was only now realizing just how much Eduardo had shielded her from challenges that would have grown her strength.

That thought alone kept her standing.

She'd grow whatever she had to grow, cultivate with her last breath. She was not going to succumb to acceptance of the life her father had created for her. Had already started the battle three months before when she'd planned her own middle of the night escape and had successfully maneuvered hours of freedom for herself. Relying on the help of people with whom she'd become acquainted through her own efforts. People who'd never met her father.

And who Eduardo had not known.

So how did one of those people end up with a longer term Wagar association? She had to tell Harc. Just needed a minute to breathe before going down into the dark abyss with him.

He'd have questions, rapid-fire, which would require a clear mind and steady hands to go with all her resolve. To figure out how to more efficiently access the well of strength that had been boiling inside her for years.

To silence the fears.

Something she was now beginning to see Eduardo had also cultivated within her. From day one everything had always come down to one thing: Her safety. A trip. A school. A toy she wanted. The kind of lights on the Christmas tree. Even the bed—the room—she slept in.

She'd thought all of that showering of concern, the watching out for her at every turn had been a result of the great love he felt for her.

"He kept me weak, under his control, by making me afraid," she said aloud then, standing up straight as the light flashed inside her. All the studies she'd done, the work with domestic violence victims…mental manipulation was a huge part of that. She'd studied, lectured, she'd talked. She'd listened to women tell their stories to learn more, to be able to help others in their living reality. And she hadn't seen that she was one of them.

The fear that was threatening to suffocate her was in her mind as much as anything else. And something that she could fight. By not thinking about it. Dwelling. Re-munerating.

She had to concentrate on the moment. The tasks directly in front of her. And let the future wait for her to affect it.

Approaching the opening of the cave and the back of the man kneeling over boiling water in a pot, she noticed how Harc Taylor's shoulders nearly spanned the width of the temporary abode, and took strength from them, too. She wasn't in the world alone, even if it felt that way.

She wasn't fighting her current battle alone.

He hadn't responded to her words. She wasn't sure he'd heard them. Or that he'd even needed to do so. But she made sure he heard what he had to know. "I've been having moments of panic for as long as I can remember. They always come *after* I get through whatever it is I'm doing. Never during. I long ago deemed it the *fall-apart aftermath*. And I also always work my way through those times. Thank you for the moment to do so."

He'd seen her at her worst. She was back.

He'd accept her or he wouldn't. He wasn't going to stop her.

Not that after her work that afternoon, she had the choice to give up and go home. She'd set retribution in motion.

"I find that focusing on menial tasks helps."

What? She stared at his back. He expected her to believe that… "You have panic attacks?"

The shoulder shrugged. "Probably not in the same way you're describing. I have doubts."

"Doubts that create negative feelings?"

He shrugged again. And then said, "Wagar flew into San Diego by private jet this morning."

Pulling out their camp forks and water filters, she attached the latter to the water bottles Harc had filled earlier. Didn't ask him how he'd gleaned his information. "Conveniently after the explosion last night," she said, warding off a shiver.

He turned, handing her the plastic bowl that held the prepared Alfredo with peas that had been little more than dried crunchy pieces vacuum packed into a pouch fifteen minutes before. He hadn't asked what she wanted for dinner.

Didn't much matter. He had what he had. Enough to feed them for over a week. More if he was able to catch any fish.

"I found a username today that is of note," she said slowly as she chewed and swallowed. The pasta pieces were the right texture, the sauce palatable. She needed the nutrition. Focusing on dinner rather than the conversation staved off latent churning inside her.

Harc, who was seated on his blanketed mattress across from her, stopped chewing. Holding his bowl up by his chest, his spoon suspended in air not far from it, he looked at her.

And she looked back.

At the thick blond hair, the focus that was evident in his posture, his stiff expression as much as his eyes. She was on the right course.

The sensation brought by the thought wiped any hint of fear from her system as she said, "B M Megee, all lowercase. The email address of my mentor in college. A woman who has been instrumental in shaping my lectureship engagements, but more, one who I trusted explicitly."

Which was the most key point.

He put down his bowl. Stood. Walked to the edge of their enclosure, looked out, and then going back for his bowl, returned to the entrance and stood there sideways, looking between her and what she supposed was the horses. "What does she know that we wouldn't want Eduardo or Wagar to know?"

And a slice of fear returned, shooting through her before she shut it down. With a dose of anger toward those who thought it was okay to take control of lives that were not their own.

Okay to get rich by hurting people.

"Nothing that I can specifically recall," she told him. "I

was always careful not to mention my father or home life. A choice instilled in from my earliest memory. And in college, I didn't talk about it because I'd developed a sense of guilt over how easy I'd had it all my life, while so many struggled just to put a roof over their heads. But with Barbie…in a low moment… I could have expressed feelings that others could use to manipulate me."

And there was the crux of the day's panic.

Along with, "The woman was everything I'd ever hoped to be. An acclaimed academic who gave her life to studying societal problems, with an emphasis on women in society and finding current-day, in-the-moment solutions where she could."

Another bite on the way to his mouth, Harc stopped it midway, nodded. Jutted his chin for a moment and asked, "Dedicated enough to take financial support for her causes? If, say, the father of one of her star students wanted to contribute but do so anonymously? So his daughter wouldn't find out?"

Of course she would have. The answer didn't have to be spoken. Its force swirled around the cave.

"And knowing Eduardo, once she'd accepted the assistance, she'd have been on his hook. He never gave something for nothing. He'd have studied her vulnerabilities and hit her where it would squeeze the hardest."

He scraped his bowl. Took the last half bite and held it and the spork as he said, "We have to assume she was reporting to him from the very beginning."

The culvert in her gut was telling her the same.

But she finished her dinner. Handed him the dish he'd wash along with their meager cutlery and got up to roll out her sleeping bag.

She'd made her bed and was going to have to lie—and maybe die—in it.

* * *

Pieces flew around Harc's air space, sometimes moving into line to orbit there, sometimes all just randomly floating on their own. Wagar's timing on leaving and reentering the country had him greatly concerned.

It was like the guy had a psychic telling him when to come and when to go. Apart from that, how could he have known that Eduardo's capitulation was eminent when none of the players bringing him down knew? If the good guys didn't know, how could a mole among them have tipped him off?

And now the professor—he'd done his homework on her that night after dinner—and didn't like what he'd found.

A bankruptcy from years before. A cantankerous divorce. And a son with a jail record. All rife for making one vulnerable to what looked like easy money for doing nothing wrong.

Working as an unofficial, undercover bodyguard. Helping a wealthy man keep his only daughter safe while she ventured out into the world.

It could be more than that. The woman might have been an old lover of Eduardo's who'd been in his camp for years. Perhaps her husband had been doing business with Eduardo for years and the woman had been blackmailed.

Maybe she'd just needed money for her son and knowing how wealthy her mentee's father was, had sought out Eduardo for help.

And it could be less, too. Because Barbie MeGee had been Charlotte's mentor, it was possible that she'd just been on Eduardo and Wagar's radar just as someone to watch. The woman might've not even known.

As soon as he'd gleaned what he could quickly, he'd shut

down the satellite signal that could potentially lead someone to their vicinity.

The goal he ultimately wanted.

To see who showed up, get them temporarily incapacitated, and turn them in.

Not in the middle of the night if he could avoid it.

The body's ability to regenerate was important.

Other than a few necessities—like the gun and ammo
that never left his reach when he was working—all their
supplies were packed in the saddlebags that were already
attached to the two saddles on the ground just inside the
door of their cave.

And in the backpacks that they'd put on when they arose
before dawn to head out.

The packs would make saddling the horses a bit more
awkward but much quicker, too. Time was of an essence.

As was the woman sleeping just a couple of yards away
from him. Unless she was as good as deepfake as he was,
the deep, even breathing told him she'd drifted off almost
as soon as they'd laid down.

She'd made a soft comment. Something about the light
of the moon shining into their space. He'd been spending
the half hour since, trying to get his body to forget she was
there, while his mind focused on keeping her alive and by
his side until the job was through.

His body needed a good sleep, and he watched the display of randomly floating words behind his closed lids as
he drifted off.

Imperial's hoof. Lifting. Lowering…

Harc sat straight up in his unzipped sleeping bag, gun
in hand and cocked by the time he was fully awake. And
heard the sound again. Imperial scraping the ground.

"Nicole. *Charlotte,*" he hissed the name that was more

likely to be recognizable to her unconscious mind as he slid into his waiting boots as he stood. She sat up. He heard the movement, saw it, too, out of the corner of his eye, on his way to the cave's entrance.

By the time he'd had a full screening of the land encompassing their little hideaway, she was right behind him, her sleeping roll under her arm.

Just as he'd described when he'd told her what to do if they had to leave in a hurry. She'd washed up before bed. He'd left her alone inside to do so. But he'd insisted that, like him, she sleep fully dressed.

She didn't ask questions. Just dropped the bag and went back for his. He heard a hiss as air left mattresses.

"Quickly," he said to her, fighting an urge to do it all himself, in order to keep his eye on the horizon. It was dark, and he knew what to look for.

"Gun loaded and in your waistband," he added.

And as soon as she appeared next to him a second time, he grabbed Mahogany's saddle. When he returned for Imperial's she'd already used the branch he'd left by the door to sweep the area of any random marking they might have left behind and was in her saddle, ready to go by the time his horse was saddled.

He shoved the two boulders, and within a minute, they'd left the space behind and were already heading upward, keeping cover in brush, behind tree clusters, as they rounded the mountain.

Other than some tamped-down grass where the horses had grazed the day before, there'd be no sign of any habitation at their campsite. And the grazing could have been done by numerous wild animals sharing the landscape with them.

Including mustangs just like Imperial and Mahogany.

Perhaps even biological relatives of theirs.

After several minutes of riding, they came to an area wide enough to ride side by side, and he slowed Imperial until Mahogany was abreast of him. Harc glanced over at Nicole. "You doing okay?" he asked.

They'd had an hour less sleep than he'd planned, but he'd rested. And hoped she had, too. He couldn't tell much in the darkness.

"Other than needing to pee, yes," she told him, speaking as softly as he had.

Yeah, he had to go, too. Would have liked for them to get farther up the mountain from any potential ping to the satellite they'd been running but didn't relish dealing with wet trousers, either. He found a place to dismount, insisted that she do her business between the two horses while he moved behind a rock.

Privacy, modesty didn't matter a hell of lot when death was knocking.

Less than two minutes later, they were on the move again. And while Harc couldn't speak for Nicole, he didn't feel the least bit awkward for their stop.

The mission they were on, the lives they'd come from, the futures they were fighting for, and the powers trying to prevent them from reaching their goals had stripped away so much of what defined usual social conduct.

Or even the ability to be bothered by their lack.

He continued to keep close watch, to listen, and to pay attention to Imperial. The horse, who'd had nostrils flaring when Harc had exited the cave, seemed to have calmed down.

Which meant "We might be escaping a meandering bear. A mountain lion. Or pack of wolves, not necessarily a human predator," he told Nicole. Didn't really believe that to be the case. But hoped it was.

He felt fully confident in his ability to handle any encounter with mountain animal life.

He'd also been careful not to leave any trash or hint of food smell out, and unless they were cornered or rabid, most of the animals would steer clear of human scent.

"But we're escaping something," she said, her tone concerned but not betraying a hint of fear. More like a determined need to know.

"That's my belief."

"On what grounds?"

He glanced at her, looking for some sign of doubt in her posture. Her expression. The fading moon didn't help much. And dawn wasn't close enough to shine any light on the moment.

"You doubting me?" he asked. Didn't much matter to the case at hand. Except that he had to know that she wasn't going to question his authority the next time he said *Move*.

"Not at all. I'm just done being content with being kept in the dark regarding the dangers that lurk. I don't want protection. Or rather, I do, but I want informed protection. I need to be prepared to protect myself."

The woman was eleven years younger than him and yet continued to surprise him with her wisdom.

He'd been about to tell her exactly what tipped him off, but she spoke again. "I don't want to be told what I can't do so I don't get hurt. I need to know the risk and how best to handle it so that I don't get hurt."

He nodded. And said, "Horses have a hearing range of two miles. Sometimes a little more. They also sense heartbeats. When they're together in the wild, on open range, the herd will synchronize heartbeats to be warned of danger more quickly. They can actually hear a human heartbeat from four feet away."

He was going around the block with the explanation. But with what she'd just said, he felt compelled to tell her not only what had triggered him awake but why.

"Studies have shown that this happens with domesticated animals as well."

"Which is one reason why horse therapy works," she said then, seemingly willing to travel along his tangent with him.

Perhaps not quite ready to know what he knew?

Buying herself time to process a sentence at a time?

"I'm guessing the horse can tell when the human is experiencing a surge of anxiety by accelerated heartrate," she continued.

"That's part of it," he told her. At least in his still very limited experience it was. And he then continued with, "Imperial and I have been working together, with the help of a trainer. When he senses danger, he's been trained not to whinny or make big moves. He scrapes his hooves against the ground. This calms him and keeps Mahogany calmer."

"You heard his hooves scraping," she guessed correctly.

"And I'm trained to wake up at the sound," he concluded, with an attempt at a hint of humor. Didn't quite pull it off.

Felt better for trying.

But knew he needed to include her more in his thoughts. "This is what we want. To draw him out here where we have a much better chance of identifying him. And capturing him. Even if 'him' is just hired hands."

He had ways of getting information out of underlings. His success rate had given him a reputation that was known through various agencies.

He chose not to share that part. Not unless he had to.

"And I need time to get the evidence to incriminate him," Nicole said. She'd tied back her hair when they'd stopped. Made seeing her expression a bit easier with the help of dawn creeping upon them.

He saw tension there.

"Exactly." There was more he could say, details he could give, agencies he'd have to call in when the timing was right, but for the moment, he left it at that.

Chapter 12

She'd read a lot about minimalist existence. Had thought she'd like to at least try a week or two of living that way, just to know how it felt.

Except for the constant threat of danger, Nicole wasn't hating the experience. Granted, she'd only been away from society, living with only the basics, for a little more than twenty-four hours.

And even if there were no danger and the gorgeous expanse of mountain glory eventually took on a sameness, being with Harc Taylor and his horses prevented any chance of boredom setting in.

Because it was imperative that she keep herself out of the pool of fear threatening to drown her, she was clinging to the source of good feeling in her immediate sphere.

The man whose every move caught her attention. Made more potent by his care for his horses. And his sharing them with her.

It was as though she had three soldiers marching in step with her as she fought her battle for freedom from a past she'd had little control over.

And if, while she was riding with the man, she got lost in the occasional fantasy about what it would be like to have his hands on her instead of his reins, his lips touching hers rather than sipping from the filter attached to his water bottle, who was she hurting?

To the contrary, she was helping...on a scope she could only imagine. By maintaining an emotional equilibrium that would allow her to focus and crack the code—keeping herself out of the panic mire—she'd be saving untold number of lives.

And maybe her own, too.

As she rode through dark to dawn and into full morning that Friday, Nicole became aware of another goal added to her list of things she had to accomplish out there.

Making certain that Harc Taylor made it back to his ranch. His horses.

Too late, she was seeing what she'd done to him, to the new life he'd created. She'd been so certain, based on what she'd read, that all he cared about was getting the bad guys, that, like Mike, he'd chosen to dedicate his life to making the world safer and had left his life's work due to major career fail.

Inadvertently because of her and her coding.

She'd thought by seeking him out, she was handing him what he most needed as well. The chance to succeed, to get his man. To quiet the demons with which he'd seemed to have ended his career. But after seeing him with Imperial and Mahogany, seeing the supplies in his barn, watching him in the mountains, an awareness was growing within her. Harc hadn't spent the past nine months pining for the life he'd been meant to live. He'd been finding it.

The thought spurred her to push herself, to focus more fully than ever, to block out everything except following where the code led.

They'd been riding for a few hours, climbing, then on flat ground, passing caves and laybys before climbing again—

with intermittent stops for stretching and snacks—when, on one such flat ground, Harc slowed to a stop.

"That cave," he said, pointing to a larger, deeper crevice than they'd been in the night before.

Glancing around, she liked the spot but was surprised by the stop. "It's only mid-morning."

"I don't want to bed down where the satellite signal has been used," he told her. Which made total sense. Most particularly with considering the hour early start to the day.

With her morning revelations driving her, Nicole grabbed her laptop, a satellite modem, and her water bottle and headed to the shade of a big tree, leaving Harc to take care of the horses and anything else that he deemed necessary.

Unlike the day before, she didn't hold back. Didn't go slowly, determining the lay of the land. She didn't hesitate out of fear of the fallback.

She dove hard and deep. Just as she'd been imagining she would before she'd acquired Harc Taylor's assistance. And became more acutely aware of the danger Eduardo Duran had been protecting her from all those years.

She'd wanted out of her gilded prison, and she'd most definitely accomplished the escape.

Trails led to trails. Not all of them connected to each other. But all connected, in one way or another, to the security code she'd written when she was fourteen.

Her heart pounded when she recognized Glob, too. A program she'd written specifically for her father to show all his monies in one place, while making invisible the accounts in which they sat.

"What?" Harc's voice brought her head up sharply. He was seated a few yards away, his phone in hand.

She shook her head. "I didn't say anything."

"You just hissed."

"I'm finding multiple different entities that have been

using a program I wrote specifically for Eduardo's business dealings, back when I thought they were legally held. It allows the user to set up a system by which he can see all his assets in one place, without disclosing where they came from or where they're currently sitting. It attached to his international accounts all over the world but would prevent anyone who was trying to hack him or who wanted to siphon off from him a little at a time from having access to them. He'd told me that he had separate accounting systems for every legal holding, rather than one global accounting firm, department, or entity, to prevent someone from getting greedy but more to protect them from being targets of blackmail."

It had made perfect sense to her at the time. Had made her admire and love her father more for his constant awareness of others and how being associated with him could put them at risk.

When, in truth, he'd been protecting himself from all the people, the countries, he'd been screwing over.

Harc was watching her. And while she allowed herself some of the warmth filling her at his gaze, she didn't get lost in the sensation. "What I'm finding here is frightening, Harc," she told him, business partner to business partner. "Glob is supposed to bring every interest together in one place. But in Wagar's files, I'm find multiple different global accounts. In other words…"

"We're either dealing with multiple Eduardo Durans around the world or Wagar is using the program on a different scale than your father did."

He could be right, though she didn't think so. "Dividing up his assets into categories," she went with his theory for a minute. "And having a separate Glob account for each category."

It wasn't how the program was designed to work. But with all the levels of security and firewalls she'd been working her way around, she could definitely see Wagar being paranoid. And even more cautious than Eduardo had been.

"The program worked," she said then, not because it was one she'd written but because they had to face facts. "Eduardo was not caught because of his illegal business activities," she reminded. "None of you could breach his security protocols, largely because of Glob. He was only caught because of my entering my DNA in that database and my sister coming to find me."

The reminder mattered right then. "Wagar clearly was aware of the program's efficiency," she said then. "So why am I seeing it used on files that all seem to be pointing to separate identities?"

She saw the truth dawn as a darkening in Harc's eyes, a glint, and the sharpening of his features as they tensed. "Wagar's the kingpin, not Eduardo. Duran was just one of the man's many generals," he summed up.

It was beginning to look that way. She didn't speak the alarming fact aloud. Just nodded.

And watched Harc's back as he got up and walked away.

Harc strode straight to his backpack. To the phone he'd taken out of the safe where he'd stored Wagar's files. And sent the encrypted message he hadn't expected to send.

Nicole would likely hate him.

She'd have to be alive to do that.

He'd take that as his win.

Her life over her affection.

If his source was still connected.

He couldn't just call in. Not only did he risk being pulled off the case since he was officially retired, but since he had no idea where a mole might be, he risked the entire operation he and Nicole had set in place.

And her possible cooperation. No one could compel her to work.

He waited five minutes. Ten. On guard over every conceivable, foreseeable danger that could have them in its sights.

He could get Nicole to a safe house. To a bunker. To a government building. All of which could be targeted and breached.

On the move, in the Colorado mountains—which were dense and rugged—lesser men than him had remained hidden for lifetimes. All he needed was the days, or weeks, it would take Nicole to get their evidence.

She had to have internet. His plan was still the best there was. Keep her moving. Burying used satellites in their sewage holes.

It just no longer included any attempt to lure the enemy to them.

Wagar as the kingpin was a complete game changer. Something he'd never even considered. The man was something of a boob. A privileged kid who'd grown into a man with too much power, certainly, one who thought himself above God, probably—but a kingpin?

Just didn't fit.

Arnold Wagar didn't have the ability to lead men. Or to command loyalty. He wasn't the richest man in the world. No matter how many hidden assets he held.

Harc would bet his life on that much.

So why was everything pointing to him?

Ten minutes passed in cyber silence. He and Mike Reynolds had once been two men of one mind. Where the Duran case was concerned, they'd shared a wavelength that had been unlike anything Harc had ever seen.

With Charlotte heading to a dude ranch for a week, one that Mike would have checked up on and would have seen the explosion…he'd only held out contacting the FBI agent about Nicole's name change, her coming to him, because he'd been confident that he could keep Nicole safe while they ended the last detail of the years' long case.

And because she'd only agreed to do the work no one else could do if he abided by her terms.

Her hacking of an FBI agent's computer, while a major infraction, wasn't the only reason she'd given for keeping her work secret. She'd refused to have her sister or Sierra's Web involved.

He'd truly believed—still did—that she'd stop her work, go completely off the grid, and finish it on her own someplace if she believed her terms had been compromised.

While he'd still been in sole possession of the files she'd needed, he'd had an upper hand. That was no longer the case.

And yeah, a part of him had been a bit too jazzed at the idea of riding out of the mountains with a bound and gagged Arnold Wagar hanging over the back of his horse.

Instead of being the hero, he'd just succeeded in proving to himself that he was as rogue as he'd been accused of being. Had lost the ability to properly measure risks involved, protocols, to make the smartest choices when in sight of getting the win.

Instead, he'd allowed a gorgeous, twenty-five-year-old genius, one he'd been studying for nearly a year, to get to him. To show him his weaknesses.

Except…they were on a cusp, like never before. If he could actually help end the Duran/Wagar reign of terror once and for all, he had to see things through. To walk away would disgust him worse than anything he did to see that particular job done.

He glanced over at the woman who'd gotten to him more than any other single person in his adult life. Hunched over her computer, her fingers flew on the keys, she studied, and they flew some more. Jealousy hit him.

Squinting, he focused on her more clearly. He was jealous of what? The computer keys? A screen?

The files on them?

Because they compelled such complete attention from her? Because she'd been willing to risk her life to get them?

Before his questions could lead to answers he didn't want, Harc felt the vibration against his palm. Stood behind Imperial, out of view of Nicole—not that she had attention on him—to see the message that had come in to his scrambled phone.

From the only other one that he'd open a message from on that line.

Encryption in place.

The code was their second level of security—letting him know, in the exact way the message had been composed, numbers of characters per word, even if the word itself couldn't be completed.

He finger typed to unscramble the message.

And took his first full breath since Nicole had told him what she'd just found.

A world of international generals was too big just for the two of them.

But with Mike off grid, having their backs—along with, Harc was sure, the entire Sierra's Web firm—and with the FBI agent's readiness to get several US federal protection agencies involved with a single symbol sent his way on the phone Harc held—or a twelve-hour lack of communication on same—Harc felt a whole lot better.

For his sake. And Nicole's.

Not that he ever expected her to see it that way.

Harc seemed different when he approached to let her know it was time to go. Nicole felt differently, too. Not only had they firmly entered the thick of things, but their enemy was more convoluted than they thought.

Not that she knew what Harc was thinking.

She was just glad that he was. Thinking. Focused.

They ate a quick meal—a mixture of scrambled eggs, pork, hashbrowns, and onions—that he'd boiled into edible form from their freeze-dried packs. She continued to work while she ate. He didn't demur.

She took care of personal business while he buried the satellite along with the manure the horses had deposited during the stop, and they were once again riding up. Over. And then downward, into a culvert on the opposite side of the peak from which they'd started.

Didn't matter how low they went as long they had an unobstructed view of the southern sky. He didn't have a lot to say as they rode, single file more than side by side, and she was glad for the time to assimilate all that she'd taken in during the time she'd had online. To mentally organize, categorize. To see patterns in what she knew.

To figure out the quickest way to get to what she didn't know.

Was she missing something she should already have picked up on? Or was more digging required.

Harc was counting on her. Many innocent people needed her.

She needed to make Savannah proud.

"You have any family?" she asked Harc as he slowed for Mahogany to reach Imperial's side. She was grasping, almost desperately, for conversation that would engage her. Resorting to focusing on him to revert her thoughts from places that would weaken her.

"Nope."

Just the one word. Neither the response nor the brevity of it surprised her. But it took her down a path of possible scenarios for his upbringing that distracted her from thoughts of things that would trigger panic within her.

"My folks were both military." His words fell into a full minute of silence. And she turned to see him looking out at the world around them. The mountains climbing up around them on all sides. "My father was one of the first America soldiers killed in Iraq after 9/11."

The words struck her deeply. On many levels. She'd thought they were similar—her and Harc. Islands in a world of societal acceptance. And maybe on some level they were. But he was, paternally, biologically, the complete antithesis of her.

Explained why Harc had decided on a life dedicated to protecting his country. To the exclusion of all else.

"And your mother?" she asked.

"She died on a skydiving training mission of all things. I barely remember her. I was raised by my father. And the people he hired to care for me when he deployed."

So they had some similarities. Not knowing their mothers. Having only paternal influence to guide them.

And people who were paid to care for them.

He moved, and through her peripheral vision, she could see his face turned in her direction. She pretended not to notice. Withstood the scrutiny through years of practice.

Taking an odd, and potentially dangerous, comfort from the part of their family disfunctions that they did share.

Not questioning why it mattered—that she and Harcus Taylor shared similarities—just going where she had to go mentally to maintain the emotional equilibrium that would allow her to be most productive.

"You mentioned Savannah," he said right then. Almost as though he'd read her thoughts and was challenging her choice to focus on him instead of the things that made her life seem like…a lie. Her sister welcoming her in, being a real loving family…as desperately as Nicole wanted it all, she was afraid to believe.

Didn't feel worthy.

Not yet. Not until she could get rid of the Charlotte Duran in her.

She hadn't responded to his comment. Was breathing a sigh of relief that he'd let it drop when he said, "You didn't mention your mother. Was she not as welcoming when you suddenly reappeared?"

What? Her head shot sideways, her gaze pinning him. "You think she'd shun me? The kidnapping wasn't my fault. I couldn't help what…"

She stopped. Seeing the soft look in his intense blue eyes. The slight nod of his chin.

He didn't say a word.

But she saw what he'd done.

He'd known. Not that it took a scientist, or even a trained psychologist, to figure out she had issues feeling good enough to live in her sister's world. But instead of talking sense to her, talking her through it all, he'd brought it out of her.

Truth from her own heart and soul.

"My mother passed away a couple of years ago after an extended illness," she said aloud, almost defensively.

But she wasn't taking offense due to what he'd said.

The walls were going up because in those last few moments of internal truth, her momentarily opened heart had taken a small bit of him inside.

Chapter 13

Harc didn't hear back from Mike over the next couple of hours. Didn't know what, if anything, the agent knew about the explosion at the dude ranch.

He figured Mike would check up on his fiancée's little sister's whereabouts, even though she'd demanded time away without contact. Most particularly since Charlotte had been Isaac's charge for months prior to Savannah's appearance on the scene.

But their communication, only the scrambled symbols at that point, had to remain seemingly nonexistent.

At least until he knew more.

Had some inkling who in the upper echelon of US law enforcement or government was a mole. If there was one.

He had to assume there was. It was the only thing that made sense to him that would explain how Duran had pulled off his big disappearance and a new identity that included billions of dollars, all while raising a daughter from babyhood.

The second stop that day was as close to sea level as he could get and still be within the mountain range. He'd been to the area a couple of times since he'd bought his ranch.

A structure open in the front but deep, with a ceiling that served as the base of a thriving waterfall.

In the past, the spot had been a piece of heaven on earth to him. Breathtaking in its majesty. Which was saying a lot for a guy like him.

One more prone to shoot to kill than sit and ponder life's wonders.

"This is...phenomenal!" Nicole's smile fit right in with the rainbow shining in the water tumbling down beside her as she stood by the stream flowing swiftly away from them to places unknown.

She'd raised her voice some to be heard over the waterfall and he did as well as he responded with "We can't stay long. The horses won't be able to hear as well. But I need the signals to be scattered around various points of altitude and types of interests."

Truth be told, he'd wanted her to stand in the spot that had given him his first glimpse of possibility for redemption, for a future for himself, when he'd first landed outside of the life he'd thought he'd be in forever. He'd landed like a projectile. Dazed. Unsure of next steps.

Or even who he was.

He'd thought he'd found answers since then.

The past few days had shown him differently. And yet there he was, back at the place that had provided the first surge of inner power that was the start of what he'd thought would be a good journey.

As Nicole settled in to work, he hoped maybe he'd find another jolt of clarity there that day. One that would help him end the case that had ended him.

He unsaddled the horses long enough to brush them. Let them roam free for an hour. Filled water receptacles. Boiled water for another meal.

Handed one to Nicole—who'd barely glanced away from the screen as she uttered a barely discernible "Thanks"—

then settled himself a distance away where he had the entire alcove in which she sat in sight. But could hear more from a distance, too.

With Imperial and Mahogany grazing close by him, their teeth nipping at weeds growing in the rocks on which they stood, Harc used a new burner phone to search every database he could access with various aliases to touch base with entities known to have been associated with Eduardo Duran and Arnold Wagar.

He'd been through them all. Ad nauseum. Was merely checking for updates.

And looked for more on the explosion at the dude-ranch cabin, too. It had been deemed an accident. The result of a minute gas leak.

He'd had to dig deep to find that much.

Because the minor blow had turned out not to be big news?

Or because it had been buried? Like so many of Duran's activities had been?

To an onlooker, he could be just another vacationer, a backpacker, enjoying the serenity on a peaceful Friday afternoon.

While every muscle in his body, every sense was on high alert. Undercover work at its core. Pretending to be one thing, while living another. Spending hours, days, weeks, months even, posing. Appearing to relax, to enjoy beers with friends, to sleep with his girlfriend, even plotting kill a compatriot, all in the name of making the world safer for those who had no idea about the underworld threatening them.

For their children.

And now for Nicole Compton, too. He checked on her most often. Just to see that she was still there, focused.

Two days on a horse in the mountains, and she still looked…elegant…to him. The long dark hair she'd left down glistened with health. And her demeanor, the way she held herself and her movements seemed to glide—there would always be a part of the wealthy atmosphere in which she'd grown up about her. In her.

A complete contrast to the simple life he and his father had shared, in a home without any hint of a woman's touch. Chairs to sit on. Beds to sleep in.

Clean. Put away.

No niceties.

As though knowing that he'd been thinking about her—and himself—in the same process, she suddenly exclaimed, "Oh my God!" and glanced up. Finding him.

Immediately on his feet as Nicole's words reached him, Harc flipped the safety off his gun as he glanced quickly in her direction and then, with the gun pointing the way, scanned the entire area around them.

With a glance at the horses, who were grazing contentedly, he hurried over to his temporary work partner. "What did you find?"

"Chats, Harc. There are a plethora of them. I'm just beginning to see the various chains. All different users. But not chatting with each other. The only commonality is the protocol being used and—" she met his gaze, communicating a fear that sliced into him "—one source that is the same."

"Wagar."

She nodded. "He's got these seemingly completely protected private chats going on with all these different people who don't seem to know about each other."

"What are they saying?"

She shook her head. "I haven't gotten that far yet. Everything's encrypted." Glancing from her screen back to him, she said, "But they're coming to his portal from all over the world."

He frowned. Glanced at the letters, figures, symbols on her screen, understanding none of it. "Including the US," he said, knowing it was true in spite of his ability to see for himself.

She nodded. "At least a dozen of them, from what I can see so far."

Chin tight, he asked, "Do you recognize any of the usernames?"

She was frowning—and shaking her head—as she looked at her screen again. "There's nothing as obvious as usernames. Everything is coded. I'll break it. I just haven't gotten that far yet."

He was sure she would, but not right then. The mission's scale was compounding in ways he hadn't expected. Or planned for. Any number of entities could be watching for signs of breach. "Time to go," he said, waiting for her nod before he went for the satellite, retrieved his shovel, and buried the unit in rocks deluged by the waterfall.

And while she took a second to pee, he quickly pulled out the scrambled device he and Mike had purchased—in double—together, typing cryptically, saddled Mahogany, and was saddling Imperial by the time she'd returned.

So much for his bizarre hope that Nicole would be able to absorb some supernatural healing power there.

She'd taken herself further into hell instead.

And he was paving the way for her to do it.

She'd wanted autonomy.

Even before she'd found out that her entire life was a big

lie, she'd been busting at the seams for her freedom. Arnold Wagar being thrust upon her had just been the last straw.

And she hadn't been allowed a single life lesson upon which she could draw to give her strength. Her entire existence had been about weakness—multiple dangers surrounding her from which she needed constant protection.

Teaching her to rely on it being there.

Not how to be strong against the onslaught. Or how to endure hardship.

That was coming at her crash-course style. Her ability to pass the test remained to be seen.

"You can take me back if you'd like," she told Harc as they rode further into the dense Colorado mountains. The man had created a good life for himself. She was only just beginning to see how completely inappropriately invasive her descent upon him had been.

Spoiled little rich girl.

His gaze was searching as he looked sideways at her from atop Imperial. "You want to go back?"

She searched his expression, too. Couldn't tell what he wanted from her. Her entire life, she'd known what was expected of her. And gave him the truth. "I want to do what's best for you."

He shook his head. "That's not how life works," he told her. "Every situation, every person has a choice. You can only make your own."

She almost snorted at him. "I know that," she said. She'd been sheltered. She wasn't a child. "My choice is to regret having brought you into all of this."

"Without my files you wouldn't be in it."

Was the man deliberately trying to frustrate her? Irritate her?

Or was she egging him on? Because more than anything,

she needed to engage with him. She couldn't explain it. No amount of higher education or intelligent quotient could make her reaction to him clear to her.

Other than a few glances at her, he was on constant surveillance of the area around them. As always. But he didn't seem a bit distracted from the conversation when he said, "So what do want to do?"

"I want to get these…" She broke off before the off-color remark escaped her lips. Surprising herself at the vehemence that had burst up from within her. "How about you?"

"Now more than ever." Not even a second passed for him to have considered the response. He was that certain.

So… "Tell me how to help you watch for danger," she said, then added, "I know to pay attention to Mahogany and Imperial. I've been doing that since this morning." When he'd told her why they'd left their beds so suddenly.

"It's more about keeping us from being seen," he said then. "If anyone is onto us, is out here searching, we can count on them having state-of-the-art equipment. High-powered binoculars. Optimum tracking devices. So we destroy the satellites ability to be tracked. And we keep ourselves in the shadows. Out of the sun's glint. Behind trees. The mountains in this state are known for being a great place to hide. For being a difficult place to find that which doesn't want to be found."

She took it all in. Verbatim. And asked, "What are you looking for when you scan the horizon?"

"Everything from movement or glints that could be indicative of lenses pointing in our direction, to weather conditions, sun's location, and landscape. Things that will affect how others stay hidden from us and how we hide."

Wisdom brought strength. She'd taught the concept to

women who were learning to recognize signs of abuse, along with ways to escape the same.

And yet…she'd never recognized the extent of her own.

The thought brought her down another notch or two but didn't stop her from paying attention over the next couple of hours as they traveled, mostly in silence.

All four of them listening. Paying attention.

And she thought about the code she'd seen that day, too. Different scenarios were occurring to her, things that she could check offline. In the files themselves.

And that's where she found her strength. Inside her own mind. It was up to her to control where it dwelled. She'd studied psychology. She knew. Anxiety was a fear of the future. Of what could happen. A lot of times depression came from looking into the past. Her job was to stay focused only in the present. Where she was. Why. With whom.

With whom. As overwhelming as present moments appeared to be, there was one major factor that just felt good. With whom.

No past. No future. Only in the present.

The man with whom she shared a very unique set of circumstances—who they'd been, what they knew, and the skills they'd honed—to stop a major source of crime where no one else had.

A sound cracked in the distance. Echoing through the canyon yards to her left. Nicole barely registered the single blast before Mahogany reared up, her front hooves moving through the air.

Fear sliced through her, she slid backward and threw herself forward, clutching the saddle horn with one hand before throwing both arms around the horse's neck.

She had to stay on. Nothing else computed. Just staying on Mahogany's back.

"Whoa!" The deep voice, soft, but firm reached her as her feet twisted in the stirrups, and she squeezed her legs as hard as she could against the gelding's sides.

"Whoa."

Nicole clung to the sound, to the horse, and almost fell off when Mahogany's front hooves returned to earth and her neck lowered with them. Unbalancing Nicole, who's arms went down with the horse, while her boots, legs, and butt stayed in place.

Hands tangled in the reins, she held on. Grabbed frantically for the saddle horn. And felt hands on her hips, steadying her.

Then guiding her down to her feet.

Heart pounding, she stood on shaky legs, knees weak, and caught her breath as she looked up at Harc.

She'd managed to stay on.

Was still grateful for his steady hands at her waist. Wanted to thank him.

But got lost in the intensity shining at her from his blue eyes. As though under some kind of spell she couldn't look away.

"You okay?" his words broke through her to her.

She blinked. Stepped back. "Yes," she told him. Brushed herself off, went for Mahogany's reins. The whole thing had taken less than two minutes. And they had to go.

"Someone's shooting at us," she stated the obvious.

And was so busy getting ready to remount, she almost missed the shake of Harc's head. He was still there, his hand against Mahogany's neck. Calming the horse. "Not at us," he said then.

She climbed back up on the horse anyway. Took the reins. Running her palm against Mahogany's neck. If they'd been closer to the cliff edge… "How can you tell?" She stopped the fearful thought with conscious effort to focus on the moment.

"Came from the west, heading east. We're south."

She didn't ask how he knew. Let relief flow through her. And then said, "But it could be someone whose looking for us and thought they saw us."

His shrug gave a sense of unconcern, but he said, "Could be. Could also be a hunter."

"But it was definitely a gunshot."

Harc moved back to Imperial, who was pulling at weeds. "I can't say for sure. But it sounded like one to me."

He was back in the saddle and turned to look at her. "You okay to go on?"

Not completely. But she wasn't there to please herself. "Of course." She would make herself okay. If for no other reason right then, but to appear in a good light to the man who was beginning to mean way more to her than just a source of life-saving files.

Chapter 14

He'd almost kissed her.

Absolutely not what he needed to be thinking about five minutes after a gun shot rang out. But Harc's gut was telling him that the shot hadn't been meant for them.

Someone whose operation was sophisticated enough to avoid international agencies with the best people on the case, wouldn't blow their presence—their cover—by shooting unless they were absolutely certain they had the target in sight.

And someone dealing in illegal arms would have a sniper rifle, which would not only bring the target clearly into focus but wouldn't sound like the crack of a twenty-two-caliber handgun.

Something else he kept from Nicole. Not to be cruel. Exactly the opposite. The next shot could be aimed at them, from a sniper's nest, and she could be dead. She still had time to get out. To go to the police. Get herself...where?

Without knowing who was working with Wagar, they had no idea where to put her to keep her safe. The man might have been willing to let her move about freely for the time being. Keeping an eye on her, but nothing else.

But not now that she'd breached at last some of his security walls. In a way that would have told him that she was the one doing it.

No one else could dismantle her code. Harc needed her aware of the danger. Constantly alert. It was the only way she'd have a chance of defending herself if the need arose.

Deliberately choosing a path that would keep them side by side, he said, "There's a peak not far ahead, an overhang, and, if I'm right, a decent-sized cave with a stream running in front of it. The flow rate is low, meaning not a lot of sound, but it's wide. You have to go through it to get to the cave."

She frowned. "So…the stream runs parallel to the mountain?"

He nodded. And she asked, "You're telling me we're going swimming?"

Her tone of voice, as though she was preparing herself to comply, not argue, almost brought a chuckle. Along with another dose of admiration. "No, Mahogany and Imperial will be able to walk through it. But no one will be able to get to us without alerting us they're there." Which was the key point he wanted her to know.

The danger was acute. But there was some inherent safety around, too.

"You've been there before?" she asked.

He shook his head. "I've been studying topographical maps of the area."

"Since you bought the ranch?"

He gave her a shrug that time, the flannel shirt sliding against his sides enough to raise the sudden acute desire he was finding himself fighting where she was concerned. "Just since you showed up on doorstep. Prior to that, I was content to do my own exploring."

Her glance was longer than he'd have liked before she

asked, "You know exactly where to take us after studying maps for less than two full days?"

She needed to be watching her surroundings at all times, not focusing that mesmerizing gaze on him.

Paying attention to everything. Like he was doing. Which included noticing her every move in his peripheral vision. "I have a photographic memory," he told her.

The information wasn't a secret. It was in his file someplace. Something Mike would have had access to.

"Now why doesn't that surprise me?" The question was clearly rhetorical, and he let it go. Or tried to. The tone of voice in which she'd said it kept reverberating as he pulled ahead of her to traverse the slope ahead.

Made him want to show her other, more physical, talents he had.

Something else he'd been known for undercover.

And another reason why he'd walked away.

Nicole got to work as soon as they'd made it to the cave where they'd be spending the night. Harc had insisted that the entire alcove be a no-internet zone, and she'd been in complete agreement. But only because she'd been mentally working through enough code-cracking ideas to keep her busy at the computer with the files she'd already downloaded.

She had some puzzles she had to solve before she dared move deeper into Wagar channels. If he knew she was there, he'd be scrambling to get new protocols in place. To prevent her from discovering a lot of what she needed to know. Was probably already doing so.

She was gambling on the fact that she was better than anyone else he could get to try to stop her. Otherwise, he wouldn't still be using fourteen-year-old Nicole's program.

Her goal was to get enough information to move on him before he realized how deeply embedded she was. Which meant that she had to figure out how to be someone he chatted with without him knowing that she was posing as that someone.

Her personal dealings with the man had shown her the one thing she could use against him. He'd drastically underestimated her. Or overestimated himself.

Either way, having known him was going to work in her favor.

Even if the bullet earlier hadn't been meant for them—and the explosion in the dude-ranch cabin had just been an accident—even if Wagar didn't yet know she was fully onto him, he would know. There would be attacks. And bullets would be flying.

Nicole focused like Charlotte had never focused before. Every sense on high alert, she studied, typed, and tried again. Inching closer to understanding the chat encryptions. She'd chosen to focus on them first. Something was telling her that within those files, she would find what she needed to know to bring everything down. A name, something to get her started as she unraveled the many layers of protection, of hiding places within hiding places that she was finding herself up against.

It wasn't all brilliant. Some of it was downright sloppy. But that was its own protection. It was hard to decipher something that was filled with mistakes.

Harc inflated her air mattress. She moved into the cave to sit on it while she worked. At some point he brought food in. She ate without taking her eyes from the various windows she had open on screen.

Darkness started to invade the cave as the afternoon wore on. Light shone from outside, but the sun had moved behind her mountain cave, rather than shining over it. She was on the cusp of something. Could feel it. Was finding words hidden inside words. Translating symbol combinations into letters, finding words that coincided with other symbols.

She could be on the brink of success, or merely forming her own sets of formulas that matched various symbol placements. She had to think like someone who thought they were the best but might not be. Because it made sense to her that Wagar would have surrounded himself with like-minded soldiers.

Using her newest version of the multifaceted formula, she typed into the decoder she'd devised, hit Enter.

And stared.

What the hell? Mouth open, she read again. Then, with shaking fingers, entered more data, hit Enter, and read some more.

"What is it?" She heard Harc's voice from a distance before she became aware that he was approaching. Glanced out toward the stream. Saw him. The horses. Before her gaze returned like glue to her screen.

She didn't want him to see.

He had to see. Someone had to see.

With shaking fingers, she typed some more. There was nothing in front of her that was actionable. Nothing incriminating in terms of arrests.

"What's wrong?" He'd been on the other side of the stream. His feet sloshed as he hurried toward the cave's entrance.

She shook her head.

"You looked like you'd seen a ghost."

Staring up at him, all she could think about was wet

socks and boots for a second, while her ears roared. He'd
need his footwear to dry before they rode again.

We can manipulate her.

It's his mess. He'll clean it up.

We're keeping him safe. Minimum security. All the perks.
His call.

He couldn't even get the damned proposal done. He's out.

We can manipulate her.

Nicole typed. And read. Growing sicker, feeling weaker,
by the minute.

But couldn't stop. Driven beyond anything that affected
her personally, she had to keep going.

Not following any one conversation she just continued
to put the random bits of coded messages she'd been using
into the formula that was working. Taking what came.

He couldn't even get the damned proposal done. He's out.

Certain phrases kept interrupting her thoughts. Shouting at her as she attempted to move on.

Harc was there. She smelled wetness. Saw the toes of
his boots. Unless he sat down right next to her, back to the
wall, he wouldn't be able to see her screen. Pulling more
from one chat, she typed.

Watch her.

I'll take care of him.

She's too visible. Surrounded. Too risky.

Make a deal.

Scrolling through code, she saw that the last, the deal part, came right before We can manipulate her. All one set of code.

It didn't show up that way. But with what she'd deciphered, she was beginning to piece together full pieces.

While she was falling into them.

The mattress dipped. Harc's weight.

"I'm in," she told him.

And closed her computer screen.

Dread filled his gut as Harc watched Nicole. She'd had a shock. He could figure that much. Needed so much more.

But knew better than to push.

He was learning her.

She'd talk as soon as she had a moment to breathe. He pulled out his gun. Safety on. Set it on the mattress beside his right leg. Away from her. Kept his hand on it.

Listened for the horses tethered up just outside the cave.

Hoped to God that they had time assimilate, to act on whatever she'd found before they were acted upon.

"Arnold Wagar isn't the man we're after." Her first words fell baldly, no intonation. That was her shock?

It wasn't at all shocking to him. He didn't like the news. Meant he had no idea who he *was* after. Meant that all those months on Wagar had been a waste. But it made sense to instincts that had been leaning in that direction.

"Who is?" He went for the most key information.

"I don't know."

He nodded. Felt tension tighten his jaw.

"Other than some key points, a lot of what I've got here isn't even conversation between the same two people," she told him. "I've got about thirty sentences so far. Pulled from several chats. But one... I'd recognized something—CD and ED. It's what my father used to call us. In the chats, they were symbols, turned backward and interchanged, with other symbols between them—but I saw them in the midst of the coding and tried a formula that deleted the symbols in between them. Random symbols. Not the same ones. It was a long shot."

He was aware of the horses. Of the night that was on its way—due to throw them into darkness within the hour. But every sense was tuned to her.

The words she was saying. What she wasn't telling him yet.

Her eerie stillness.

Until she looked straight at him for the first time since he'd glanced up from across the stream and had seen her in shock, mouth open, in the distance.

He'd been setting barriers around the alcove, traps that would catch a toe, and make sound, if stepped upon. Fishing line, invisible at night, that would cause tripping. Falling.

And had nearly fallen himself as he tromped through the water to get to her.

Would have imparted any and all of it to her right then, had she not been looking at him as though she'd never seen him before.

She blinked. "I've got a lot of work to do," she said then, both hands clutching her laptop.

"Not until you tell me what's going on." That was not negotiable.

"I'm not sure yet," she started. Then, never looking away

from him, she said, "I think I've been a pawn since I was a baby. A way to ensure my father's loyalty."

Harc coughed. "You're telling me Eduardo Duran—*Hugh Gussman*—is innocent?"

"Hell no. Just that I think he had such a superior opinion of himself that he refused to deny himself what he wanted. Which let them, whoever, know his weak spot." She shook her head. Frowned. Then said, "I don't really know that yet. But it makes sense. I'm just putting pieces together as they're coming to me. It seems pretty clear that his one mistake was bringing me with him. And somehow he thought marrying me off to Wagar was going to fix that?"

Opening her computer back up she tapped, typed, scrolled, and turned it so that he could see the screen.

Could read what she'd compiled.

And while there was nothing concrete in what he read in terms of their quest, their cause, the job he'd set for himself—he felt her shock.

Could only imagine the horror of knowing that her entire existence had been formed by a selfish man who chose to take what he wanted rather than leaving his daughter to have a normal life. And somewhere along the way she'd become a bargaining tool. Never being treated like a human being.

"As narcissistic as Gussman seems to be, as avaricious, it's also clear from this that, in his own way, the man valued you above all else."

"As a prized possession," she said, her tone flat. "I gave him legitimacy. Made him approachable. Seem warm. Even likeable."

"You adored him." He said what he knew had to be eating at her. Because it was eating at him, and he was as far an outsider as one could get. Then he finished with, "You adored who you believed he was." He told the more accurate truth.

And while he wanted to stay beside her in the cave, sit with her as she ached, he knew he couldn't. Feelings, other than gut instincts, didn't have a place on the job.

She hadn't found anything actionable yet, but she'd unearthed another game changer, and he had to get word to Mike.

Nicole absorbed Harc's warmth. Reminded herself that she lived in the moment. Not the future. Not the past.

And started to find her strength again. She couldn't help who she'd been born to. Nor what her father had done with her life. But she could completely shape every moment she resided in as she was there. By taking what she'd learned in the past—good and bad—and applying it to her present.

She had to get back to work.

Almost as though he'd read her thoughts, Harc stood up. "I'm going to take Imperial and do a more expansive perimeter check."

Her stomach tightened painfully, but she nodded. Understood. Wanted the reassurance of him knowing what was out there.

And she was scared to death of sitting in that cave in the mountains all alone. Except that the worst that could happen, her dying, wasn't as bad as being the weak, over-protected daughter of an international criminal. "I'm going to be sitting right here, working," she told him, paying more attention to her laptop than to him.

Being in her moment, not her fears.

"Where's your gun?"

The question sent another slither of fright through her.

She reached into the backpack right beside her. Pulled out the weapon enough to show it to him.

"Get it out," he told her, still standing over her. "Have the safety off and by your right side, ready for you to grab in an instant."

She took the gun out with a shaking hand and said, "Scaring me is going to slow down production."

He didn't seem to move a muscle. "Not as much as having you incapacitated would do." There was no apology in his tone. Or compassion, either.

"Listen for Mahogany," he said as he headed for the cave's exit. "He'll let you know before anyone has a chance to get close enough to hurt you."

"Unless a sniper has a gun trained on me from farther than two miles away." She was being facetious. Didn't quite manage the smile to go with the words.

But looked up to see Harc shaking his head. "There's no straight shot into the cave," he told her. "Look around you—the only distance you can see is sky. Ten yards beyond that stream is down. Behind you there's up. And in here you're protected on both sides."

She nodded. Looked back at her computer, dismissing him to matters more important than comforting her.

But as he turned to go, took a couple of steps outside the cave, she called softly, "Harc?"

And when he turned, said, "Thank you."

The nod of his head brought the smile she'd been unable to find.

And a prayer that he'd return safely.

Chapter 15

Sierra's Web had eyes on Arnold Wagar, in real time, electronically, and by watching those he was known to be connected to. Bodyguards.

Work-for-hire goons he was suspected to have had associations with in the past.

And a well-known problem eliminator with mob associations who'd just been released from prison after the first of the year.

All but that last bit had put Harc at ease as he'd ended the scrambled messaging communications he'd ridden down to receive. And then buried the satellite device he'd brought with him to ensure transmission.

Sierra's Web's vision was acute. The best there was. Mike had just assured Harc that not only would they be watching Wagar, they'd be doing a thorough deep dive on who could be pulling Wagar's strings.

And Mike had agreed with him, that Nicole's time frame to create the miracle they all needed was growing critically short. Sierra's Web tech expert, Hudson Warner, and his team had detected someone other than Nicole looking at Wagar's online security.

The FBI agent hadn't mentioned Savannah, and Harc hadn't asked about her. Since the woman was a partner in

Sierra's Web, it stood to reason that she was fully briefed, but the lawyer's skills weren't needed on the front line.

And Mike and Harc didn't ever cross that line.

Still, as he pushed Imperial to hightail it back to Nicole, as he considered all that he and Mike had discussed, he knew a growing sense of unease regarding the secret communication.

Which unsettled him far more than it should have.

He'd spent his entire adult life living two lives at once. The one those around him could see, and the one that worked in secret to solve heinous crimes.

Heart, emotion—soul, even—were sacrificed in order to succeed.

Which made it hard to explain why he felt almost light-headed with relief as he and Imperial climbed the last half mile to the cave, careful to avoid the traps he'd set, and meandered across the stream toward Mahogany. And Harc could get eyes on the woman sitting up in the cave.

The gelding left behind was watching them, his long tail giving a wave, and Nicole...didn't even seem to look up. Engrossed in her computer screen, she was typing, then studying. Just as she'd been doing most of the afternoon.

Decrypting, he assumed.

Figuring that she hadn't moved since he'd left.

Until he got close enough to see the tamped-down marks in the patches of brush and dirt where Mahogany had been left to graze. Human-sized footprints that Harc hadn't made.

Watching the dark-haired head at work, Harc's heart gave a warm lurch new to him. Unsettling him. Changing him somehow.

When she didn't react to his return, he left her alone. But was aware of every move she made. Knew when she watched him fill the pot with water from the stream to make their last meal of the day. He was turned sideways and could see her with peripheral vision.

He was fine to pretend that his absence hadn't been a big deal, for either of them.

Liked it better that way.

Darkness was going to be fully upon them soon. And while they'd have some moonlight at the opening of the cave and the solar charges had enough juice to keep Nicole working, they needed to rest. He had a feeling the next day or two would not play out as the last two had.

The closer they got to Wagar, the more pressure the man felt, the higher the chance that he'd be sending hungry hounds trained to kill straight for them.

Harc was ready for them. He wasn't sure Nicole was.

Or even could be.

While she'd had survivalist training, and was freakishly smart, she didn't have the mindset of an agent. He'd seen the panic on her face. The way she had to fight to find her inner strength—formidable as he suspected it was.

Life hadn't prepared her to take on the evil that would be coming at them. Ironic, since her father had born and bred it, too.

He approached the cave just as the sun made its last dip. "Dinner's going to be ready in two, and then we need to get rest," he said, as though they were having just another day on a leisurely backpacking trip.

She nodded. "Shutting down will give my laptop time to charge." She closed the device as she was speaking. Set it aside.

He'd hoped for a bit of reading material to take him through dinner. And to prepare him, too. Had expected to be scrolling through random chat-room comments, akin to what she'd shown him earlier. Needed to see for himself, in case he recognized something she didn't. An alias. A code word.

She reached to her side, and he noticed the gun still lying there. Wondered if she'd taken it outside with her during her sojourn with Mahogany while he'd been gone. Didn't ask. The woman had spent her entire life with bodyguards watching her every move.

The hand by her gun reached out to him. "Here. I saved the day's work for you to have a copy, too."

He took the small plastic case containing a micro SD card. Nodded. Deposited the gift in his pocket. And while she rounded a boulder behind which he'd dug her personal hole, he gathered sporks and water bottles and had dinner waiting upon her return.

They were temporary partners. With different skills and responsibilities.

Not two people finding a kinship with each other.

With a burner phone offline, and plugged into a battery pack, Harc slid her micro SD card into a slot and read while they ate.

She'd expected him to get right on it. Just hadn't thought he'd do so while sitting two feet from her while she ate. With only the beam of a flashlight for her to see by.

Leaving her far too much space for the past to creep in on her. The things she'd discovered…about Wagar, proof that he was answering to someone who had ordered him back to the States to clean up his mess.

And before that…the reason he'd asked her to marry him.

There'd been more than she'd surmised, but she hadn't

been completely off, either. The knowledge gave zero satisfaction.

Harc would be homing in on the more pertinent facts. Wagar had another contact in the US who was calling shots. Someone other than Hugh Gussman.

And one in another country as well. She was thinking El Salvador, but until she could get back online, she couldn't verify much more than that.

She ate because she had to keep up her strength. The beef stroganoff wasn't gagging her, as she'd thought it might.

Partially because she was letting herself enjoy the view she had. Pure distraction. She knew it. Acknowledged that she was resorting to base humanity in an unbecoming way. But did it anyway. She'd found Harc attractive the first time she'd seen him.

Studying the rugged, very-different-from-anything-she-was-used-to masculinity wasn't hurting anyone.

Better that than let the darkness suffocate her, while the reality of having no life crushed her. Because she'd been fighting both possibilities since the first encryption that had included *CD. Charlotte Duran*. The initials had been the key to unlocking information that would hopefully end a quarter of a century of criminal activity.

They'd also deadened something inside her.

Had she really been holding on to hope that a man who'd stolen millions from the government while a trusted employee, who'd abandoned his wife and child, faked his own death, kidnapped his other child and fled the country, had been capable of loving her? Selflessly? Unconditionally? As a child should be loved.

As Savannah had been. As she'd have been had Hugh left her with the mother she'd so desperately needed growing up.

As her sister loved her still.

Because when Savannah looked at Nicole, she saw the baby she'd been. Savannah hadn't even known the woman Charlotte had become when she'd risked her life to save her.

Harc reached for his water bottle, a foot away from hers. His knuckles brushed against it. Knocked it over, and she caught it. Handing it to him.

And got caught by the glint she could see in his eyes as he focused on her. She wanted to stay there. Feeling... okay. To forget everything. The world she'd lived in. The one waiting that she wasn't sure she'd ever fit.

She wanted those slightly opened lips to touch hers. To wipe out thoughts. And replace fear with something better than that.

Then he took the bottle, sipped, and glanced back at his phone and she realized that he hadn't been caught in the sensual web with her.

She'd been there alone.

In a world that wasn't real.

Just as she'd been her entire life.

Harc needed answers. He needed Nicole online, working her magic, getting more. He needed names. Places.

Account numbers.

He couldn't afford to bring a multinational, fully armed and trained devil to their door in the middle of the night with no backup.

But Nicole needed some sleep.

He was already asking more of her than she could easily manage. More than she'd been prepared to handle.

More than he'd have been able to handle as well as she was doing were their situations reversed.

While he hadn't yet read every communication verbatim, he had the gist of what she'd found. Proof without critical details.

There wasn't one kingpin. There were at least two.

Arnold Wagar was not one of them.

If the man didn't get rid of Charlotte Duran, permanently, in a way that couldn't point back at him, he was toast.

Judging by earlier chats, most of which had stopped three months before, Wagar used to have the ear of one of the kingpins. And ran some pretty powerful shows.

Neither man in charge appeared to be involved in the chats. Nor did they seem to be aware that they existed.

Wagar had recruited someone new. Someone he'd been lying to, but also filling in so he'd be up to speed. Which was how Nicole had managed to find out all that she had.

The chats alone were probably enough to give them Wagar.

But they'd be no closer to ending the reign of terror. Just as bringing in Hugh Gussman had not done so.

They were closer than ever. And as far away as they'd always been.

"If I hadn't put my DNA in that database, I'd still be living in a mansion, thinking I was adored by a generous, decent, extremely successful businessman." The words brought Harc's gaze from the screen he'd already ceased reading—had just been staring at—to the face of a goddess who appeared to be on the verge of being beaten.

Even as she sat upright and ate freeze-dried food to give her strength.

He hurt for her worse than he'd ever hurt for himself. Even as he knew he couldn't possibly know how she was feeling.

And he had to ask, "Would you want to go back there?"

"No." The response was immediate. Emphatic. And he hurt for her some more. Wanted to go back to staring at his phone, to escape from himself and his compelling desire to take her in his arms and let her feel what it was like to be loved.

Because...all he knew how to offer her was the physical stuff. He could bring joy, and experience it, in the moment—he was certain of that. Could give her a sense of being adored and cherished.

But only for the moment.

Which was no better than her father had done.

Instead, he cleared away the empty dishes. Took them outside to wash them, dumping the dirty water in his hole. Checked on the horses.

Put away everything he'd taken out of the packs. Had them ready by the cave's entrance.

Fully synced with the life his plan had created. Just like always. His chameleonlike skills had made him an excellent CIA agent. Not a great man.

But he had to try. She was sitting in the middle of her sleeping bag–covered mattress looking more lost than he'd ever felt. Which was saying something.

Bending over to secure the latch on the last pack, he said, "Maybe you sent your DNA in because you sensed that something was off. Inside, you knew. Which is why you were so desperate to find other family."

She shrugged.

"That act alone was the catalyst that brought down an entire portion of a bad empire," he reminded her. Because stuff like that mattered to him. Pulled him out of funks.

He glanced over as he stood. Saw her watching him in the beam from the flashlight. Decided they should have more water for the night. Reached for his bottle, filling it from the jug he'd carried in from the stream earlier. Glanced again, to see her…still watching. Seemingly following his every move.

And when she caught him watching her, she said, "Mike was there. He'd have found something eventually."

Maybe. Probably. But with no guarantee that it would have been enough to end Duran's reign.

She was still watching him, and he stood there, feeling like an idiot, loath to reach in for her water bottle, as she said, "Did you read the part about Wagar being ordered to marry me and then decide to return home to El Salvador permanently as a way to get me and Eduardo out of the country without looking like Eduardo was running away? Without raising suspicions? They wanted me out of reach of Savannah's search. And, if need be, once over there, they were going to keep me under lock and key, if I didn't comply with their wishes. They wanted me pregnant, with a child of my own, so I quit yearning for family, and they intended to put me to work creating more superior code. And to keep an eye on my previous work, to make certain that it wasn't being breached."

He hadn't read it all. But he'd had the gist of it. Felt useless as he nodded.

Held the jug on his lap as he sank down to his own mattress. Needing to be there for her. To find a way to help.

And feeling utterly helpless.

Not a familiar state for him. And not one he liked. At all.

"And because you refused to marry him, Arnold Wagar is now going to be on the run from the very powers he helped build." He said the words before he thought them through. Which was why he'd known he should back up and quit trying to be more than he was.

He saw the twist to her face as she said, "Unless he delivers me up." And felt the weight of his mistake.

Leaning forward, he reached for her water bottle. He'd fill it. Turn out the light. And hope to God she could find some respite in unconsciousness for a while.

But had to say, "That's not going to happen. I always get the job done, and right now, the job is protecting you." All bravado. Mixed with a dose of truth. He'd only ever failed on one case, and it was because he'd quit. As it turned out, that one failure had come back to give him a second chance.

The only way she was going to die was if he went first.

She stood as he was filling her bottle. Grabbed some things out of her pack, and flashlight in hand—pointed at the ground, not out, as he'd taught her—she headed just outside, behind her boulder. Getting ready for bed, thank God.

The sooner she found escape in sleep, the sooner he could hope to do the same. Even just for an hour or two. They'd have to be on the move before morning.

Even if they returned to the same camp at night, he had to move her elsewhere to get online. And had a better chance of doing that under the cover of darkness.

She could nap in the afternoon if need be.

Feeling more like himself as plans for the next twelve hours or so started to solidify, Harc put away the jug and grabbed a fresh filter to apply to Nicole's freshly filled water bottle.

Had just tightened the lid when she came back inside. Waiting while she repacked her things, he tried not to notice the freshly brushed hair or the lighter-colored jeans she'd donned with a black long-sleeved T-shirt that made her braless state more obvious than the looser shirt had the night before.

He didn't need to know that while she was sleeping in

clothes as he'd said, she'd opted not to keep her chest bound up as well.

Either the previous night had been too uncomfortable for her or she'd quickly donned the bra while he'd been saddling the horses before dawn that morning.

As his body reacted to the thoughts he was trying to obliterate, Harc dropped to his own mattress, still holding Nicole's water. To have done otherwise would have meant getting closer to her as he handed it over, when what he needed was a trip out to bathe in the stream.

He was working.

On the job.

The reminders did little to help his current situation.

More times than not, undercover, he'd taken lovers as part of the job.

And beyond that, where Nicole was concerned, he'd already crossed the line between work and personal.

Even if he wasn't willing to accept the fact.

Chapter 16

The nightmare wasn't ever going to end. Eduardo had stolen her life from her when she'd been just a baby. All the time he'd claimed to have been protecting her, he'd been caging her to protect himself. The more she dug, the more encompassing his deeds became.

She wasn't just the property of one criminal. Untold numbers, without names, were staking their claims on her. She knew too much.

And too little. She was in the race of her life, she got that loud and clear. Unless she figured out who they were before they found her, she was going to die.

But she wasn't going to go without reclaiming her life. She would not die as Eduardo had made her live.

Not ready for the one beam of light to go out, to leave her alone with the moon and the dark while her traveling companions got their rest, she took her time getting her toothbrush, paste, and body wipes neatly in their designated pocket inside her backpack. Her mind, her body were too fraught with the day's revelations, still reeling too much to allow sleep.

Shoving her folded dirty clothes in the plastic bag she'd packed in her suitcase in Phoenix for just that purpose, she placed it in the separate zippered portion at the bottom, thinking maybe she should just wash them and give them several hours of night air in which to dry. Except that would keep her companions up.

And then, with nothing else to do, she dropped from her knees to her butt on her mattress in the near dark and asked, "Do you know how horses sleep standing up?"

She did. And she knew why, too.

"Stay apparatus. A series of tendons, muscles, and joints that lock into place."

She nodded. There was more, but he'd summed up the gist of it. "And they do it because it takes them a bit of effort to stand from a lying position, which makes them vulnerable to prey."

She was babbling, engaging him in it and not feeling any more prone to sleep herself.

"They do lie down to sleep as well," he said, as though willing to engage in the inane with her. Shooting a smidgeon of warmth through her frozen soul. "In their stalls. And I've wondered if they ever did when they lived out here full time." He was slowly turning her water bottle around in his hands.

He glanced down as she watched him and held the drinking container out to her just as she reached to take it from him. Their fingers collided. The bottle dropped to the ground between them, and they both leaned in to rescue it.

Her fingers got to the bottle milliseconds before his did, and already in flight, his hand wrapped around hers.

Changed by the warmth of his touch, she didn't move except to look up at him. To hold on. It was as though, the day's frigidity melted away. Showing her that she was more than what her father had grown her into.

That she had choices yet to make that could define who she was.

That she was already making them.

Feelings more than actual thoughts, the impressions came at her as she held his gaze. Her eyes started to focus more in the moment. She saw the blue in his. The intensity. The…wanting.

And she wanted.

To make her own choice. To indulge. To find forgetfulness. To feel good. To know him. All of him.

To be held by him.

Leaning in a little further, leaning on the water bottle she still held, Nicole brought her lips closer to Harc's. She didn't kiss him. Just closed in, her eyes still locking gazes with his. She wouldn't force anything.

He had to want it, too.

He moved closer, stopping with only a couple of inches between their faces. Giving her time?

She couldn't tear her gaze from his. Had to stay connected. Until he looked down at her lips. As though telling her what he wanted but wouldn't take without her permission.

As though asking if he could kiss them.

Her answer was just as silent as the question. She leaned in those two inches and pressed her lips to his.

Molten desire raced through him, transporting him from rational thought to instinctive action. She'd touched him with an opened mouth, and his lips met hers fully ready to engage. He tongued her right out of the shoot. No finesse. No foreplay.

Just a hunger that had to be satiated.

There was nothing tentative about her lips. Or her intentions.

And he didn't intend to disappoint her. Leaning toward

her, he wrapped an arm around her waist and lifted them both to her mattress, lying down with her in the softness of her sleeping bag. And kissed her. Again and again. Softly. Exploring. Tender. And hard and hungry, too. He couldn't stop. Couldn't get enough.

Half on top of her, he tangled his fingers in her hair. Got hotter by the way the silky strands seemed to restrain him. Chain him.

Right where he wanted to be.

Until she moaned. He slid to his side, his pelvis pressing against her thigh, his chest up against her ribs. Saw her eyes open, read the slumbrous heat there. "You okay?" he whispered.

"I've never been better." The words were a treasure. A gift.

A truth so stark that he felt as though he'd just heard from the depth of her heart. Heard it calling out for more.

As though he, the one who'd sold his own heart and soul, could help strengthen hers.

Harc had made mistakes. A lot of them. He had to get this one right. And she'd lived in that gilded cage.

"You've done this before?" he had to ask. Not to say he'd stop if she wanted to go on, but…he'd do some things… differently.

She nodded. Smiled again, seeming so mature and sexy that he had a hard time containing the explosion pressing for release. "I dated a med student," she told him. "We did it in the university lab." With another grin she said, "My bodyguard never entered classrooms with me."

The life she'd lived, the fact that she'd not only gotten herself out of it but was embracing a chance to be who she chose to be—someone who'd risk her life for others, to right wrongs—mesmerized him.

She traced a finger around his lips. "I've never felt like this though."

He wanted to nip at the finger. Restrained himself because it wasn't about him. "Like what?"

"Physically ignited. Not caring about anything beyond right now. Hungry."

"You want more?" he asked. She was in charge.

Completely.

"A lot more," she told him, looking him right in the eye. "I want to keep feeling like I feel right now. I want to want. And to get what I want. I want to be wanted. And to give until you cry for mercy." She stopped then. Blinked. As though she'd just shocked herself. And then smiled. "Yep, that's what I want," she said, her arms around his neck.

He kissed her then. Softly. Pulled back to look deeply into eyes partly in shadows with the flashlights dimming beam. Searching. Needing to know how best to make the next moments as perfect for her as possible.

"I want to be strong," she said then. "And…for a little while…just to be me. To forget what was. To let go of fear of what comes next. For some reason, you make all of that possible."

The declaration exploded in his chest as much as the feel of her was engorging him in other places. Harc lay there, awash in unfamiliar emotion that was swirling throughout the desire burning through him.

Nicole reached up to run her fingers along his brow. To touch his lips. "And I want to know what you want," she whispered, lifting her head to kiss him softly.

He had no words to give to such a moment. Came up blank. All he could do was gather her close. And show her.

He wanted her. More than just sex, he wanted to be something she would never forget. Something good.

The bridge from her old life, giving her an unforgettable, emotionally and physically mind-blowing passage into whatever her new life would be.

He wanted to hold on tight. To see her naked. Touch every part of her. Be touched by her. To know her completely.

To be the best she'd ever had.

Before he had to let her go.

Morning was going to come. The fact drove Nicole higher. Sometimes faster, sometimes slower as she explored the most magnificent male form she'd ever imagined. Harc clothed had been rated-X fodder. His body without clothes was perfection.

Art.

Muscles that were big enough to proclaim powerful strength but not overbuilt and getting in the way. More, they were rock solid. All over his body. She explored every one of them. Head to toe. Prolonging the natural euphoria flowing through her. And she was pretty sure through him, too.

Every touch, every move, they were in sync. Pleasuring and being pleasured. The onslaught to her senses consumed her, driving her, until…finally, she had to climb onto him and have it all. Helping him with the condom he'd pulled out of the wallet in his pants pocket, she caressed his hardness. Sliding herself down onto him, she practically exploded just by the hungry, appreciative look in his eyes. By the fact that he was watching her, entering her and taking her in, too.

She wanted to take it slow, but their bodies were in control and did what they had to do. She moved, he did, and together they rode higher and higher until she couldn't help herself any longer. Convulsing around him, she closed her eyes, savoring wave after wave of exultation as he spasmed inside her.

Then…it was done.

Just as Harc had known that Nicole needed him, he got quite clearly that reality had returned when he came in from his hole a few minutes after the most incredible sex he'd ever had. Already inside her sleeping bag, Nicole was fully dressed. An assumption made by the lack of her clothes on the ground with his, and what he could see of the shirt covering her shoulders.

He didn't rush to dress, some perverse desire inside him driving him to take his time. Whether she was watching or not, she'd be aware. He was certain of that.

But when he buttoned the last button and picked up his gun, to place it by his hand as he lay down, he was all agent again.

Turned off the flashlight. Closed his eyes. And heard, "Thank you." Softly. Contentedly. And his chest flooded with warmth again.

His glib *Anytime, ma'am* turned into "You think you can sleep now?"

And when her "Mmm-hmm" reached him, he smiled.

For a minute. Maybe two. Until he heard even breathing coming from her direction and his mind flew to the danger he'd helped her walk into.

He should have known that things were bigger than just Duran and Wagar. All those months undercover in El Salvador, he should have uncovered more.

Self-conflagration came. And…went. Just…left.

No explanation.

Other than that, he had a job to do and couldn't waste

time on that which couldn't be changed. Unless he wanted to continue to live amongst the mistakes.

Listening to the breathing of the young woman who'd come barreling into his life with such indistinguishable force, he knew she wasn't the only one who'd gained more than sex from their encounter that night.

From their acquaintance overall.

She'd come from something terrible. And had the courage, the determination to make the future different.

To *be* different in it.

She wouldn't let herself be wholly defined by who she'd been, but rather, was taking out of it what would suit her, and forging ahead one choice at a time, to be someone she could live with. He had to do at least that.

And more if he could.

He had to do whatever it took to see that she got the chance to make all the choices she had to make, to get to the future that promised to be everything she'd ever needed.

As young as she was, she was just getting started on carving out the rest of her life.

The eleven years between them sat heavily on him as he lay there, hands behind his head, listening…and coming into focus, too. His ranch was his life. He honestly wanted to get back to it. But not until he succeeded on his final mission.

Running through facts in his mind—those he'd known for more than year, and those just recently acquired—he looked beyond the shock, the emotions, the not knowing to pieces. Letting every piece of information floating around in his mind bump into each other. Trying to find what fit next to what. With what.

How it fit.

Looking for a mole, mostly. That was his ultimate key.

Who knew Hugh Gussman back then? Who benefitted from the man's theft?

Who was sitting at the head of the empire?

How did they capture an unknown enemy? How did they stay alive when they didn't know who they were fighting?

So many agents had been through all the information at their disposal. Sierra's Web was getting a fresh look.

And the person was still undetected?

How could anyone be that good? For that long?

Pieces floated. They landed. They floated some more.

Harc drifted off. Woke up. Drifted off some more.

And then woke up.

Sat up.

Listening.

Chapter 17

Harc's gaze shot to Nicole first. Her head was turned toward him, face seemed relaxed, as best he could tell. Her covers moved up and down regularly, evenly, with her breathing.

He immediately switched surveillance to the moonlight and shadows outside the cave. Picking out Imperial and Mahogany first. Both standing. Quietly.

Not on edge.

Nothing looked out of place. Even the stream flowed easily. The night, their small part of the world seemed peaceful.

He'd woken with a start.

And it hit him. A missing piece that was preventing him from putting together the puzzle.

Wasn't missing. They just hadn't seen it.

His subconscious had, though.

Hugh Gussman had been a regular guy. A husband. A father. He'd bowled in a league. And he'd been incredibly bright. Climbing up the ladder in the IRS, but bored with his job. To the point of trying to see if he could steal money in order to report the breach possibility and gain himself a larger promotion, sooner.

Instead, he'd been mesmerized by his ability to gain a lot more money, a lot faster, by taking the darker route.

After he'd amassed two million dollars, he'd reported his own work to the authorities, agreeing to name the perpetrator if he could be assured that he and his family would be safe. He'd been on his way to supposedly testify the day he'd turned up dead.

Except that he'd not only been alive and well, he'd had a one-year-old baby with him and managed to…disappear.

How?

Until three months ago, no one had even known Gussman had been alive. There'd been no "how" in existence.

And when he'd confessed, Gussman had written that he'd slipped over the border to Mexico and paid for new identities.

Lying back down, Harc let the facts flow in whatever fashion they would.

Wagar had been his main focus for the entire case— the reason Nicole had even sought him out—and because Wagar was the one with the most to lose if Nicole lived, the man's relationship with Duran kept resurfacing.

In Gussman's confession he'd said that he'd met Wagar the year before, at a black-tie charity function in Los Angeles. But that had clearly been a lie. Charlotte's security program written at fourteen had been in use in Wagar files for longer than that. Two years that he knew of so far. Could have been more. A lot more.

Arnold Wagar had been a kid living in El Salvador when Hugh Gussman was supposedly murdered. A teenager. Barely an adult. He'd grown up in wealth. Came from a well-respected family.

And his father had been a Salvadoran dignitary in the US at one point.

Which point?

Had anyone checked?

There'd been no reason to do so when they hadn't known about Duran and Gussman being one and the same. Gussman...who'd worked for the government.

Upright again, Harc itched to get a message to Mike. To have someone check for any associations from a quarter of century before held by Dignitary Wagar. And look to see if young Wagar and Hugh Gussman had ever crossed paths.

The conversations Nicole had found, decrypted... Wagar could have been talking about his own father—the elderly, well-respected patriarch of the family's century-old wine business—when he'd mentioned being toast if Charlotte Duran wasn't dealt with.

The elder Wagar was the CEO and president of a billion-dollar business that had well- and long-established international shipping capabilities.

Was it possible that the spoiled son wasn't the only one who'd gone rogue? Could Wagar's father be the kingpin?

A man with a private jet, with high clearance in the United States government, whose spoiled, weak son had befriended a genius with two million dollars...

The elder Wagar had had a lot to lose taking on Gussman. And for what? Two million was grocery money to a man of the elder Wagar's wealth.

Unless his wine business had been in trouble?

Or his son had been. Had Hugh rescued Arnold from some trouble in Washington when the family had traveled there with his father? And the elder Wagar had done him a favor for having aided his son? Helping him escape and then obtain new identities for his daughter and him?

Hugh could have lied to him, too. Told him that he'd been threatened. That he was a widower with a young child...

Or the Wagars could have been using their winery as

a cover from the beginning. Could be a long-established criminal family. Even the head of a cartel.

Perhaps they'd recruited Gussman.

Heart pumping, Harc's mind continued to fly, his photographic memory showing him full documents he'd read, and he knew—with the certainty that had led him to close so many cases without loss of life—that he was onto something.

Maybe not cartel or even the elderly Wagar. But something.

When Charlotte told her father that she'd entered her DNA into that database, Duran had known that he could be exposed at any time. That not only Arnold Wagar, but perhaps an entire mob family in El Salvador, was also at risk.

Or someone else entirely. Someone closer to home.

Or further away.

But someone.

And it started with how Gussman got out of the country and became Eduardo Duran.

He'd lied about having just met Wagar the year before. Slipping over the border to Mexico could just as easily have been concocted.

Gussman had also claimed, in his confession, that the only reason he'd agreed when Wagar had asked for Charlotte's hand in marriage was because he'd simply wanted his daughter's future protected, with a prenup that gave her half of her husband's wealth were he to divorce her. In exchange, Wagar not only got a beautiful young wife with excellent skills he could use, but he got a sizeable chunk of Duran's legitimate business dealings as well.

Or would have.

If all had gone according to plan.

But from what Nicole had found the day before…that

had all been a lie. The marriage had been designed to get him and Nicole out of the country legitimately. And to lock her away from Savannah. Or anything else she might want out of life that didn't include plans that had been put into place when she'd been an infant.

To the point of satisfying her need for more biological family, by providing her with children of her own. Through her marriage to Arnold Wagar.

Children of her own. The thought brought slamming back his time with Nicole hours before. The sex. The thought of Arnold Wagar having had his hands on that body…against Nicole's will…made him want to kill the man with his bare hands.

Glancing over at her again, he was shocked to see Nicole watching him. Eyes open, she hadn't moved. And wasn't smiling.

She deserved children of her own. With a man who would light up her world. Which most definitely left Harc out. Not that he'd considered being in. What they'd done… didn't even figure in to the moment that had yet to come.

Sex on the job was always that way.

Turning on the flashlight, he met her gaze, braced himself for what was quickly going to become her low opinion of him, and said, "We need to talk."

Nicole sat up. Opened her mouth to assure Harc Taylor that he needn't worry that she was going to build the night before into anything more than it was, but sat with her mouth open as he got in first with, "I contacted Mike Reynolds."

The shock to her system was uncalled for. He'd never said he wouldn't contact the FBI agent. His agreement to help her after she'd laid down her stipulations had implied that he'd abide by them. At least to her that's what it had implied. He'd never actually said he'd respect her mandates.

Her mistake. Trusting someone she didn't even know.

A CIA agent.

Who'd quit his job.

Fear shot through her then, and reaching for her gun, she stood. If he was about to...

His hand clasped over her gun hand. Not hurting her, but holding tight. Keeping his grip steady, he rose to meet her face to face. "I'm sorry," he said, looking straight into her eyes. She wanted to lower her head, not look up at him—wanted to never look up to him again—but knew that she needed him.

And nodded.

As much as she hated having put herself in a position of having to do so.

She couldn't even think about what she'd done with him the night before. It hadn't been meant to be more than a way to get through the moment. And she had to let go of it.

Her chances of finding her way out of the mountains alone, without Harc's supplies, were negligible. And she wasn't ready to die.

"So Mike has known all along where we are? Where I am? What we're doing?" she asked as, heart in cold storage again, she focused on the tasks at hand.

Another skill she'd learned over the years of her growing up among her father's employees.

Harc's headshake surprised her. "I contacted him yesterday. We need his and Sierra's Web's help, Nicole..."

He'd contacted them before he'd had sex with her. Granted, she was the one who'd instigated the coupling. But had he complied, not out of a real desire for her or any emotional connection in the moment but because he was more like her father and Duran than she'd realized? Had he hoped, as Arnold Wagar had, to control her with the intensely emotional physical connection between them?

Had he been buying her cooperation in whatever he deemed came next?

The thought came. And went.

Even if he had been appeasing her, to what end? The one they both wanted. Obliterating everything Eduardo Duran had created, or been a part of. And if he gave her that, he gave her everything she'd come for.

Glad she'd held her tongue, she stood there, feeling betrayed by him anyway but knowing that her reasoning wasn't fair. She was falling for the guy. Not at all what he'd signed on for.

And not his fault that he hadn't slid a little bit in like with her, too.

Still. "You shouldn't have contacted him without letting me know," she said, her tone low, holding a smidgen of the anger she wanted to unleash.

On him, a little bit. But mostly her father. For playing her for the fool her entire life. Manipulating her to the point that she wasn't sure she'd ever be able to fully trust anyone.

Including herself.

"I weighed the risks," he told her, unblinking as he let go of her hand and stated facts as though in a courtroom. "I couldn't risk you knowing and going off the grid to do the work on your own, as you threatened to do. I understand why you didn't want Mike, your sister, or Sierra's Web involved. I've been at this gig a long time, Nicole, and I'm good at what I do, but I'm good because of the people who have my back when I'm in the field. Because of the information they can get for me, that I can't get myself without risking my cover."

The explanation was more than he'd had to give. She nodded again. And stepped away from him, reaching for the articles she'd take outside with her as she prepared for another day of work. Knowing that more was coming. He wouldn't have just confessed a day-old communication without reason.

He'd said they needed to talk. The line rarely boded well.

Setting her belongings in a pile on her mattress, she sat down and looked up at him, waiting.

"Knowing that your father isn't the kingpin, finding out that Wagar has been far more involved that we knew, he could be the head of a set of international generals. And I took that further—if not Wagar, someone else is—so we need more intel. I'm charged with keeping you safe. This entire thing might end up resting on what you find…it's bigger than who you fear putting in danger or someone losing a job, Nicole. With the head of this thing still out there, Sierra's Web is probably already in danger. You're public knowledge. People know you moved to Phoenix. Who you're related to. They have to assume that if you haven't already shared your expertise with the firm of experts, then you will."

She nodded. Stood. Toe to toe with him. Attempting to push back against the dread his words had instilled within her.

Savannah. Her firm…all that had been good in the three months since her life had literally imploded…stood to be hurt because of her.

Their little DNA match had become like a nuclear time bomb.

Because Charlotte had listened to her heart and reached out for family.

Harc's gaze seemed personal somehow as he looked her

in the eye. "Just so you know," he said, "Mike and Sierra's Web were already delving into things. He'd been keeping tabs on you, as Charlotte, and they knew about the explosion at the dude ranch. They were already on high alert, not having been able to find any sign of life. Your license plate didn't show up on any traffic cams, your phone was off, you weren't using credit cards. Savannah was hugely relieved to know that you were okay. And with me."

Something else she should have figured—them checking up. Savannah had used the excuse of an exclusive vacation to disappear from her partners when she'd come to find Nicole. Nicole had just done the same. But Savannah had been a long-standing family member of the group she'd left. Nicole had only been around three months. And her father had been an international criminal. She could see how they'd think she needed watching over. And she probably would have too, if she'd ever had reason to think beyond her own small, protected world where she stayed cloistered, using her education and means to help strangers escape domestic abusers. The irony of that one wasn't lost on her.

Nor was another one. Sierra's Web hadn't been able to find her. "I was successful in putting Charlotte to death," she said. Not at all happy to know that she'd probably managed to accomplish the feat because of living with that international criminal all her life. "Which means that Wagar and whoever else will be having trouble finding me. It's like, whoever set that explosion, if it *was* purposeful, did us a favor. I could be dead."

Harc nodded. But then shook his head. "Anyone with means for a deeper investigation would be looking for a body—even if just a single piece of one that could prove DNA."

Hoping that the switch from nod to shake meant that he'd

reconsidered the idea of just letting her believe the latter, to be wholly truthful with her, she said, "I hate that I didn't see the danger to Sierra's Web simply by their known association with me."

"Why would you have? We all thought that Wagar was a smaller fish in your father's pond. And the government had eyes on him."

He was right. And she appreciated the reminder. But he'd still betrayed her trust. "Going forward, I am an equal in *this* partnership. You talk to me. I talk to you."

She expected to see his chest puff up at the very least. Or for him to glance away. Instead, he continued to hold her gaze and said simply, "Agreed."

The force of that one word gave her backbone some much-needed support.

He started to talk then, unloading on her so quickly, she had no time to feel. Only to focus. Follow along. Think.

She wholly agreed that the answer they were seeking led all the way back to Gussman's escape from the United States with a baby girl and gaining respectable new identities out of nowhere. Hated that she hadn't already reached the conclusion herself the day before.

As soon as she'd read Wagar's take on the wedding that was supposed to have happened between him and her, she should have known. Instead, she'd allowed herself to become overwhelmed by the proof that even in his supposed confession, Eduardo had lied. His written reasons for the wedding had been altruistic. To continue to protect her.

Had she really still been holding out some kind of hope that she had meant enough to him that he'd sacrifice anything for her? As she had so many times for him.

Was she really so desperate to be loved that she'd needed

to know some of the closeness they'd supposedly shared had been real?

"Does Mike know that Wagar isn't the one running things?" she asked, when the ex-agent paused in his dissertation.

He nodded. "But I have to get with him as soon as possible. We need them all to do a deep dive on Gussman's past. To see if there was any chance Gussman and a young Wagar could have come in contact twenty-five years ago. And we need to know who else the Wagars, father or son, might have known then. This could be the source of our mole. Or could lead us to him."

"Or it could be the kingpin," she said, for want of a better word to describe the fiend who was still out there, running the show.

From what she'd gleaned, they'd thought, with Eduardo out of the picture, with his full confession, it would only be a matter of proof and then paperwork to take down Wagar and the rest of the operation.

She...through Harc...had been the source of the proof. It had all been so clear. And clean.

"Eduardo Duran was playing us all along," she said. "He lied about the reason for trying to force me to marry Wagar. And now that I've found my older code, we know he lied about just having met the man last year. The entire confession could be false. Every bit of it." Fear struck anew as she looked up at him.

Saw him nod as he said, "I reached the same conclusion about an hour ago. So say it's all false. To what end?"

Was the question rhetorical? Had he already figured out the end, too? Nicole told him what came to mind anyway. It could matter. She knew Eduardo better than anyone. "Maybe he's so well connected that he knows he's not long for prison. Whether there's a prison escape plan already in place or something working within the court system, he could be out and sitting in a country that doesn't extradite within hours. It's not like he hasn't successfully disappeared before."

With a baby who hadn't had a chance to know any better, let alone stop him.

Staring into Harc's blue eyes, still finding strength within them, she asked, "Do you really think it's possible he's that connected, that valuable?" Because she did. The one thing she'd always been able to count on was that Eduardo always got his way.

Until she'd entered her DNA in that database.

And had refused to marry Arnold Wagar.

Harc's shrug wasn't the instant denial she'd hoped for. But she wasn't surprised when he said, "Depends on what incriminating information he has on whom."

The words instilled renewed drive. Along with the time bomb they now had to assume was ticking at their backs. "I need to get online," she told him. "Since it's no longer just you and me needing to find and pull together all the pieces, I'll turn over the rest of the chat decoding to Sierra's Web. I've got to dive as deep as I can as quickly as I can with the code that only I know. Just tell me where and how we make that happen fast."

She thought, for a second, that his gaze warmed. In the dim light of the flashlight beam, she couldn't be sure.

But was positive she didn't want to know.

Either way.

Chapter 18

If Hugh Gussman was still in the picture as largely as they were beginning to suspect, Nicole was in one hell of a lot more danger than Harc had ever imagined. No one knew her or could predict her thoughts, choices, and actions as well as her father could. The man had spent Nicole's entire life controlling, teaching, and manipulating her.

The thought was foremost on Harc's mind later that morning. They'd cleaned up and left camp to set up a very temporary base to get the satellite set up. Nicole sat beside Harc on a boulder by the horses, watching his screen right along with him as he passed scrambled messages back and forth between himself and Mike. First and foremost, Mike had obtained clearance for Harc to officially work the case.

He felt his partner in the wilderness stiffen. And then relax. Wanted to know what she was thinking, how she felt, and shook himself. Neither thing was pertinent to the moment.

And while he was glad to know that he had the authority to do what he had to do, he wasn't all that pleased to be back under protocols.

Not that they'd ever stopped him on a job in the past. He'd just vowed to be done with tightrope walking where right and wrong were concerned.

And yet his mind was swirling with facts, dangers, potential unknowns, and ideas when the next message came through.

He held out the burner, and he and Nicole read simultaneously. She turned to look at him, so close he could see the darker rim of brown around her iris as she said, "They want you to devise the plan."

She appeared to be pleased with the idea. But he needed to be sure. "This one is your call, Nicole. You put this whole process in motion. You're the one with the skills that have the capability of stopping this thing."

"You know Wagar," she told him without hesitation or even looking away. "You know the case. And your professional record for successful missions is exemplary. Which is why I'm out here with you right now."

He was the one breaking eye contact. To scan the horizon. And closer in, too. To keep a sharp eye on the horses. Assuring that they were remaining calm. "You're out here with me because you needed the files that I had," he reminded her.

"I had the files a couple of days ago." And she could have left at any point. It wasn't like he'd have shot her for doing so.

He was one of the good guys.

Mostly.

The thing they weren't talking about, the big elephant that had been on their table all morning, was like an invisible wall between them. He couldn't consider what they all were asking—that he take over an official case, take point—with walls he couldn't scale right in front of him. "This isn't because of last night, is it?" he asked.

Her expression stilled, blanked. Her shoulders dropped. "I resent the fact that you even had to ask. I'm trained in self defense, Harc, not combat. Or physical warfare. But

I'm far wiser than you give me credit for if you think, for one second, I would let the weight and scope of what we're facing, the lives of all of the potential innocents out there who have yet to be harmed, rest on an hour of sex."

Her disdain was as clear as his path forward.

But he didn't think he was ever going to forget the initial surge of very personal disappointment that had sliced through when he'd first heard the words.

They were staying in the mountains. Harc's initial plan to draw out the players in a quarter of a century long, very evil game, made the most sense to both of them. And ultimately to whatever small team Mike had had with him during their scrambled communications. She didn't ask if Savannah was there.

Couldn't allow herself to believe in the dream life her sister had promised over the past three months. She'd tried to let herself live it. To fit in.

But until she'd wiped their father from under her skin, until she could atone for the years she'd spent with him, she didn't belong there.

Law enforcement agencies from all over the world had been pursuing the crime organization that had made Eduardo Duran a billionaire. They'd thought they'd won, albeit only leaving Wagar's illegal arms branch, but from what Nicole had gleaned in the past couple of days, they hadn't stopped whoever was at the top. The kingpin had escaped pursuit yet again. And so they weren't going to chase him.

They were going to show him how dangerous they were to his operation. To force him to come to them to stop them.

And the rugged, dense mountains of Colorado were the perfect setup.

Trained experts would be dispatched on the ground,

aware of Nicole and Harc's coordinates at all times. And twenty-four-hour satellite surveillance was already being put in place. With as few government and agency employees as possible aware of the moves. For op security purposes, much of the work would be put on Sierra's Web.

And while Nicole was thankful, hugely relieved, and moved by the support of her sister and the firm, she was also beset with an almost debilitating guilt, too.

She was sharp. Aware.

She should have seen. Or at least suspected.

"I spent the past five years becoming an expert in women's studies," she told Harc as, on horseback, they made their way quickly to the coordinates of the mountain alcove that Sierra's Web had determined, via satellite, was the best location to set up their operation. "I worked with victims of domestic violence, which almost always involves various forms of mental manipulation, and I never saw it happening to myself."

She felt like a fool. But more, she needed him to know her weakness. He'd need to be aware, to plan, in the event internal blinders prevented her from doing her job.

She was a potential risk.

He glanced over at her and then, with a quick nudge to Imperial's sides, hurried the horse up a short steep incline to flatter ground above. Slowing, while he watched her and Mahogany complete the climb behind him, he remained in the way of forward progress, bringing Mahogany to a stop as he said, "You were driven to hack Mike's computer. You then showed up and managed to convince a determined, retired CIA agent to turn over privileged files that only two men in the world knew existed, and to join you in risking your life to end your father's reign of terror."

She nodded. Not getting his point.

"So don't you ever doubt that you are the asset. That you will do anything it takes to right wrongs."

She opened her mouth to argue. To point out that if her mind was being played, she might unknowingly make wrong choices, but he held up a hand. Shook his head.

"Just by hacking Mike's computer, you'd already won the battle against your father, Nicole. You fought your way out. Don't give him any more power over you by allowing him to make you doubt yourself."

All well and good, but, "What if…"

He shook his head again. "No. Don't go there. Don't let him make you go there."

With a shift of the reins in his hands, he started Imperial—and thus Mahogany and Nicole—on their way. Leaving Nicole riding a horse in the mountains fighting with herself not to allow the doubt to win.

While she feared that she could get them all killed.

"We're all human," Harc turned to call back to her. And then, as they reached wider ground, stopped Imperial just long enough for Mahogany to pull alongside him. "We all make mistakes. Including you. If one is made here, by you, by me, by anyone who's just joined us in this fight, the rest of us adjust. Compensate. And continue pressing forward. That's how this life works."

This life. As a whole? Life in general? Or the dangerous and strangely compelling world of undercover work?

Nicole didn't figure a current definition of life mattered all that much.

But being there with Harc, working with him on that case did.

Satellite had shown multiple other human occupations in their portion of the vast mountain range. Some of which would be legitimate backpackers. Most particularly at that time of year. But several were suspected as being already on the hunt for Nicole and Harc.

A pair of individuals had been tracked backward, through camera footage, to the first two sites where Harc had buried satellites. They were currently at the second, so a good day behind them. If they were lucky.

But those two might not be the only pair who'd been dispatched.

Satellite didn't penetrate rock walls, caves, or even see beneath thick underbrush.

Nor was it impenetrable. Depending on who they were after—say, someone with high government clearance—their hunters could be already tracking them, aware of every move they made.

Which was why Harc had determined that the next camp they set up would be permanent. As non-changing as things could be while undercover. He'd requested a location that contained rock overhang protection for the horses as well as a deep enough cave that he and Nicole would have a chance to go farther in, make some turns, if someone penetrated their location before they could escape.

Something they *would* do. Unless the ground crew already on its way to them were able to pick off the intruders first. Which was the plan.

He had to be prepared for every step of it to fail. If one did, he'd have another plan already in place to keep the op strong.

And heading toward success.

Reaching their desired upon location before mid-morning, he unmounted himself from Imperial's back with all senses on alert, studying every aspect of the area, designating the first step of the mission complete.

And a success.

Crossing it off his list and putting it behind him. Setting up camp was step two. Completed in better time than he'd expected with Nicole's help and their immediate attendance to the routines they'd set up for the past few days.

Her mattress was set up, with bedding rolled out, on the edge of the first turn into the mountain when he entered the cave. She was checking her gun.

"It's a weekend, so there will be more hikers out," he told her. "Not that I expect anyone to make it this far for an overnight jaunt—just want you to be aware..."

"I'm not going to shoot unless whoever I'm aiming at has a gun," she interrupted him. "And not then if you're there and have already drawn. I'm backup. Period."

He nodded. Smiled. Noticed that she'd blown up his mattress, too. And laid out his bedding.

Also by the turn. But separate from hers.

He'd had a thought or two about pushing them together.

So he could dive on top of her if he became aware of intruders at the last second in the night.

And maybe do other things. If she needed the escapism.

While he'd been standing there, wasting invaluable seconds, she seemed to have been completely unaware of him, pulling out her computer. Was already back against the wall with the thing on her lap.

Awareness of his brief lapse, of her lack of one, shot Harc into full focus and the next two hours passed in complete compliance with the plan. Never a waver.

The horses were set, both for their safety and for their ability to alert Harc while inside the cave. Holes were dug— Nicole's behind a boulder and up against the cave wall, providing her complete privacy but safety as well, since her ablution activity was the one instance when he didn't have eyes on her.

He set up traps around their perimeter, mapping each one to show to Nicole so she'd be aware and prepared.

The stream he'd insisted upon was only yards away from the horses, and he caught, then cleaned lunch. Needing to give them both some real sustenance, even if just for mental-health purposes.

And while the fish was on a small camping cook pan, on the one small propane burner they had, he settled down to his own cognitive work. Delving into various files that occurred to him to seek out. Memorizing as he read. Trying to build a profile of the case from the new perspective they'd gained. Looking for connections.

Nicole opted to eat lunch inside while she worked, and he joined her. Asking for a rundown of her morning.

Her head shake wasn't encouraging, and he breathed back a hint of impatience. Not at her. At all. But at instincts that were screaming at him about the brigade coming for them. It wasn't far off. His best shot at keeping Nicole alive was if she found the masterfully hidden definitive proof they needed, accounts and names, before they were found.

"I'm in deep," she told him. "I've stumbled upon a couple of more sophisticated messaging protocols. But nothing that means much to me. Mostly just confirmations. Literally. Just says, Confirmed. Assuming I'm decrypting them correctly. I've made a list of dates and times, in case they correspond to any activities any of you are aware of that took place immediately prior to them."

Taking a bite of fish, he said, "Send it to Hudson Warner, and to me, please."

She nodded. Putting down her spork, she typed. And then said, "Done." Before turning her screen around.

Thinking she was showing him confirmation that she'd completed the task as requested, he barely glanced at it, until she said, "Here's the gist of what I've pulled out. I'm cutting and pasting like before. I just see nothing here except security protocols."

Setting his metal bowl on the mattress beside him, he grabbed her device. Noticed battery level and reached for a new one. Then got up and went outside, checked the solar chargers. Both of which were almost at full capacity.

Which he'd already known. Of course he'd known. He'd set them up.

He'd just needed a second outside the cave. The wave of doubt he'd seen in Nicole's eyes as she'd taken one last glance at her screen before turning it to him…mirrored by what he'd heard in her voice…had sent such a flood of anger through him, he'd had to vacate. To breathe.

Eduardo Duran was a lucky man, being locked up in prison and not the one heading into the mountains to try to stop Charlotte Duran from exposing too much. Harc wasn't sure he wouldn't kill the man if they came face to face out there.

All the heinous crimes the man had committed over the years were enough to put him down. But the fact that he'd taken an innocent baby, stolen her life from her, to the point of the genius being unable to trust herself, stealing her confidence even when she was risking her life to do good…came close to unhinging him.

Something he'd never experienced before. Not on a case. Not ever.

With a glance at the horses, he took a deep breath and headed back inside. To the computer Nicole had left right where he'd set it.

Her bowl was empty.

As he sat down, she headed outside, behind her boulder.

And with both ears in full listen mode—a state he often slept in—he focused on the screen.

Traveled through the first page and halfway down the second—aware that Nicole was reentering the cave.

And froze.

Letters, some upside down, interspersed within various groupings of caps and lowercased code and symbols, jumped up at him.

Turning the screen as Nicole resumed her seat, he said, "What's this?"

She glanced, looked up at him. "It's garbage code. A series of parts of various security protocols that, as they're written, actually do nothing. Except confuse hackers."

Tense, he stared at her. "Are you certain? Exactly as they're written? These are all recognizable to you?"

She nodded. Then said, "All of the code is. And the series of letters, interspersed upright and upside down. They're placeholders in the event someone wanted to go in and put the protocol into place. They'd replace the nonsense with missing code to make it live. It's actually something I designed. Eduardo didn't need as many levels of security on some things and didn't want them to slow him down. I took them out of working order but left them in place in case something changed. Mostly, I was a kid being lazy and didn't want to delete it all only to have him ask me later to put it back."

His gaze sharpened. "You did this? In this file?"

She shook her head. Which eased the intensity tightening his jaw absolutely none. "No. I wrote this when he was having some employee complaints several years back. It was a way for leaders to keep him apprised of various activities without anyone else tapping into the conversation.

But whoever used my code obviously didn't understand it. They just copied and pasted here."

He nodded. Chin jutting as he scrolled.

"Why? What did you find?" The worry in her tone cut into him. A feast for his own escalating concern.

"Because these letters, when you put them all together, spell a name I recognize."

Moving over to sit next to her, between her and the entrance to the cave—more as a protective move toward her than anything else—he pointed to the letters and characters he'd been referring to.

And spelled.

"Henry Villanosa," she said slowly, putting them all together. "Who's he?"

"An IRSCI—IRS criminal investigator." A man who'd been on the job for thirty years. Who—according to the Gussman case file Harc had read the day before—had been involved in the investigation of stolen funds case in which Hugh Gussman had been set to testify. Except the star witness had disappeared. And the money had never been found.

But Villanosa's name just had been. Hidden in stolen code in Wagar's files. Dated over a year ago. Just after Charlotte Duran had entered her DNA in the family-finder database.

He pulled out his phone.

Messaged Mike.

And had to physically restrain himself from taking Nicole into his arms. Shielding her from danger. As though any bullet that hit him couldn't just pass through him into her, too.

Sitting there knowing so much more, and still not enough, how could he possibly devise a failproof plan to keep her safe? To help set her free to find the life she deserved to have. If he could just do that—give a gifted and kind young woman the freedom to be whoever she wanted to be—maybe, just maybe, he'd find a piece of his soul again.

In that moment, in that cave, that *if* seemed larger than any obstacle Harc had ever faced.

For the first time in his life, he felt helpless.

At a time that was never going to matter more to him.

Chapter 19

Henry Villanosa. She hadn't tried to unscramble the letters into a name. Had seen the old lazy code and had accepted it for what it was.

But as a team, she and Harc, with their different perspectives, had managed to find another piece to the seemingly impossible to unravel dynasty her father had been involved in.

And yet her one innocent act—sending in her DNA in the hopes of finding maternal family—was bringing wolves out of the woodwork. First Wagar. And then Villanosa.

She didn't waste time joining in Harc's communication with Mike. Agitated and driven, she went straight back to work. They were making strides. But were racing the clock to get enough.

Harc might've thought he and Sierra's Web, even the whole damned FBI, could keep her safe. She knew Eduardo's true power. And if he wasn't the kingpin and Wagar wasn't, that meant someone with even more connections was also after them.

Someone they didn't know. Couldn't guard against.

Someone who wanted her dead. As soon as he got to her, she would be.

She'd made a lot of progress that morning and typed fast. And then faster. Copying and pasting data as she went.

Within twenty minutes, she had confirmation that she'd been found out. They'd assumed, wanted it to happen, to draw out their enemies, but when she reached a wall of security that none of her tricks would breach, her heart started to pound. New protocols had been put in place the previous night. While she'd been having mindless sex with Harc Taylor.

The security code was good. Really good. She was better. Got through it in less than an hour. And then another. She'd made it through four completely different walls before she got back to information hidden behind them.

When actual accounts flashed onto her screen, she started to shake. To feel the snakelike fear ride up through her again. She didn't stop, though. Fully focused, she pushed forward. Copying and pasting as rapidly as possible, aware, every second, that she could be shut down again.

She didn't stop to access the information she was gathering. To read through it. There was no time. And reading was not what anyone needed from her. Harc had an entire firm and a team of agents to assess the information. Her job was to get it for them.

And then to somehow rest that night knowing that their campsite would be known to their aggressors.

She'd agreed to the plan.

Would find the strength to persevere as long as she had breath.

Scrolling from the page she'd just pasted to the next she needed to copy, Nicole froze. The words…they jumped off the screen at her. Almost literally. She stared.

And screamed, jumping so hard that her computer slid sideways off her lap, when Harc suddenly hurried into the cave. "I've been on with Mike," he said, his expression grim. His focus so intense on whatever was on his mind that he didn't even seem to have noticed her own bad moment.

Unless…he already knew.

She felt sick. Queasy. With butterflies turning to bees buzzing and stinging inside her abdomen.

"He had agents posing as you and me, chosen because of their physical resemblance to us, at the last site where you used the satellite yesterday. They were accosted an hour and a half ago…"

Her breath caught. She dragged in air past the tightness in her chest.

"The agents were able to take them down, to arrest them. They're refusing to talk, but Sierra's Web has already run backgrounds. They're both recent parolees, have been incarcerated for more than ten years. They're new hires, Nicole. And it's starting to look like that's part of the pattern. Has been all along. Which is why it's been so hard to break up the organization. While its fingers reach to the ends of the earth, it thrives due to a major outsourcing program that never uses the same people for more than a job or two, rather than relying on a loyal crew. The operation itself is likely quite small."

His words computed even as her skin grew tight. Hot. "You're saying it's going to be nearly impossible to get those we want to catch, to come to us. We've just got independent hitmen after us." Smart. Savvy.

And all Eduardo.

Staring up at Harc, aching everywhere, Nicole almost wished she was already dead.

It only took a second, one look in Nicole's eyes to know that more was going on than the news he'd just brought in to her.

While they could figure that anyone who came after

them wasn't going to be able to give them the names and dates they'd need to convict whoever was involved at the top with Eduardo Duran, they'd just gleaned a very important piece of information. Had new lines of investigation they could now pursue. Someone would know some little thing that would tip the case.

If he and Nicole didn't succeed, that was.

Was that the problem? She was freaked out to learn that Wagar or whoever ruled him had sent thugs to get them? That their plan was working?

She'd spent her life looking at things on paper, from a very protected luxury fortress. Prior to coming to him, she'd been in the trenches for one day and one night in her entire life, running away from pressure to marry Wagar and then confronting her father. One day and one night when she'd believed herself the protected daughter of a well-respected decent living billionaire.

"You want to call it off?" he asked, standing there watching her right her computer. Adjust it on her lap. And do so again. "We can get a helicopter in here to pick you up right now."

He wasn't quitting. Walking away had been the worst thing he'd ever done. All the lines he'd skated, the tightropes he'd walked between right and wrong…he'd done for selfless reasons.

Walking away had been selfish. And weak. He'd been afraid that he wouldn't be able to keep himself in line.

He'd given in to the fear.

When Nicole finally raised her head to look up at him, he recognized some of that same fear. The kind he'd seen in the mirror. Fear of self.

Doubting your own mind.

Dropping down to his mattress, with the horses in full

view, Harc pulled his gun from his waistband and set it beside him. Resting against his hand. "Talk to me." The words came of their own accord. Straight from his heart.

The look she shot him then was something he'd seen before. The day she'd come to meet with him. When he'd been acting like an ass.

Not at all what he'd been expecting.

Seconds passed, he withstood the look. It didn't change.

"Did you, while you were on a job, sleep with a woman solely to get closer to someone with whom she'd been acquainted?"

Everything stilled within him. And without. He was on high alert. Had agents in the mountains, risking their lives to protect Nicole as well as apprehend anyone connected to Arnold Wagar or Eduardo Duran. He had to know how she came upon the information. "Did you find further Wagar conversation? On top of what you sent to Sierra's Web?"

Her chin lifted. "You didn't answer my question." The look in her eyes…there might have been sadness there.

More, he felt as though he was looking at someone who was hiding something. Not a woman with whom he'd slept accusing him of being first rate scum.

And remembered more of their first meeting. The woman wasn't going to give until she got.

"I did," he said. And for complete clarity, but for no good reason that pertained to the job, he said, "More than once." Not liking how that sounded, and with the night before continuing to rear itself in his mind, he added, "I entered relationships with them. After they'd been vetted. And always used a condom."

He knew what that made him. Had known when he'd quit his job that the things he'd done precluded him from having a regular life in normalized society.

He'd broken all normal boundaries by which good guys were judged. Had proven himself impossible to trust.

When she'd come to him seeking his help, when he'd agreed to work with her, her trusting him hadn't even been on the table. Nor had he had a hell of a lot of trust in her, either, for that matter. She'd found him by hacking into his friend's computer.

And she was Eduardo Duran's daughter. Someone he'd been watching as a player in the man's criminal organization.

So why was it hitting him so hard to lose what he hadn't had to begin with?

She'd glanced down, farther than her screen. Almost bowing her head, but after taking a deep breath, met his gaze head on. "And did you turn on one of your own agents? Disclosing his cover to Wagar's people, in order to prove your own loyalty?"

His mind sharp, he ran through ramifications of what she knew. Considered how long she might have known. What it meant that they were having the conversation right then, with killers in the mountains, looking for them.

When she was supposed to be using the skills that only she had to find evidence no one else had to end the years-long reign of terror.

"I did," he said with a tilt of his head. Didn't bother to add that he'd also saved the man's life.

Her nod back hit him oddly, considering the topic of conversation. Almost as though she cared more about his response, than in the less than stellar actions she'd been grilling him about.

Because she'd known all along?

And the night before had changed things between them? Making his unsavory life choices matter more?

He'd given her what she'd wanted. Now it was his turn.

"How long have you been waiting to ask me about those things?"

She shook her head.

"Have you known since you first came to see me?" He couldn't imagine Mike would have kept a dossier on him. She'd have had to thoroughly read multiple case reports. Which, based on how she'd described her hacking incident to him, she hadn't had time to do.

The stillness about her.

Almost a sense of defeat.

Acceptance laced with fear, he amended, remembering the way she'd yelled out and jumped when he'd first come in.

Fear...or guilt?

He almost felt as though in the time he'd been outside, she'd become someone else

"What's going on, Nicole?" He wanted to reach the woman he'd held the night before. His tone was all agent.

Lives were at stake.

And not just theirs.

"I think my father is talking to me."

Adrenaline raced through Harc. His right hand covered his gun. And though his mind told him he could have been living with the enemy the past few days, his instincts told him to offer help.

He just wasn't sure anymore if the instincts guiding him were work related—offer help as a means to find out all he could—or because he'd fallen for a woman he thought was incredible. No matter who she was or what she'd done.

He'd placed his hand over his gun. Was ready to move with it.

But he hadn't aimed it at her.

Why she noticed, or why it mattered, Nicole wasn't sure. More, she was using that hand, the gun as a distraction from the harsher reality in front of her.

"I broke into a new system this morning. It allowed me to view one bank account." She swallowed. Couldn't look back at the screen.

Was still fuzzy headed with ramifications. Trying to find her way out to focus, think clearly. To not let panic rob her of her ability to act wisely.

To protect herself. And others.

She'd get there. Was going to accept nothing less. She just had to find a way to speed up the process. Not get lost in minutia.

Like finding out that the man you'd slept with, the man you'd opened your whole heart to, slept with the women he got close to on the job.

And that he'd turned on one of his own. Could even have been Mike.

Or her, for that matter.

"Nicole?"

She heard Harc's voice through the fog. Left it out there.

Would her heart always lead her astray?

As it had with her father?

The thought, more than the voice, brought her upright. The man whose genes had given her life had robbed her of the life for which she'd always yearned. To be a normal kid in a regular family. To have a mother.

She hadn't even dared dream of a sibling.

Eduardo had stolen all that opportunity away from her. He'd robbed her of a chance to know and grow up loving and being loved by her mother.

He'd made her dependent solely on him. Giving her no

chance to love anyone but him. Even her nannies…they'd come and gone on a regular basis.

He'd taught her to think like him.

But the blood in her veins was akin to Savannah, too. The big sister who'd risked everything, who'd nearly died, just to find Nicole. No strings attached.

Eduardo's entire empire had been run by him pulling the strings he'd injected into everyone around him. He'd been the master puppeteer.

No more.

"Nicole?"

"The account is mine." Or rather, "It has my name on it. Solely. With my—Charlotte Duran's—social security number and driver's license attached. The address is the post office box that I set up, and transferred all my accounts to, after moving to Phoenix."

"He doesn't know about Nicole."

The words weren't at all what she'd expected. They drew her gaze to the familiar intentness in Harc's blue eyes.

And yet…from a distance. They'd spent a few days in the mountains, as work partners. Had had sex. And if they survived the current situation, they'd go their individual ways. Never see or speak to each other again.

Thinking only about what he'd chosen to bring out of the hellacious mess she'd played right into, she said, "Or he does and he's just not yet ready to reveal the information," she said.

"How much money is in the account?"

Yeah, that was more to the point. "Over a billion dollars." And holy hell to that.

He didn't react. Just asked, "When was it established?"

Yeah, that, too. "Right after we moved to the States."

His gaze narrowed. She glanced over the several yard

distance to their newest cave's entrance. Couldn't see much of the outside from her vantage point. Wasn't sure she wanted to do so.

"You're telling me you didn't know about the account?"

Hard to believe, right? She shook her head. "I knew of an account he set up for me, of course. I knew he made regular deposits to it, for my own security, he'd said. He had me pay the property taxes out of it, but otherwise the funds just sat there. Accruing. Three months ago, I emptied the money out, donated everything to women's shelters and a national domestic violence hotline number, and then closed the account."

He could believe her or not. She wouldn't blame him if he didn't. Didn't much matter.

She could hardly believe how naive she'd been. How she couldn't have known...because she knew him.

Better than anyone.

Chin up, she glanced right at him as she said, "This account is offshore." Watched his expression sharpen, his brows narrow.

"And it always held that much money?"

He was getting there. Maybe.

Could be she'd be the only one who ever would.

She shook her head. "He opened it with half a million."

"And deposited to it over the years?"

She nodded. "A quarter of a million a year."

Which didn't reach anywhere near a billion. Even for someone not great at math.

She and Harc were both top notch in that area.

"But it grew to a billion?"

She nodded.

"When?" The billion-dollar question.

Part of her was relieved that he got there so quickly, as

she said, "The day I told him I put my DNA in that database." See, that had been her mistake.

Telling him.

She'd played her hand. Letting him know, by the admission, that he owned her. Played right into his. Had she not given him the heads up, he wouldn't have had a year to prepare. To notify Wagar. To get people on Savannah.

Her sister might have shown up, tipped off Mike—who was already in residence and clever enough to have seen a stranger tracking his charge—and once they'd told her, she could have helped Mike infiltrate her father's dealings and end the entire nightmare right then and there.

There'd have been no Wagar proposal.

No running away.

No one shooting at Savannah.

But Eduardo would have had her.

He'd known it then.

And believed it, still.

That was how they were going to get him.

Even it meant taking her down with him.

Chapter 20

Nicole wasn't his lover. Or even his friend. She was no longer a work partner. Not because he deemed it that way, but her demeanor, her tone, everything about her spoke withdrawal from him.

He'd expected as much. He'd slept with her on the job. As he'd done with other women.

He'd ratted out a fellow agent to prove his cover's loyalty.

He'd come full circle. With a difference. He was no longer running away. He was back in. One-hundred percent.

Reaching for his computer, he held out his hand. And when she just looked at him, he asked, "Can I have the flash drive?" It was how she'd passed every bit of information on to him.

She shook her head. "I haven't put anything new on it."

Okay, he got it. She didn't trust him. Resented him, too. But the situation they were in went way beyond letting hurt feelings get in the way. The one thing they could count on with each other was their shared passion to bring down the entire empire that had made Eduardo Duran—and they had to assume others—very very rich.

"I need to see that account, Nicole." He didn't pretend to ask. Or talk like a friend, either. "I need to send it on to Mike. They can trace account numbers, perhaps find out what bank it's sitting in, which opens a hell of a lot of doors."

When she didn't move, except to shake her head again, and didn't look away, either, he took a step back from the situation. Sat there assessing her.

Couldn't get a read.

She was her father's daughter.

And…he suspected that Gussman *was* the kingpin. With assistance, to be sure, but still…the man had managed to steal two million dollars from the United States government a quarter of a century before. Money that had never been found.

It wasn't that much of a stretch to realize that the genius had things over powerful people, keeping them loyal to him lest he expose the conceivably large portfolio he had. He'd already heard back that Villanosa was off the grid.

Because Gussman, Wagar, or someone else working with them was watching Nicole's progress online. The bad guys knew what they knew.

Villanosa was either in the wind, starting a new life under a new identity…

Or he was dead.

That was how people like Eduardo managed to flourish for decades.

It also meant that the organization was minus one powerful person. A man who'd had strong governmental influence—and classified intel, too.

Harc had to find a way to capitalize on the weakness.

Gussman was diabolically smart. A manipulator unlike anything Harc had seen before. He'd cold-bloodedly chosen to leave one daughter behind when he'd taken the other from their mother. Had even put a hit out on his firstborn when she got too close.

As Harc sat there, in visual battle with Nicole, pieces started to fall into place one after another. Gussman's confession hadn't been for Charlotte's sake. It had been a preplanned move devised long before Charlotte and Mike had shown up at the mansion that night. Designed to manipulate everyone involved.

Which was what he'd been doing all along. Everywhere.

And was still doing? With Nicole?

The truth hit Harc like a punch in the gut. Delivered by a heavy-weight boxer. He stood up, taking his gun with him. Shoving it into his waistband, he said, "I need to see that file."

Her head shake, the raise of her brows was clear. Almost deliberate. "I've closed the chain," she told him. "You can take my laptop, have anyone you want analyze it—no one is going to find the information I had up on screen. And no one can compel me to show it to you, either. I'm not under arrest. And I know for a fact that you don't have anything on me to be able to arrest me."

He missed a breath or two. Couldn't believe that he'd been wrong about her over the past few days. Eduardo might have made her in his image.

Perhaps he'd taught her how to act in any situation.

But the man hadn't sent her to Harc. There'd been no reason to do so. Nothing for the man's empire to gain by exposing it to more scrutiny.

By exposing the lies in his confession.

But what about Nicole? Was she back under her father's control? Had she ever completely left it? She'd been devastated. Angry.

Didn't mean she didn't still love the man.

Staring her down, he said, "So does this mean you're done? We're through here?"

He wasn't. Not by a long shot. But there was no point in being sitting ducks if they'd gained all they were going to in their current rendition.

The sudden widening of her eyes, before they narrowed in on him again caught his attention. Stuck.

Had she overplayed her hand? Did Eduardo need her to continue playing Harc, her sister, the FBI, Sierra's Web?

Or was something else going on? Something less easy to pinpoint. To understand.

Was she in trouble? More so than he, or anyone, knew?

As in, far more involved in Duran's operation than she wanted anyone to know? But then why seek him out? And more to the moment, why even tell him about the damned account she'd just supposedly discovered?

Because while she was somewhat in with Duran, he'd hidden too much from her for her to carry on without him?

She'd needed access to Wagar's files to find out what her father hadn't told her?

She hadn't answered his question. He wasn't backing away from it. "We done?" His tone held more threat than question.

Nicole raised her chin again. "No."

If he wasn't mistaken, there was a tremble in her chin, if not her voice.

Wishful thinking on his part?

"Then what? You continue to work, we all protect you while you do so, but you don't help us end this thing? You don't give us the information we need?"

At that, strange as hell, her face cleared. Setting aside her computer, she stood, eye to eye with him. "I swear to you, Harc. I will continue to share. I will give you everything you need. Just not information about that one account."

He held her gaze a long time. Delving deep. Mercilessly. She didn't even blink. And he believed what she'd just said.

Maybe he'd grown soft. His ability to do his job might have left him in the dust during his time away.

He didn't think so.

"Then let's get back to it," he said.

And walked out on her.

She had to do it. Nicole knew as well as she knew that she was no criminal, that she was the only one who could stop Eduardo Duran.

The only one who could think like he thought. The only possession he'd ever coveted and lost.

Standing alone in that cave, watching Harc's back as he headed toward the horses, she couldn't conceive of any way she'd succeed without his help. Mike and Sierra's Web—they were the icing on the mud she'd been served up. But Harc, he was her lifeline.

Her proof that no matter how much you'd lived in darkness, or consorted with thieves, you could still do good. Succeed.

Find love—even if only with animals who sensed a caring heart and didn't judge beyond it.

Would Mahogany and Imperial know that she'd crossed over? Even if only doing so undercover?

Harc no longer trusted her.

Which was for the best.

With that last thought, Nicole did some stretches and then sat back down. Opened her portal to the dark web, dove deep, and started to type.

Fearing that, even if she lived, she was going to lose herself for good.

She'd let Harc and Sierra's Web think that she was working toward finding them intel. She'd continue working on things she'd already accessed and downloaded that morning. Before the new portal had appeared on her screen.

She just couldn't be "seen" online poking into Wagar/ Duran business.

Instead, she was going to accept the olive branch she knew her father had just offered her. Attempt to have him help her play both sides. And hope that she didn't get herself killed.

Harc messaged with Mike. Who immediately brought Savannah into the scrambled conversation. He was going forward with Nicole, no matter what the others thought, but he would not involve them unknowingly.

He wasn't all that surprised to have almost immediate confirmation that they were choosing to stay fully on board. With a note from Savannah to please watch her little sister's back more closely than ever.

And acknowledgment that, considering the brainwashing with which she'd grown up, they couldn't completely trust her.

He unscrambled the last bit with dread filling his gut.

They all knew they couldn't they let her go. Even if she'd been completely turned by Duran—or had never really left his camp—she was their best chance at getting the evidence they needed to bring down the rest of his empire.

Harc was in one hundred percent.

No matter who Nicole turned out to be—and great move to change her identity as a sign that she'd left Charlotte behind, to hide the fact that she hadn't—she hadn't been dealt a fair rap in the beginning. Being manipulated and brainwashed from the time you were a baby…just not right.

She was smart, though. Well educated and then some. And an adult. Fully aware of the fiend her father really was.

The choices she was currently making were on her.

He left her to whatever she was doing for another hour. Until he got another message from Mike. Marked urgent.

In light of the information Harc had given them pursuant to the loaded offshore account in Charlotte's name, and at Harc's request, Mike had sent an agent in to have a discussion with Eduardo. Part of the man's plea agreement had included cooperation with authorities.

After which he'd always claimed to know nothing about whatever they'd brought him. Or took all blame on himself. He'd been in solitary confinement for weeks, giving him an opportunity to rethink his position.

Unscrambling took seconds. Comprehending what he was seeing, less than that. Shooting off an urgent reply to get more bodies in the mountains and watching the satellites for any and all movement, he spun on his heel and headed back to the cave that was beginning to feel more and more like a jail cell.

Nicole's. Not his.

He was the only guard.

Nicole was still waiting for a response to pop up from Eduardo in the minimized window she'd kept open, and continued to check every few minutes. She needed him to see her there. Waiting. Picturing her pacing. Her face tight with worry. Needed him to get an immediate response from her when he did send her his acceptance of her own olive branch. She had to give him the relief and gratitude he'd expect from her.

Without going overboard.

In the meantime, she was doing her best to find anything

she could in the morning's work that would gain her some traction—and trust—from Harc. And the others. Mike. Sierra's Web.

She couldn't let herself think about Savannah. Couldn't feel their connection. Not if she hoped to succeed at convincing Eduardo that meeting up with her sister had been a mistake. That they were nothing alike. That she didn't fit in with Savannah's world. That her sister was like their mother. She was Eduardo all the way. That he'd been right to leave them behind. And to pick her.

A series of numbers popped up in the decryption code she'd made up minutes before. Digits that, while different, mirrored the account number Eduardo had shown her earlier in the day.

And she knew…she'd just downloaded that information an hour before Eduardo's veiled message via a new portal exactly like the ones she'd been looking through—but with different encryption—had popped up. He'd set up security measures to have someone notified immediately if any accounts were breached.

There were no defining letters attaching. Nothing that she could see that identified the account owner. And she wouldn't expect there to be. The information would be hidden in another file. With different code.

Another part of a system she'd set up for her father. In her teens, she'd loved making up intricate codes for everything. Challenging him to decode them.

Even in the birthday cards she'd given him.

She shuddered at the thought of how much she'd adored the man. Was downloading the account information to the flash drive she'd pass on to Harc, when he came striding into the cave. His expression foreboding.

To say the least. Whatever was about to come at her…
wasn't good.

She wanted to take it standing. Didn't trust herself to remain steady enough on her feet to pull off her ruse.

"What?" she asked, as though they were who they'd
woken up as that morning. Or even who they'd been before
they'd had sex the night before.

Either was far better than the stranger looking down at
her as though he'd never seen her before in his life.

"Seriously, Harc. If you're going to shoot me, just do it.
Or tell me that you're leaving and taking both horses with
you." She wouldn't blame him for either.

And wouldn't stop what she'd started, either.

"Did you know?"

She blinked, shook her head. "About the account that
seems to be lodged at the same bank as the one I found for
myself this morning?" she asked, eyes open and honest as
she met his stormy gaze. "I told you I would share with you
everything I found." She pulled out the flash drive. "I just
moved the information over for you. And you'll be able to
see exactly when I accessed the information. And when I
found the decryption that unlocked it for me."

Frowning, seeming almost lost for a second, he leaned
over and took the flash drive. Then dropped to his butt on
the edge of his mattress, knees up, his boots in the dirt between them, and with his arms on those knees, moved the
drive from one hand to the next.

Then pocketed it. Pulling out his gun. Laying it down,
with his right hand beside it.

Not touching it yet.

She took that to be a good sign.

"Did you know that your father was in solitary confinement?"

She frowned back at him. Seriously concerned for a moment that he was trying to make her as simple minded as her father had done. "Yeah, I knew," she told him. "Mike told Savannah he was refusing to cooperate—in his way, of course—meaning they couldn't do anything to prove it. Why? You think I purposely didn't tell you?"

"Stop!" His raised voice upset her. The note of pain she heard in it, almost unhinged her.

Blinking back tears, fearing he'd see them as the ploy they could have been had she been in Eduardo's clutches all along, she said, "Harc. I'm sorry I can't show you that account. Until this is through, I have to protect myself. I thought you'd understand that. If Eduardo has framed me, I can't be sitting in a jail cell right now. I've got to get this work done first. And with Mike and the FBI officially involved and you on protocol again, I can't take the chance that someone would have to arrest me." There was far more truth in the words than he'd ever believe, if he knew what she'd done.

He raised both arms to his knees again. Studied her. As a person communicating with a person. Not an agent on the job. "Why did you tell me about the damned thing, then?"

And she gave him the truth. "I didn't mean to. Didn't think I should. But... I couldn't keep it from you."

If Eduardo were monitoring the conversation, he'd be proud. As long as he couldn't see into Nicole's heart. Know how she really felt.

It hit her then that that was where Eduardo Duran had failed. Every time. He'd never understood that Charlotte wasn't exactly like him. That she didn't just live in her mind but was driven by a compassionate, caring heart that needed to love and be loved.

He'd seen her lectures, her philanthropy through his own

critical lens. There was reason for everything he did. And every reason led to bolstering either his bank account or his stellar reputation.

Harc was still watching her. She wanted to crawl across the distance separating them and into his arms. To get lost there.

And never be found again.

But she had a role to play. Had to end things with her father, once and for all. End them in the world. Not just her life.

"Why are you upset that I knew Duran was in solitary confinement and didn't tell you?" she asked then. Needing to find some place where they could share the same ground again. To be on the same team.

He shook his head, then dropped his chin to his chest. Looked up at her. Then lifted his head to meet her gaze as he said, "They went to bring him out of his cell for questioning this afternoon. He wasn't there."

Heart pounding, she felt the blood leave her face. Felt her head swim. Thought she was going to pass out. Forced herself to focus long enough to ask, "The cell was empty?"

The diabolical man could walk through walls? And still show up on body checks? And eat food and send the empty container out?

Harc shook his head. "There was an off-duty guard there. One who swears he knows nothing. Says he was bound and gagged and blindfolded, dragged there, and left."

"When?"

It mattered. More than anyone knew but her. More than they could know.

"Today. Mid-morning."

Right about the time she'd accessed that file.

Eduardo had had a plan.

And when she'd breached a certain predetermined point, someone on the top tier payroll with a whole lot of clout and ability to manipulate had set it in motion.

Eduardo. Even in a cement cage behind a locked steel door, the man had the ability to control his world. Whether he ruled those in power with intimidation, threat, or, more likely, huge amounts of money and promises of protection—twenty-five years of getting what he wanted proved he was a master at it.

Shaking, Nicole feared that she was never going to be free of him.

Or be able to stop him.

Chapter 21

She wouldn't share the account because he'd gone official on her and she was afraid it would incriminate her. Get her arrested before she could find the proof to end the empire her father had been involved with her entire life.

Harc wanted to believe her. He didn't…quite.

Outside making dinner, all senses on alert in spite of the many trained defenders on the ground surrounding him and Nicole, Harc believed that she hadn't meant to tell him about the account. But hadn't been able to keep the secret from him.

Mostly.

With the caveat that she was smart enough, savvy enough, had read him enough to have concocted the story to get back in his good graces. About why she wouldn't share the account. And about why she'd told him it existed.

The near tearful state—the same.

But the way the blood had drained from her face when she'd found out Eduardo was nowhere to be found—that hadn't been faked.

Even if she was in cahoots with him, she hadn't been happy to hear that he was likely free.

Because she feared him?

Or because he was leaving the country without her? And she feared her fate on her own?

He hated the not knowing.

After looking over the new information she'd down-loaded to the flash drive, he believed that she'd just found the second bank account. Had already passed on the information to Mike. With any luck, they'd have the name of the bank soon.

Could begin digging from there.

He also believed that Nicole wanted to find evidence to eradicate the crime organization. Why else would she have come to him? He just wasn't positive she'd turn over the information to him once it was found.

Her father could have put her onto Mike and Harc. To get rid of evidence that only she could find.

She'd been shocked and hurt to find that second program she'd written. The one Wagar had been using. Meant even if she was working with Duran, he hadn't told her everything.

Perhaps just his way.

And it was possible the man wasn't sure he could trust her. She might be in the middle of a test of some sort. One which, if she failed, could get her killed.

Bottom line, some purpose with life-risking strength had driven Nicole Compton to breach Harc's privacy. He had to stick with her until that situation was resolved, one way or another.

The possibility that she could die in the process also weighed on him heavily.

He couldn't let personal thoughts get entangled with the facts or he'd lose focus.

A point he lost sight of when, two bites into dinner, Nicole—who was sitting on the ground nearer to the cave's entrance, facing the horses—said, "I'm finding myself less able to concentrate because I'm bothered by something."

He continued to eat. To maintain a semblance of calm. As all senses went on high alert. With a one shoulder shrug, he swallowed a bite and said, "You want to talk about it?"

Innocuous. No pressure. And an insult to her intelligence. Why else would she have brought it up? He took another bite of the stroganoff they were repeating for a second time.

"Not really, but I can't afford to be less than my best when every minute counts." She was eating, too, albeit more slowly than him. She was calmer than he liked, considering that she could be playing him.

All of them.

"The chatter I found this morning, between Wagar and… whoever…indicating that you slept with a woman close to Wagar when you were undercover…"

His gut dropped. He put down his bowl. Done eating. The utensil was nearly empty anyway. He'd seen bits of the messaging…had consumed everything she'd sent him. He'd only seen that he'd slept with a woman close to his subject while undercover. No specific mention of Arnold Wagar.

And nothing of note from the agents assigned to watch the man, either. Wagar was in the States. In California. Lying low.

But then, when the majority of your business took place on the computer, behind seemingly unending layers of encryption, you could be blowing up countries and who would know?

"I know I came on to you last night…"

Her words grabbed his full attention. His gaze shot over to her. Collided with hers. Was she looking for an apology?

Her eyes were clear, focused on his as she said, "I just need to know why you responded."

Really? He almost said the word aloud. Paused, not sure what she was looking for. Some kind of reassurance that she was attractive?

In the midst of the intricate and hellacious situation they were engulfed with?

He shook his head without responding. The answer was too obvious. Didn't need saying. Yeah, she'd had the ability to get him off track. To consume him mind and body for a time.

He'd thought he was helping her through some rough moments. Helping them both.

Maybe he hadn't thought at all. Clearly, not enough.

And was getting hard again just thinking about that hour. One of the most pleasurable he could ever remember.

"When you're working, you sleep with a woman to get what you want from them," she said then. "To get them to confide in you, maybe give information that seems harmless to them but that you need for reasons of your own that you aren't disclosing to them. Or to get them to introduce you to someone."

And...boom. He got where the conversation was going.

Started to blurt the truth. Held his tongue while he considered the angles. What she might be seeking. If indeed her concentration was being affected by the not knowing. And he had a flash of her face the night before as she'd looked him in the eye.

There'd been no subterfuge. To the contrary, the lack of even a hint of walls between them had been completely new for him. No walls. Not from her. But not from him, either.

And that was when Harc knew that the job he was on

had become personal. There was no way it couldn't be. No matter what he found out, he'd fallen for the woman.

And even if she was in trouble, he was going to do everything he could to see that she got out of it. Including killing the fiend who'd fathered her, if that was what it took to free her from him.

She shouldn't have asked. Nicole knew, most particularly in light of the duplicity she was practicing with her escaped father—a man who could be right there in the mountains with them ready to snatch her away again, that her sexual situation with Harc mattered not at all.

But twice since their pre-dinner conversation, she'd found herself staring at code instead of working to decipher it. While her mind was on Harc.

On duping him. Her chances of success there.

And on whether she could even pull it off. The man was different than anyone she'd ever met. Granted, she hadn't had a ton of experience in the dating field, but she'd been in the company of the male sex her entire life. If her father ever entertained women, it had been outside Charlotte's purview.

She'd been acting as his plus-one at charity and social events since she was a teenager.

She finished her dinner. Cleaned her own thin metal bowl. Took care of personal business. And as she headed toward the cave, saw Harc standing just outside it. Watching her approach.

Guarding her?

Or keeping an eye on the area in general?

She went to pass him, to head back in to work while there was still an hour of daylight, was choosing not look at him when she heard, "Nicole."

She wanted to be unaffected enough to ignore the soft, almost apologetic tone in his voice. She wasn't.

Stopping, she looked over at him. She didn't need his pity. She'd been desperate for escapism. Had known she could get it with him. She'd thrown herself at him.

She'd known the second she'd woken up that morning that she'd made that particular bed, and it was up to her to climb out of it.

"The women I've slept with while working—there were only three—the relationships were predetermined as part of the job. Not the sex…that only happened if it became obvious that I'd lose their interest if things didn't go to another level."

He was telling her something. His gaze said so. She still felt numb.

And hurt, too, which made no sense.

"Last night had nothing to do with this mission we're on. It was personal. Because you asked and I didn't want to reject you…" She paled. "…but also because I wasn't strong enough to find a noble high ground and deny myself the chance to share that with you."

Oh. For the first time since she'd awoken that morning Nicole felt warm. Inside and out.

She blinked. Look at him again. Didn't smile with her mouth but felt as though both of their gazes had shared a grin. Said, "Thank you." And, bowing her head, went back to work.

Spurred on by the possibility that the sooner she got through more layers of frustrating blocks—or heard from Hugh Gussman/Eduardo Duran—the sooner she'd have a chance to sink into some more incredible forgetfulness.

With a man she was never going to forget.

Even if he ended up hating her.

* * *

The evening was too eerily quiet. Horses had grazed to their content. Harc brushed them, communing, and neither one of them gave him any cause for anything but calm.

As in before the storm?

Feeling like eyes were on his back, he couldn't help but concern himself with what was coming their way.

And how soon it would get there.

One thing he knew for certain, to his core, was that he had to sleep half-awake. And be at his most vigilant. Their campsite afforded more protection than most anywhere else they could be. Unless a chemical bomb landed in the middle of their small compound, they shouldn't be breached without warning. Every move they made outside the cave or the tarps he'd set up for personal business was being picked up by satellite.

As were the areas surrounding them.

And as one who found ways to get around procedures, he knew that nothing was foolproof. If he was on the other side of the barriers that had been set up, he'd find a way to get to that cave.

His task was to figure out how he'd best do so. And prepare for the eventualities.

Sourcing out the weakest spots, he set underground barriers to alert them in the eventuality of intruders. Littered the area with leaf covered TNT poppers set on hard ground or rocks.

His last messaging with Mike was frustrating in its lack of any hint of closure. Wagar remained in his California home. Eduardo hadn't shown up on any of the hundreds of traffic and other surveillance cameras Sierra's Web personnel had accessed, starting with the prison in California where he'd been held and expanding from there to Phoenix to southern Colorado and at all airports in between.

The BOLO had gone out to all agencies, both federal and local.

For all they knew, the man was holed up under the care of a plastic surgeon, changing his looks as he'd done in the past. With new identification papers already created.

He could also have been transported out of the country. Could be sitting on the beach somewhere without extradition, drinking mai tais on the beach.

That fact that Wagar was still in the States told Harc that Eduardo had remained in the country as well. An assumption with which Mike agreed. Believing as they did that the underground network of which the two were a part was small, and going with an agreed upon theory that Eduardo Duran was the kingpin, as they'd always assumed, everyone was on high alert, with multiple crews working round the clock, resting a lot of hope on Nicole's ability to get to the root of the operation before Duran got to her.

They'd traced the account number Nicole had given them to a bank in the Cayman Islands. But didn't get any further than that. Winchester Holmes, Sierra Web's financial partner and head of their entire financial team, was familiar with the bank. And with many who'd banked there. It was exclusive, refused to work with American authorities and was also known for their less-than-savory connections. He believed, based on the little he'd been able to determine from the finances Eduardo had turned over as his entire business portfolio upon confession, that the man had no go-to bank. But, rather, that he had a portfolio that appeared to be complete, while hiding any number of untold accounts in any number of untold locations.

The man was a genius.

So was his daughter.

And so were they—each in their own fields.

Mike sent the reminder at the tail end of the conversation.

Truth was, though, that Duran was just that good. Which was why he'd been eluding authorities for more than twenty-five years.

Harc was up against the case of his career, of his lifetime, one in which he'd developed a personal affiliation—and he didn't like, at all, how far away he was from closing it as he went inside the cave for his toiletries and fresh clothes before turning in for a while.

His rest would be intermittent. He'd lived that way for months at a time during various points of his career. That prospect didn't faze him. Sharing the small space with a woman who'd slipped by defenses he'd had up his entire career did.

Eyes wide, Nicole glanced up at Harc as soon he'd taken enough steps inside the cave to indicate that he was heading back her way. She just as quickly turned her gaze back toward her computer screen, stomach roiling. She'd heard back from Eduardo, just as she'd known she would.

Had information for Harc. Something that was going to hit him hard. If she delivered it, the teams backing Harc up would be all over it instantly, and Eduardo would know that. It would be her sign to him that she was working for him.

That the plea to come home, to be with the only person who really knew her, who loved her, to be where she'd always belonged was legitimate. She'd further strengthened that plea with a condition of her own—Wagar being permanently removed from anything to do with her.

She knew how to play Eduardo's game. Was making him choose, too.

The fact that the information she was staring at but hadn't yet downloaded to the flash drive Harc had returned to her earlier would also prove to Harc that she was on their side was part of what was stopping her.

The second she passed on Eduardo's information, Harc would never be able to trust her again.

Something he wouldn't know at first, of course, but from that point on, she'd be counting the days and hours until he turned on her.

If her plan succeeded, he'd also have everything he'd wanted. Duran done. His organization demolished.

He reached for his toiletries. Would be heading out, leaving her to sit there in a battle she couldn't personally win, either way.

She had to be brave. Strong. To see the plan through. No matter the sacrifice to self.

And she couldn't afford to alert anyone else. First because no one knew how Eduardo was managing feats like a magician. Who was paving his way.

Or on his payroll.

Second because she wasn't sure she could pull the whole thing off if she wasn't on an island by herself. Eduardo knew her better than anyone. He'd know if she felt secure. She'd let some nuance slip. Something.

Let alone the fact that the more people who were brought in, the sooner Eduardo would figure out that she'd turned on him so completely.

She was on the hook. And so afraid that Eduardo would manage to slither through official protocols again.

And again.

Unless she stopped him.

"Harc?" She made the intonation rise on the last part of the syllable. Like she was just discovering something. Hit Save on the download so the timing of his file would verify the information had just appeared.

Rather than having been sitting there for more than half an hour as she'd vacillated with herself. Trying to figure out which of the horrible choices in front of her made her a better person. She went with the one she could live with. If she survived.

He turned at the entrance of the cave. Took a few steps toward her. "What's wrong?"

"I just found a whole series of conversations between Arnold Wagar and someone who was working for him," she said, shaking inside, her chest tightening like a vice over her lungs as she got close to the big reveal.

The one that had had her near tears and frozen on the one screen since she'd first read it.

Pulling out the flash drive, she reached it out to him. "They're with Clayton Abernathy," she said, her gaze meeting his as she delivered the name of the agent he'd double-crossed on his last assignment.

He'd taken the drive but froze as she said the name. Was staring in her direction. She wasn't sure he was seeing her, though. "You got word that Wagar needed you to prove your loyalty before being granted a meeting with him, right?"

"I wasn't sure it was Wagar," he said then, snapping into focus as his right hand rested against the gun jutting from the side of his shirt. "I was going to be meeting with him or a top lieutenant," he said, studying her. As though she'd been there. Had something to do with what had happened when she'd been busy lecturing and wishing she could live without *Isaac* at her heels every second of every day.

"Abernathy told Wagar that you were an undercover

cop. CIA. The test of your loyalty was supposed to have ended your life. But you didn't act as they expected. You went for Abernathy, who you thought was in the range of fire, and escaped the bullet that was meant to have killed you." She held his gaze the entire time she delivered the news. Willing him to not only believe her. But to know that she felt his pain.

That she cared.

Personally.

He seemed to get the message. He held on to her gaze, too. His eyes glistening with intensity. He nodded. And his "Thank you" was more of a caress than mere words before he said, "I'm going to message Mike," and walked out.

Nicole wanted to follow him. To be with him, a hand at his back, as he delivered the newest detail to Mike. Her knees were so weak, she hadn't been sure she could stand.

But she'd be ready for him when he returned. Inviting him in again, consoling him as he'd consoled her the night before. Filling her soul before it went completely dark.

Loving him for the short time left before he found out she wasn't to be trusted.

Because she knew, with the same certainty that dictated Eduardo's successes, that Harc was going to find her out. Like Hugh Gussman, Harc was just that good.

Exhausted, she shut down her computer, readied herself for bed, and was lying awake in her sleeping bed with a small flashlight putting a soft glow over the darkness that had fallen by the time Harc returned to her.

She didn't ask how his scrambled message conversation had transpired. The answer was pretty much a given. Mike and the agencies and firm involved with the investigation would be arresting the CIA agent and bringing him in for questioning.

At which time he'd deny knowing anything about which they were speaking. But this time, with what she'd downloaded and given Harc, the authorities would have proof to make the claims stick.

The double agent would be prosecuted. Sent to jail.

And unless she did her job right, he'd end up disappearing from his cell, too. And given a new life someplace of his choosing...

She needed Harc. To feel his touch. To lose herself in him until everything but thoughts of him were obliterated long enough for her to breathe.

Almost as though he'd read her mind, he pulled his mattress over and dropped it next to hers. Shoving it up against hers with his foot. And then dropping down to it.

Desire ignited inside her, swam through her veins as she watched him settle his gun under the top corner of the mattress. Thinking of how much more accessible and comfortable things were going to be with twice the space—on fire even more for him having thought of it—she reached out a hand to him.

Felt it flounder in dead air as he lay just out of reach, on his side on the edge of his mattress, his back turned toward her.

And she realized he hadn't moved the mattress over for pleasure. He'd done so to put himself between her and the cave's opening.

He was doing his job.

He wasn't going to be doing her.

Chapter 22

Harc came to with a start, fully aware of the direction from which the pop had come. Gun in hand, he stood, heard Nicole rustle, and put his left hand behind him, signaling for her to stay back.

He couldn't hear the horses. His gut tightened.

"Get your gun," he whispered. "And stay put as long as you know where I am and am still standing. I shoot from behind as quickly as I do forward."

Something he'd already told her. And bore repeating. She hadn't seemed to take it to heart at the time.

He took another step forward, heard her take the safety off her pistol—a Glock—smaller than his, but powerful. He stepped soundlessly, quickly, to the side of the cave's opening.

Sliding outside, he kept himself covered, by rock overhang above, brush around him, keeping his back to the mountain—just as he'd planned. Got close enough to the horse's cover to see that they were both there.

Lying down as they did when they slept in their stalls. Relief was brief. He wanted to believe that Imperial and Mahogany had taken to their new shelter as they had to the nice roomy stalls he'd had built for them at the ranch.

He knew better.

Nor did he think that someone had gotten close to them. Imperial would have given the loud sniff with which he'd been trained to alert Harc.

Usually when Harc's tension was escalating, but any time the horse sensed danger. No way the former wild animal would have lain down to sleep in the former mountains that had been his home.

Had it been him, he'd have dropped a treat for the mustangs from above—something light like pieces of banana—that had been shot with something to make them sleep. Quiet. Inobtrusive. Nothing that would alert them or wake him.

Something for which he hadn't planned.

But looking up, he saw exactly where the culprit would have been to successfully complete the feat. Knew, too, that in the amount of time it would have taken the horses to eat and then lie down to sleep, the fiend could be right there with them.

Watching. Waiting.

He had no idea how many were out there. Or how close Mike's agents and Sierra's Web's protectors might be.

Counted on the perp or perps not being visible by satellite.

Something much easier to accomplish in the dark. Based on the moon there was another couple of hours before dawn.

If Harc could hold the enemy off until then, he'd have all the help he needed. Coming at the intruders from behind.

Frozen in place, he kept watch. Ready to shoot at any movement around the entrance to the cave. Waiting to hear more pops. Watching the two locations he'd also scouted for best ways into the camp.

One involved climbing up the mountain from over a mile below.

The other, going up half a mile and scaling down. Either would require skill and equipment. Something a professional would already know and have prepared for.

And would require arrival one at a time.

Giving him one chance to take each one down before the next appeared.

Unless they came from both locations at once.

Temperatures had dropped from the balmy seventy during the day to the thirties that were expected for late spring. Sweating, he welcomed the chill.

Couldn't shun his awareness of the so-special woman in the cave just yards away. Trusting him to keep her safe.

Needing him to keep her safe, even if she didn't trust him.

Attack was imminent. His gut, his soul, and his mind were all clear on that.

As he told himself that he could single-handedly take down anything that came at him in however many numbers. That he was fully prepared.

That good at what he did.

And prayed that help was there, guarding his back.

Eduardo Duran.

Picturing the man behind his desk in the home in which she'd grown up, the completely confident and self-assured look on his face as he dealt with one irritant and another—getting rid of them without raising his voice or losing his charming smile—Nicole shuddered. Adjusted the gun in her suddenly sweating palm.

She'd known he'd act quickly. That her clock had been ticking. She hadn't expected him to pounce within hours of the making of their deal.

As she stood against the wall of the cave, near the entrance so she could keep Harc in sight, realization hit.

Harc had messaged Mike.

Authorities had moved in on Abernathy immediately.

And that had been Eduardo's cue.

Every move a preplanned piece on the chess board of life.

With such forethought and precise planning that checkmate was inevitable. The man was only going to die when his physical organs grew so old they could no longer be revived.

And he was coming for her.

He'd had his proof that she was working for him.

And he had her.

But not without a fight.

He was the kingpin. She had no doubts there anymore.

The lack of information she'd been able to find, other than what Wagar had been using for his own deeds—none of which had led to Eduardo Duran directly—told her that there *was* no one else. There'd have been a virtual connection someplace.

Or a clear lack of one. A void.

She'd found no void. Just dead ends when it came to actually getting to the money. Most of what Eduardo had done wasn't on paper.

Or spoken about over modern technology, either.

Which is what had made him so successful.

He'd been word of mouth. Fistfuls of cash for those who were willing to keep their mouths shut, to make one thing happen quietly, low risk, in order to get rich fast.

He'd been the brains. Millions of successful plans carried to completion. No two exactly alike. That would have bored him.

Days of staring at her own misused code, living in her father's head, and seeing the end of her life in sight, brought clarity.

A strange kind of peace.

She knew.

No more doubts.

There'd be no proof. Not without finding every tiny dealer out there who'd been touched by Duran money once or twice. And was willing to talk. But even then, the deed would be too small on its own, the evidence nowhere near enough to bring down an empire.

Duran knew that. He'd styled his business that way from the beginning.

And when he'd needed bigger help, he'd chosen well. A CIA agent. An IRSCI. The spoiled, avaricious son of a foreign dignitary.

There could be more.

While Nicole stood there, gun aimed and ready to shoot at any movement that wasn't Harc, her senses focused so completely on those yards of land before the drop-off and around both cliffs to the sides of them. She knew that when the case was over, when the mountains were clear of Eduardo's men and Harc went home to his ranch, Eduardo's world would be unchanged.

He'd probably move.

Maybe not. Maybe he'd fight the court battle, to prove that he wasn't guilty of convictable crimes. His confession had already been shown as false. She'd proven that.

The financial details he'd given would be bogus, too. She had no doubt of that.

He'd say he was protecting her.

She was his scapegoat.

The realization was new. And yet…felt like she'd known

forever. Everything that he'd ever done could be explained by his need to care for his baby girl.

On some level.

He was a fiend. A murderer. A thief and an abuser. And smart enough to have come up with the perfect crime.

Which he'd repeated countless times in the twenty-five years she'd been alive. Right under her nose.

Using her technological creations to transfer funds and then make the tracking of such impossible. He hadn't just used them. He'd manipulated them in such a way that even he wouldn't know how to trace them. It was all random.

Except for the Wagar part.

He'd be next, after Harc and Nicole. She was sure of that, too. The man's cry for help the other day…maybe that had been directed at her, too.

Wagar had failed to keep Nicole in line, to romance her and give her and Eduardo a legal and clearly understood passage out of the country when Nicole screwed up and entered her DNA in the database.

The man would do better, surrendering himself to the police.

Nicole started to shake. From standing frozen in one position, but also with the thought that struck. Keeping her senses tuned outward, she kept her gun in hand as she retrieved her computer. Dove into Wagar's private channel and told him to go to the police.

Told him that Duran's plan was in motion and he wouldn't live out the night if he didn't get protection immediately. Banking on the selfish man's weakness, his desire for life over death to prompt him to make the call.

If he saw the message in time.

And so he'd know it was her, she repeated, in an offhand fashion, something he'd said to her months ago when he'd tried to force her to kiss him on the back grounds of her father's mansion.

He'd said that she would be his. And she'd like it.

I'll never be yours. And I never liked you, she typed.

Then punched in the code to send through the security protocols.

Gun in hand, she left her computer on the ground. Took up her previous position, standing guard.

Heard a shot ring out.

And knew her time had come.

Harc got the one whose head popped up to ground level from down below a single second before the arm bearing a revolver appeared. Got him before the guy's shot went off.

He spun in the next second, saw no movement slithering down from above. But heard the land as another one of his TNT pops went off. He shot behind a boulder that protected him from the second attacker, at least for a few seconds. And saw the second head coming up over the edge of the cliff, was ready for the gun to appear, aimed right at him.

"Stop!" The voice was female. He hardly recognized it. Didn't turn. Couldn't take his focus off the head. "I go willingly, as long as Harc Taylor is left alone. The second he is harmed, I shoot myself, and the program I wrote and have set to go live will do so as planned."

What in the hell was she doing?

He took his gaze off the man hanging onto the side of the cliff—gun in hand but not currently aimed—long enough to confirm that Nicole was standing in the middle of their encampment with a gun pointed at her head.

He scanned for the dropper. Saw no one.

Glanced at his known shooter again. The gun still lay

on the ground, within the grasp of the hands and arms hanging on.

"Daddy?" the woman called, her tone unrecognizable to him. "You're here, aren't you? You wouldn't leave me out in the night to do this all alone."

Harc didn't breathe. Waiting. Neither of the horses had moved. He prayed the drugs kept them down a little while longer.

"I need to see you, Daddy. I've missed you so much." Harc heard the familiar sound of tears in the voice. Recognition hit him like bricks in the gut.

And he knew. She wasn't crying for the man who'd robbed his daughter of her right to a life of her own. She was crying for what she'd almost had.

What she'd wanted—that for which she'd started to grow a tiny bit of hope.

No one had moved. Which was Harc's clue that she was right. The hired thugs knew what Nicole did—that Eduardo was there. The man's one weakness had always been the child he'd mistakenly thought he owned. Because she'd been from his seed. His daughter.

Hugh Gussman wasn't going to let this one go down without him.

Even if, ultimately, she had to die.

"I answered the second I saw your message, Daddy," she continued to stand there, gun to her head, calling out in an almost childlike tone. "I did as you asked. I'm so sorry I didn't want to marry Wagar. And that I entered my DNA into that database. I was just lonely, Daddy. I'm so, so sorry." She started to cry then.

It took everything Harc had to leave her standing there, alone, with her sobs.

But she'd just given him clues as to what she was doing.

Playing out a scenario she'd kept from him, from everyone. Eduardo had contacted her.

And she'd gone back to him. In cyberspace.

Leading to the horror playing out before him.

He had to trust her. To let her show him the way.

Unless…had Duran manipulated her into getting herself killed?

Or even killing herself?

Some kind of sick version of Munchausen syndrome?

He had to trust her. And keep his focus on saving her life, too.

"Daddy? I'm sorry! Please come get me."

Harc saw the head on the ground move slightly. In the direction from which he'd heard the most recent pop. Just as a voice came from trees above it. "Taylor, drop the gun, and my daughter lives. Don't, and you both die."

Harc set his gun on the ground at his feet.

He had a smaller pistol in an ankle holster. Nicole had seen Harc strap it on that morning. When they'd barely been speaking. Both pretending that they hadn't spent part of the night naked together.

She held on to the thought, letting it feed the tears that were her only chance at getting Harc out of there alive. As much as her father saw her as a possession, one he'd likely kill if he felt justified in doing so, he also prided himself on lavishing her with fulfilled wishes. And being able to console every pain she'd ever felt.

Thinking of Harc kept her purpose strong and the tears coming. Eduardo didn't like her tears. They panicked him. She'd learned young to suck them back. Her inability to do so would knock him some.

The shaking was not part of the plan. Not that it had been all that intricate to begin with.

Saving Harc. Exposing Eduardo. Perhaps dying in the process. She'd just known that it had to end.

And that she could make it happen.

Her father knew full well she could have put a program in motion. He'd want to keep her from letting it go live.

He couldn't be sure what all she knew. She'd lived with him a long time.

Eduardo's voice had come from above. The ensuing silence told her that he was either aiming for a big final moment. Or on his way down to her.

She braced for either.

The man at the cliff, athletic build, several inches shorter than the CIA agent she'd fallen in love with, had climbed all the way up and stood, gun aimed toward Harc. She prayed he had his little pistol in hand and would get the first shot off if the man moved to shoot.

In daylight, she'd put her money on him every time. But in the dark…discernment of a small muscle move could prove impossible.

Still, it was clear that he was waiting further instruction. Her father was still at the helm.

But his ship had definite leaks in it.

Wagar was a wild card.

And two of Duran's powerhouses had been exposed.

He was a pro at taking hits and making them appear as bonuses. New ways to conquer. To win. But he'd taken a lot of them recently. One after another.

He had to be aware of the chinks hitting his armor.

He'd have known that if Harc Taylor or any other authorities had enough on him to convict him without a confession, they'd never have accepted the plea deal.

Or at least figure them for being smarter than that.

And her deep dive into his protocols would have told him that they were still looking for that evidence.

There had to be something there he didn't want her to find. The thought filtered down through her very deliberate continued show of weakness. Almost wiping the tears from her face.

Not much. She was certain she'd been right about any lack of findable proof. For the most part. But something that would end him.

"I found it, Daddy," she called. "It's in the program I wrote tonight. It will go live unless I stop it." She hiccupped. Caught a whiff of his cologne. Dropped her gun arm from up by her head down to her thigh. Then, in a weaker tone, said, "And I'm so sorry about that, too."

Truth seeped into her despair.

He'd arrived.

And she *was* sorry.

Because the last piece of her own puzzle had just come to her.

As much as she hated Hugh Gussman and Eduardo Duran, she loved him, too.

Chapter 23

She'd been communicating with Duran. Behind his back. Shock and disappointment hung in the air Harc was breathing. Mixed with more.

She'd made provisions for him to live.

He had no time for feelings. Processed all information as it came at him. Fully focused. Nicole was using the strongest weapon she had—her mind.

She might've been working with her father. But she wasn't working against Harc.

Filling in the blanks from there, Harc saw what was coming. Weighed options.

"Daddy…" Running to the man as he appeared around the corner, Nicole wrapped her arms around his neck, hugging him close. When the older man's arms circled his daughter with equal fervor, Harc's emotions went into deep freeze. He calculated.

Came up with several responses, all equally valid, depending on circumstance.

Duran was impressive in person. Even in darkness illuminated only by the moonlight. Tall, lithe, athletic, the man commanded respect in the middle of the night after rappelling down a mountain side.

He was also armed. Harc noted the bulge in the man's

jeans beneath the hooded sweatshirt Duran wore. Suspected there was an equal one in his waistband.

He could relate. Figured a third gun on the man's ankle and a knife slid into a sock on the other leg. He knew the drill.

Lived it. Even on the ranch. Some habits didn't die.

The goon at the cliff still had his gun trained on Harc. Second hired man still hadn't shown himself. That one worried Harc some. He didn't like not knowing.

No sound from the horses.

Nor any sign of agents on the ground.

The hug ended. Hugh Gussman's arm remained around his daughter's back. Claiming ownership. The man never glanced in Harc's direction. He took a step.

Nicole did not.

"Not yet, Daddy. Harcus Taylor goes first. As soon as I know he's safely with authorities, I'm yours."

"We don't have time to play games, Char," the man said. "I give you my word he won't be touched."

The man was good. Too good. Forcing Nicole to trust him. Or admit that she didn't.

Go. He willed her. His mind clicking, crossing off scenarios, bringing others up to play. He could take the guy at the cliff. Didn't know how many others there'd be.

"You gave me your word by coming down here," she told him. "I need to know I can trust you to do as you say, Daddy. I'm not a little girl anymore. It has to work both ways."

He wasn't going to kill her right then and there. She seemed to know that.

Harc was beginning to suspect the man wasn't going to kill his daughter at all. He really thought he had enough control over her to be able to keep her. His prized possession.

He wasn't as sure that Nicole had fallen back under his spell.

She was fighting too hard for Harc. But requiring the show of trust was a good call.

About ready to pop out of his skin with his need to do more than just stand and watch the woman put her life on the line, Harc took her cue. Kept his place in the game. A pawn. Standing on the same square. Untouched.

"How do you know I wouldn't have him shot the second he's out of ear range? Or quietly captured before he's ten feet away?"

"Because I'm trusting you." Four words. Said so softly Harc barely heard them. Lined with love. There was no mistaking that. Then, more loudly, she added, "And because that program is going to publish in the portal, like I said, but the information is also going to be hitting key inboxes if he doesn't make it back to safety. You taught me well, Daddy. Respect has to work both ways. I let you down. But you betrayed me, too."

She was good. Impressive. And hadn't looked at Harc once.

He could hardly believe it when Eduardo bowed his head. More than a nod. Clearly a sign of acquiescence. Whether genuine or not, Harc had no idea. Couldn't take a chance on thinking that it was.

He saw the man give a nod toward the man at the cliff. Was already reaching for the gun he'd dropped to the ground when he heard...movement. But no shot. Glancing up he saw cliff guy holster his gun.

"Get your gun and go," Eduardo's voice aimed at Harc was filled with authority. And warning, too.

Harc was only going to be given one chance. Gun in hand, he held it tight. Took note of the fact that any bullet he'd shoot at the older man would hit his daughter as well. Eduardo, still holding on to Nicole, had put himself between her and Harc.

Not just a defensive move to save his daughter. Harc got the message. Eduardo would always be the wall between Harcus Taylor and Nicole Compton.

He was also going to let Harc walk out of there. Whatever Nicole had found on him was a game changer.

And she hadn't shared it with him.

The thing they'd come to the mountains to find—something that could end the kingpin's twenty-five-year reign, close down his organization permanently—and she'd found it. But hadn't turned it over to authorities.

"How do I report in when I'm safe?" he asked. "What number do I call?"

"You call me." Nicole's voice. Not her father's. "On the phone you supplied."

They were the last words he heard her say.

Of all the ways she'd envisioned herself heading out of the mountain—including in a body bag—on foot with her father hadn't been one. The enforcer at the cliff fell in right behind them, making good on Eduardo's choice to let Harc go. When a second man appeared as they rounded the cliff and led the way in front of them, Nicole took a breath filled with relief.

They were really going to let Harc go.

She'd saved his life.

And if that's all she did, she'd die on a good note. A decent person. Who'd been born to the wrong man and had to pay for his sins.

She'd been eerily calm since her father had appeared. No panic. No shaking.

She didn't want to die. Wasn't giving up.

To the contrary, the burst of success filled her with more strength than she'd ever known. She didn't try to break free of her father's arm around her waist. To the contrary, she wrapped him with her own. Allowing herself those moments in the woods to think about reasons why she'd loved him.

"You never missed a Christmas," she said aloud. "No matter where you were or had to be, you either took me with you or you made it home." They'd walked off the way she and Harc had come in. And were taking things carefully.

Eduardo gave her side a gentle squeeze—a hug, not a hold—and said, "You're my princess."

He didn't sound right to her. There was a lack of something…confidence? Or maybe it was the presence of something. Worry.

She'd never heard him with a tone of doubt underlying anything he said.

And it wasn't that either, she realized as she replayed his words and realized they'd been laced with sadness.

Because the easy days were over?

Or because she was?

"I'm assuming we're leaving the country," she said then, talking softly enough that those behind and in front of them couldn't hear.

"A car is waiting to take us to a helicopter that will land us on a yacht. From there we take another helicopter to a private air strip. And on to Morocco."

Morocco. Not El Salvador.

She didn't ask about Arnold Wagar. Didn't want to know.

What mattered to her was the man would not be touching her again. She'd die first.

Die. Death. The words, the concept…it was like they

were guiding her. As though she had some kind of wish to end her life.

She stumbled. Her father caught her, steadied her. And it hit her. He'd protected her. But he'd never let her have her own identity. She'd been raised in his image. But she wasn't him. Wasn't even all that much like him.

The past three months, the past days, she'd been defining herself. She knew what was worth living for.

And what was worth dying for, too.

Choices made from the depths of a soul that had been smothering for most of her life.

She didn't want her life to end. It was just beginning. But if she had to die, she was right with herself. A concept she'd never even considered before.

And should have. Long before.

As the strip they were walking along narrowed into a climb, Hugh Gussman fell into step behind her, a hand at her back as needed. She slid some, clawed some, made her way upward. And wondered if her father felt right about the life he'd lived.

She didn't ask. Nor did she question him further about their plans. How long were they going to hike without sustenance? Would they make it out of the mountains yet that day? On foot?

Just like their escape from the country, he'd have it all planned.

Unless he chose to kill her as soon as she deadened the cyber messaging she'd told him she had scheduled to publish. She wasn't going to make that easy on him. He'd taken her gun, but he'd seen to it that she had one hell of a lot of self-defense training, and she'd use every single aspect of it in a fight for her life.

She'd stay calm. Use her mind. The one weapon she had

that just might be more powerful than his. It wasn't less—she believed that much.

And if he intended to let her live, to start a new life with him, she might go. Just long enough to nail him.

She had other family.

A vision of Savannah smiling at her from her raft in the pool in her big sister's backyard flashed into Nicole's mind. Followed by others. One in the middle of the night. Just a head above the covers, eyes wide and filled with love, as Nicole lay with her head on the next pillow, trying to comprehend that her entire life had been a lie.

Savannah—whose only family were her partners. They'd welcomed Nicole into the fold, and Nicole wanted to be a contributing part of it.

She also had a heart that had just done a speed course on falling in love. She'd always been a quick learner.

Giving herself a mental shake, she shied away from any other thoughts of Harc. Every step was working toward his freedom from harm. With agents on the ground in the mountains, she expected a call from him within the hour.

Half of that had already passed.

She hoped they weren't trying to come after her. Eduardo would have men posted every step of the way. He didn't follow protocols other than his own. He played dirty. And he'd spare no expense, stop at nothing to get what he wanted.

She had to pee.

And was going to need water.

Dawn would be breaking, and then what? Satellite vision would increase tenfold. No way was Eduardo unaware of that possibility. Nor would he allow himself to be caught in such a basic way.

He had to keep her alive, though. Until he could be certain that she hadn't found the one thing that made him vulnerable. On and off as they hiked, she'd been trying to figure out what it was. Had been taking a huge risk threatening him with it when she hadn't known for sure that it existed. Just, knowing him, it made sense to her that it did.

He'd already be out of the country otherwise.

Ordering whatever hits he wanted made.

They'd come to a clearing. A flat area in between towering mountain peaks. As soon as she stepped onto it, uniformed guards appeared, rifles pointed.

Her heart started to pound. Until, in the darkness, she made out the helicopter.

With a US Army seal.

The guns weren't protecting Eduardo. They were pointed at him.

She started to shake. And to cry.

Harc had saved her.

Eduardo's entourage had won. They'd made it to the clearing before Mike's teams had. Tearing up inside, Harc moved stealthily down the tree trunk, taking in every aspect of the flat ground he'd had in view from his branch for the past fifteen minutes. Dim view.

Cursing at himself for the night binoculars in his pack and not on him, he counted a dozen bodies with rifles. Falling with precision into two lines forming a pathway to the opened door of the copter.

A stolen vessel. Made possible with the equally pilfered credentials of one double agent, Clayton Abernathy, who'd been found dead sometime after midnight.

Duran had used him one last time. Served him up to Nicole and then had him murdered. Leaving no forensic evidence behind.

And if Nicole got on that helicopter, there'd be no trace of her for Harc to find.

Mike, multiple agencies, and Sierra's Web had been online with him since the second he'd walked free of the encampment. Agents in the area had been following intruders since before Harc came out of the cave.

The ones who'd drugged the horses had already been apprehended with paraphernalia found on them.

Over a mile away.

That arrest had just happened when Harc first called in.

Imperial and Mahogany were still out but alive and breathing steadily, he'd been told.

Somehow he had to provide the same fate for Nicole. Alive and breathing steadily.

Him against a dozen armed hitmen.

Nicole had just arrived at the door of the helicopter. Was being helped up. Harc's phone buzzed. Agents were two minutes away.

He didn't have that much time. Harc aimed his gun. The machine's props were already turning. Ready to lift off. Once Eduardo was on board, the thing would be in the air.

The criminal mastermind lifted both hands up to the opening in the copter.

And Harc pulled his trigger.

The blast deafened her. Falling from the bench she'd just perched upon to the floor, Nicole shoved her body underneath the seat as far as she could. Shaking hard, she remained frozen to the spot, listening to the shouting, both inside and outside the aircraft.

Followed by a barrage of gunfire.

Booted feet passed in front of her. A door slammed.

Covering her ears, she braced for a bullet. And prayed that Harc had made it to safety.

He hadn't called.

And Eduardo was leaving her there to die. If she didn't explode in the helicopter, he'd make sure she got caught in the gunfire.

He'd bested her after all.

She'd known the possibility was there.

Tears dripped from her eyes down her cheeks. An awakening of sorts.

She wasn't going to die while hiding in fear.

As the gunfire continued to rage outside, though with less secession and maybe fewer guns, she slid out from under the bench and saw one of her father's go bags.

The helicopter…it had been his.

She'd climbed aboard thinking she'd been saved—because Harc had been. Instead, she'd been on her way to meet her fate.

The go bag.

It held at least one gun. Always. Less than a minute later, armed, she made her way toward the side door of the helicopter. Keeping herself hidden inside, she took a quick look outward.

Her breath caught, her heart pounded through her lungs, as she saw Harc, gun raised and pointed at one of the men she recognized from the trek through the woods. But Eduardo was coming up behind Harc, armed and aimed.

"No!" The scream ripped out of her. Renting the air.

Guns went off. Hers. Others.

And she fell to the edge of the door, shaking, watching as though in slow motion as bodies fell.

Eduardo's. The guards'.

And Harc's.

* * *

Winded, Harc lay on the ground for the couple of seconds it took him to realize that it was over. And then his gaze focused on his gun where it had fallen when he'd been hit. He started to reach for it.

Had to get to Nicole.

"Harc!" He heard her scream in the midst of the fray, over voices calling orders, feet rushing. And closed his eyes in gratitude for a brief second.

She was alive.

They'd done it.

Nicole heard all about how Harc had saved her life. His shot at the cockpit, disabling the instrument panel, had been dangerous. A few inches either way could have blown up the aircraft. Instead, he'd given agents on the way to the clearing time to arrive.

And how her scream had alerted an FBI agent she'd never heard of to Eduardo's approach on Harc, resulting in the agent killing her father.

Harc's gun had taken down the last of Eduardo's newly hired henchmen. Just as the bullet from Eduardo's gun had gone off, missing Harc's chest due to the FBI agent's bullet hitting him.

She listened while everyone talked around her. Both in the helicopter ride out of the mountain carrying an unconscious Harc with a tourniquet tied around his leg, and in the private waiting room she'd been shown to upon arrival at the hospital in Denver.

The bullet had hit an artery. And while an agent on-site had managed to stem the flow, Harc had lost a lot of blood.

Was in surgery.

And she was…numb.

Couldn't feel a thing. Except a lack of air. She could draw breath. Just couldn't seem to get enough of it to relax. Every muscle in her body taut, she sat there. She heard. She comprehended. She even nodded where appropriate. Shook her head.

Said thanks once.

She was a robot. The body leftover from the woman she'd been.

If Harc died...

"Nicole!" A jolt rent through her as she heard Savannah's voice. She'd been told Mike and her sister were on their way. On an hours-long flight.

Had she imagined the sound?

Forcing herself to respond, to look toward the voice, she caught only a glimpse of the tears in her sister's eyes before she was caught up in Savannah's arms, her sister's head next to hers. Holding hers.

Sobs rent her body. Horrible, ugly wracking sounds that hurt her from the inside out. And she held on. Tightly.

Feeling Savannah's body start to rock slowly. Side to side. Taking Nicole's with it. In a rhythm that felt...familiar to her. Not in a memory type of way.

In an instinctive one.

Closing her eyes, she gave herself up to the soft motion. While tears continued to roll slowly past her shut lids, the sobs let go of their hold on her body.

And when she was ready, she pulled away. "I'm so sorry," she told her sister. "So sorry." She shook her head. "I'm sorry."

Savannah's head shook softly as her soft fingers pushed the tangled hair away from Nicole's face. "You have nothing to be sorry for, sweetie," she said. And then more firmly, with a wide open almost steely look in her eyes: "Nothing."

She knew that wasn't true. "Harc..."

"Your scream saved his life."

The words struck a chord within her. She stared at her sister. Seeing the scene again. The body's going down. Shuddered. Saw possibility.

"He saved mine," she said then. Putting pieces together. What she'd known. What she'd heard. "If he hadn't shot the cockpit, I'd have been in the air when agents arrived."

Whisking away to God knew where with the man who'd fathered her.

"He's dead," she said then. No antecedent to the pronoun. Savannah didn't seem to need one. She nodded. Touched her forehead to Nicole's. "I know."

Looking in her big sister's eyes she said, "I loved him."

Savannah didn't look disappointed as she nodded.

And Nicole said, "And I hated him so much."

Savannah's smile denoted no happiness but a curious, comforting understanding as she said, "Me, too." And followed it with, "For both."

They talked softly then, just the two of them. Savannah told Nicole how her dad had been her hero her entire life. Before he'd "died" and afterward, as she'd believed he'd given his life to right egregious wrongs.

And Nicole told her sister, again, about Eduardo never missing a Christmas with her. There'd be more. Sometime.

In bits and pieces as Nicole healed. As they both did.

Savannah's sudden smile, lighting her face, brought a hint of hope for the future to Nicole as her sister said, "And by the way... Nicole! You chose the name Mom gave you!" Then, more softly, "And Compton..." Savannah's lips tightened, her chin clenched, and her eyes filled with tears again. "That's me."

"It's us," Nicole told her. "Sisters. Family."

Savannah opened her mouth, but Nicole didn't get to hear whatever her sister's response would be. The door opened and Mike was standing there.

She hadn't even thought about the fact that he hadn't come in with Savannah.

Standing, Nicole studied his face. "What?" she asked. She'd lived with the man as her constant companion—except in the bed and bathrooms—for months. She knew that look. He had something to tell her.

"Harc's out of surgery. Awake. And asking for yo…"

She missed the end of the last word as she ran from the room.

Harc hated hospitals. Hospital beds. And everything about being confined. He'd been told he'd be free to leave in the morning as long as there were no complications. And he agreed to abide by doctor's orders.

He'd already broken those. Was propped in the chair in his room, his left, very bandaged leg extended and braced with the footrest. The feat had cost him some sweat. No tears.

No way he was going to say goodbye to Nicole lying in some damned bed like a helpless, injured soul.

He'd barely gotten his leg settled before the door opened and she was there.

Still in the shirt he'd seen her walk into the cave in after changing the night before. The same jeans. Her hair hadn't been brushed.

She'd been crying. A lot.

Eduardo was dead.

Other than the blood loss, Harc hadn't been in any real danger. Bodily at any rate. The fact that he'd been shot in the back of thigh was going to play with him for a while.

Undercover agents never turned their backs on their enemies.

He'd just been surrounded by them...

Nicole had stopped just inside the door. Her big brown eyes filling with tears. He saw her draw breath. Straighten her shoulders.

Prepared himself to get through the next moments.

And then home to Imperial and Mahogany who, Mike had just told him, were back in their stalls, having been checked by his vet and were expected to be just fine. Both had eaten.

She took a step closer. Then another. Each one bringing them nearer to the goodbye. He had no right to make it difficult for her. Or prolong it. She was finally free. A young woman who'd been robbed of a past, with her entire future stretching freshly ahead of her.

He just had to know one thing. "What did you find on your father?" They'd been searching for years. He needed the closure.

"Nothing." She looked him straight in the eye as she said so. Coming closer all the while. He'd have backed up if his chair wasn't already against the wall.

When she reached him, she...didn't stop coming at him. She ran her fingers through his hair. Touched his face. Smiling. And crying, too.

"I had to think like him," she said softly. "And as scary as it was to find out, I was pretty good at it."

The tone of voice...he'd heard it the night they'd made love...it broke down some barriers inside him. Enough to say, "You did good. Better than good. You impressed the hell out me. And got the job done."

She deserved to know all of that. But no more. The fact

that he'd never met a woman like her, was certain he never would again, would be kept to himself.

He was a semi-retired CIA agent who'd made some morally questionable decisions, with a ranch to run. Not a young man with his entire future stretching out before him.

Kneeling down, she folded her arms over his good thigh. Making it nearly impossible for him to keep his hands to himself. "I know it's way too soon and that I have no idea what any kind of regular life even looks like, let alone how good I'll be at it, but…" She stopped. Looked up at him. With a hint of arrogance that kind of turned him on. Even in his newly out of anesthetic, but painkiller-less, state. "Actually, that's not quite right. I know a lot," she said. "I've experienced horrors unlike people in regular life feel. I've got three degrees. And most importantly, I know what I want to live for. And what I'm willing to die for, too."

He smiled. Couldn't help himself. The woman was…just that intriguing. Beguiling. Inspiring. Admirable… "What do want to live for?"

"Another night naked with you."

He coughed. With some spit attached. Not at all cool. Or even a hint of sexy. More like a guy in a hospital gown drooling all over himself.

Or the partially broken man that he was. Recently zipped up bullet hole notwithstanding.

With one thumb, she wiped his lower lip. "Why aren't you in bed?"

He wasn't going to answer that. And so he said, "What are you willing to die for?"

She nodded, as though to say, *Okay.* As though he'd just issued a challenge and she was willing to take it on.

"Another night naked with you."

There was nothing sexy in the vulnerable look in her

eyes or the soft, almost pleading tone of her voice. He couldn't look away. Or gently remove her arms from his thigh. He should. He had to.

He couldn't. "You have no idea what being with me would mean."

"I think I do," she said, sounding more like herself. Assured. Confident. "I've just spent days sharing caves with you, Harc. Voiding into holes. Eating freeze-dried food. On the verge of death. And talking about things that matter. Riding horses in a gorgeous mountain range and experiencing the most incredible lovemaking I'm ever going to know. I invaded your home. Made you defensive. Angry. If I find out you sniffle instead of using a tissue, throw your dirty clothes on the floor, or listen to acid rock…it's just not going to matter."

He was sinking. Had to stop her. "You don't like acid rock?" he asked, as though the dislike would be a mortal sin.

"No. Do you?"

She had him. "No."

With a nod, Nicole sat back. On her butt. On the floor. No hands on him. He felt bereft. Put it down to the anesthesia.

"Here's the thing," she said then. "You've spent over a decade living fake lives. Getting so completely into them that you slept with fake partners…"

Now she was getting it. He felt the truth slice clean through him but had known all along where the conversation had to lead.

To end.

"I've lived an entire fake life, Harc. Yet when you look at me, you see…me. Not Charlotte Duran or Nicole Compton. You just see…a person."

He nodded. She was right. He did.

"When nothing else seems real, you are."

He swallowed. Hard.

"You don't judge by a straight line of right and wrong. Or by action alone. You judge by motive. By heart. You don't trust what you see. Or hear. You need more. And because of that, you understand that I'm not always going to trust. And you can live with that."

"How do you know that?" She could be wrong. He'd rather lose her right away, then down the road.

"Because you were at the clearing this afternoon. You shot the helicopter. And you asked for me when you came out of surgery. I didn't trust you enough in the end," she said. "Eduardo had contacted me through a portal I'd hacked, and I didn't tell you that. Nor did I share my plan with you to play him at his own game. I went double agent on you, and...you still shot the helicopter."

"I'm eleven years older than you."

"I'm eleven years younger than you."

"I live on a ranch."

"I can't think of anything I'd like more. Lord knows, I need the therapy."

Finally, he found his out. "I was actually thinking about going back to work. In some fashion. Not undercover. But I'm good at what I do. I know things. I can help."

She smiled then. "I've already told Savannah that I want to stay on with Sierra's Web. I was thinking maybe, down the road, there could be a house in Phoenix and the ranch waiting for us when we need a break or have time off."

"Like at Christmas." The words came out of his mouth before he could stop them.

With tears in her eyes, Nicole climbed back up on his good leg. "I love you, Harcus Taylor. I'm a piece of work.

Life with me won't be easy. But I'm going to love you until the day I die and after that, too."

Harc felt moisture prick his eyes. Not tears. Something more than that. Stronger. His heart melting, if such a thing were possible. He had no more fight in him.

"You can let yourself accept love, Harc." The whispered words slid inside him.

Without allowing another second to pass, he leaned over. Put hands under both of her arms and lifted her up to his good thigh, wrapped his arms around her, and held on. "I love you, Nicole," he said with his face in her neck. "I don't trust this entire situation between us, but I can't fight it. I love you. The Charlotte part, the Nicole part, and the parts that are yet to reveal themselves."

His chest lightened with every word.

And his instincts laid back, grinning.

There'd be challenges ahead. Problems, even.

But he'd finally found the man he'd always wanted to be.

He'd been inside him all along.

Driving him.

It had just taken seeing himself in Nicole's eyes for him to understand.

* * * * *

Harlequin® Reader Service

Enjoyed your book?

Try the perfect subscription for Romance readers and get more great books like this delivered right to your door.

See why over 10+ million readers have tried Harlequin Reader Service.

Start with a Free Welcome Collection with free books and a gift—valued over $20.

Choose any series in print or ebook. See website for details and order today:

TryReaderService.com/subscriptions